He smi

'You're Amy, ⋯ ⋯em-
ber me. Are you fee⋯ ⋯ost
as if it might have ⋯ ⋯
was fantastic. I'd heard you were in one, but I
didn't know you were that good.'

Heard I was in one? Had he been asking about
me? I think I must have left my mouth open so
long I started dribbling. I could feel myself staring
at him as though he was a Being from an
Alternative Zone in the dream world of my head.
Say something, I thought.

Hmmm. Hmm. Something like 'Hem hem
nyaaaf weasel' is what came out, I think.

What I meant to say was, Yep, I'm fine, thanks.
Great night. Marvellous party. Just came up here to
chill out and catch up on a bit of Tolstoy. Of
course, I do this kind of thing a lot, in between
studying to be a brain surgeon. But 'Hem hem
nyaaaf weasel' was what came out.

And the Being from an Alternative Zone
laughed. Which is when I fell in love.

Also available by
Ros Asquith

I Was a Teenage Worrier

The Teenage Worrier's Guide to Life

The Teenage Worrier's Guide to Lurve

The Teenage Worrier's Pocket Collection

(includes *The Teenage Worrier's Pocket Guides
to Romance, Families, Mind & Body and Success*)

love, fifteen

Ros Asquith

CORGI BOOKS

LOVE, FIFTEEN
A CORGI BOOK 0 552 14777 X

Published in Great Britain by Corgi Books,
an imprint of Random House Children's Books

This edition published 2005

1 3 5 7 9 10 8 6 4 2

Text and illustrations copyright © Ros Asquith, 2005

Corgi Books are published by
Random House Children's Books,
61–63 Uxbridge Road, London W5 5SA,
a division of The Random House Group Ltd,
in Australia by Random House Australia (Pty) Ltd,
20 Alfred Street, Milsons Point, Sydney, NSW 2061, Australia,
in New Zealand by Random House New Zealand Ltd,
18 Poland Road, Glenfield, Auckland 10, New Zealand,
and in South Africa by Random House (Pty) Ltd,
Endulini, 5A Jubilee Road, Parktown 2193, South Africa

THE RANDOM HOUSE GROUP
Limited Reg. No. 954009
www.kidsatrandomhouse.co.uk

A CIP catalogue record for this book is
available from the British Library.

Printed and bound in Great Britain by
Cox & Wyman Ltd, Reading, Berkshire.

Acknowledgements

This story is dedicated to anyone who's ever made a mistake, but it also comes with very special thanks to Angela, Rachel and Lyn for invaluable feedback and support. Big thanks also to Charlotte, Christine, Vanessa and Paula and the terrific teenage mothers of Brent.

Huge thanks to all the magnificent teenagers I know and love and apologies to the wonderful Amy and the wonderful Lottie (who are *not*, repeat *not*, anything like the Lottie and Amy in the book, although they are extremely nice and so on, obviously) . . .

Even bigger thanks to Lucy, Annie, Sue and all at Random House, but particularly to Philippa Dickinson and Sophie Nelson, and also to John, who between them must have spent almost as much time on this as I did.

CHAPTER ONE

In Which Amy Encounters a Sartorial Disaster

Wednesday January 29

Coming down the high street after school today,
Lottie and I were singing *My Baby's Shoes
Are Some Jive-Ass Slippers* when two frenzied
weirdos headed straight for us, rolling their eyes
and waving their arms. One looked like a pig on its
hind legs and the other like a pissed flamingo.

'Loony alert.' I pointed. 'Who the hell are they?'

'It's us,' said Lottie in a small voice.

And it was. Hunky Horst had thrown open the
new swish plate-glass double doors of his latte bar
and there we were, reflected in them.

Checked in the hall mirror when I got home.

What a shock – a pig on its hind legs with a
school bag. Lottie skittered off to her house
swearing she would never wear a pink feather boa
again.

I was still glued to the mirror in the hope that if
I stared hard enough I'd turn into a sex goddess,

when my mother stuck her head round the kitchen door and said hello.

'Oink oink,' I said, tearing myself away from the mirror.

'Good day?' asked Mum, like she always does. 'The girls have been so sweet today,' she went on, not waiting for an answer, like she always does. Still, it would only have been *Oink oink*, so she didn't miss much.

I pointed my snout upstairs towards my bedroom and Mum nodded, smiled her mad smile and disappeared again.

FEELGOOD TIP
Keep a diary and add three positive things each day to 'feel good' about yourself.

Must remember To do This every day. After watching painT dry.

Pudding One and Pudding Two, my 'sweet' little twin sisters, were in my bedroom when I got there. In *my* room. Whence they are supposed to be banned by the subtle signs on the door:

Not that they can read, of course. They can smell though. There was a horrendous niff in the air. One Sweet Girl was green, the other was red with smoking black bits around the edges. Pudding One had thrown up over Pudding Two and Pudding Two was very unhappy about it, though she was still at the battering-Pudding-One-with-blunt-instruments stage rather than the wailing-down-stairs-to-Mum payoff. This repulsive event had happened on my bed, which was bad enough. But, hah! (*Scornful laugh.*) That's nothing. What had missed Pudding Two (which was most of Pudding One's rocket-propelled insides) had landed on my Shimmering Ebony Valentine's Night Outfit, proudly laid out on my bed to psych me up for the Great Valentine's Night Ordeal in just sixteen days' time.

A lot of things went through my head about what I might do next – bring back hanging, or torture chambers . . . or contraceptive devices that eliminated possibilities of twin sisters – but in the end I settled for letting out a scream of anguish that made Pudding Two put her fingers in her ears and bolt from the room howling her best Junior

Acting School howl, and had Mum up the stairs and through the door, clutching a hysterical Pudding Two, like something from the Jedi Olympics.

'Mum! *Look what they've done!*' I howled.

'*Amaryllis!*' she squealed, almost as loudly as me. Now, is that a name you'd like to hear broadcast all over the neighbourhood?

Then she ranted on: 'They're three years old! Something's made them sick, poor darlings.'

'Stop calling me Amaryllis,' I muttered grumpily, hoping to change the subject.

'Oooh, poor little Puddy . . .' She wasn't listening to me, as usual – she was fussing over a Pudding.

'Howwid Millis! Hit me wiv a boomerang!' wailed Pudding Two.

She has quite a good imagination for someone who looks like a giant whoopee cushion.

'Look what she's done to my Valentine's outfit!' I squealed. 'And now you're being *nice* to her for it! She'll grow up like those crack dealers over the road. It's not *fair!*'

When you say it's not fair, you always hear the answer: 'Life *isn't* fair.' It's one of the most annoying things I know.

11 p.m.

Have discovered what made the Pudding throw up. She ate my egg. I have kept that Easter egg for four years. Now it is gone gone gone.

Tom Carpenter gave me that egg. I may only have been eleven, but I knew what love was. It's nothing

4

like what I felt for Flubber, who has just dumped me for she-who-shall-not-be-named. That was just liking someone quite a lot and fancying them like mad and, to be honest, being flattered. I never felt Flubber's soul was making a beeline for mine, like I did in those few minutes I spent with Tom . . .

But I can't kid myself that Tom Carpenter felt the same – he just happened to be at the same naff kids'-party-in-the-park style Easter egg hunt. 'I'm too old for this kind of thing,' he said. I remember it as if it was yesterday.

'So am I,' I said.

'But you like chocolate?'

'Mmmmmmm.' And I tried to pout. So he gave me the egg. And a smile that turned my knees to water.

It was Lottie who told me his name, his age (he was two years older than me) and said he was a doctor's son.

I mentioned it casually to Mum that evening and she said she'd been to Dr Carpenter only last month for her varicose veins, and he was gorgeous. 'He looks like Pierce Brosnan. All the women from sixteen to sixty round here are ill all the time now.'

That night I put pepper up my eleven-year-old nose and I was so ill the next day Mum took me to the doc's. But it turned out Dr Carpenter had gone private.

'We should go private too,' I said hopefully.

'That Tom's certainly made an impression on you,' she smiled. 'But I can't see us going private on your dad's plumbing and my book-keeping.'

So I never bumped into Tom again.

But if he didn't feel the same as me, why did he give me the egg?

12.30

It is very sad to keep an egg from a boy who you only met once for four whole years.

It was mouldy, anyway.

<hr>

Thursday January 30

a.m.

The Puddings are having their usual breakfast of Oaty Pops with marmalade.

I will have to get a flat.

It is not good going to school without breakfast, but my stomach has its limits.

6 p.m.

> ## SOCIAL BUTTERFLY TIP
> *Throw a fancy dress party! Give it a theme, like 'B'. And hope there'll be people dressed as Batman, Beckham and Brad Pitt!*
>
> Or Boils, Bulimia and BoTox?

Shimmering Ebony Outfit of Starry Twinkles on Night Sky now resembles frog with skin ailment on mud bank. Washing machine has performed some evil witchcraft on it and now, instead of a little black number, it's a baggy brown and green disaster. Shouldn't have used 'fast coloureds heavy soil'.

With heavy heart, decide to ring Elsie. She is the reason why this Puking Pudding and Frog Invasion Event is a lot worse than it seems.

I'm supposed to sing at Elsie's Valentine's Night disco in a couple of weeks. Well, on Valentine's Night, actually. Shimmering Ebony Outfit was my one hope of diverting attention from my gigantic boobs, bendy legs and giant's feet and actually looking as good as I can occasionally sound when I'm singing.

I know I can sing, because anoraky people with album collections the size of the British Museum are always telling me so – with a bit of work on a few details of course. Like staying in tune, not strutting around the stage until the microphone plug pulls out, remembering the words – stuff like that. But when I sing it's like the Real Me breaking out, not the frightened, spotty, bolshie Me. As I have often told tone-deaf Mum, I need encouragement, and lessons, and somebody from a record company waving a contract out of the window of a stretch limo.

Ring Elsie.

Tell her I cannot possibly sing at her thing.

'You miserable slag! Why not?' comes this squeak from the other end.

'Nothing to wear.'

'Wear nothing. There won't be any parents there.'

'Don't be thick.'

'You can borrow something of my sister's. She's about your shape.'

Elsie's sister looks like a sofa. I may look like a pig on its hind legs on a bad day, but I am definitely losing my puppy fat.

Elsie listens to my outraged silence and reconsiders. 'I've got a great dress you could have. You might pop out of it in a few more places than me, but that would be all to the good.'

'No, no, it's all hopeless,' I moan.

'What now?'

'Spots.'

'Where?'

'Top lip. Looks like a red moustache from a joke shop.'

'Polyfilla? Or get a real fake moustache? You could pose as a guy. Why not?'

If Elsie is trying to persuade me, she's making an excellent job of it. Not.

She says she supposes she could get Xanthia to sing.

'Fine,' I say. 'Fine fine fine.'

I slam the phone down.

Xanthia Starr is she-who-shall-not-be-named. She is the girl I can't stand but would like to look like – hair like a raven's wing, silver stud in a belly as flat as a vanity mirror, legs that go up to the stratosphere, little pointy nose-job type hooter it takes her just one nano-second to look down at you from. To let her sing instead of me would be a victory for the Beautiful People. Much as I'd like to be one, I'm not going to roll over and wave my little legs in the air in defeat. It would be a victory for the Tone-deaf People too, which might even be worse.

11 p.m.

'Xanthia has a voice like a violin in a washing machine,' I tell Elsie. 'She sings over my dead body.'

'Good on ya, Amy. I knew you'd do it,' says Elsie.

So I'm stuck with it. There's only one thing for it.

> ### Make a Big Decision to Look on the Bright Side!

as it says in *Teenacious Tips*.

My spots might have disappeared by then, although new ones are always lurking, fighting for tickets to get on the zit escalator that will take them to the surface and freedom. And can always get Lottie to do my hair. Hers is like a very depressed mouse most of the time, but when she works on it, she can make it like an excited young stallion. She has magic hairdo fingers.

Midnight

Have read first sentence of *Hard Times* by Charles Dickens ten times.

I tried to sneak it out of the school library, but of course had to put up with a lot of nudging in the ribs from Ruth and Van's gang trying to convince me it was a porno novel.

1 a.m.

Crack dealers living opposite are doing plenty of business tonight – people are screeching up and down the road like something out of *Grand Theft Auto*. Never see any cops – they're probably all screeching up and down a road somewhere else, chasing people for listening to gangsta rap. Mum and Dad say we can't complain or we'll get bricks through our windows, but I think they've signed a neighbourhood petition that has 500 fearless fake names on it.

BEAUTY MASK TIP

Blend together 1/2 cup chopped cucumber, 1/2 cup chopped avocado, 1 egg white & 2 tsp powdered milk. Apply 2 tbsp of the cucumber avocado mask to your face and neck in upward circular motions.

Use leftovers for sandwich. Eat sandwich on way to chemist to buy facepack.

7.30 a.m.

Have now waited two whole days for spots to go. They are that very glowing beacon red that comes before the crusty stage that makes you look like you've climbed out of a shallow grave during the night. This stage usually only lasts a couple of days, so if I can convince myself that my mates throwing up at the sight of me isn't anything personal, it's really the light at the end of the tunnel.

Re-examine frog skin, formerly known as Shimmering Ebony Etc. Doesn't look so bad now I'm getting used to it.

Anyway, frogs do OK – maybe there will be a prince in the audience at Valentine's do. But on Valentine's Night, of course, a lot of people will be on the lookout for him.

Have developed a stinkeroony of a cold.

Do dot fadcy siggig adythig, adywhere.

But baybe it will have cleared in two weeks.

<u>**Monday February 3**</u>

Hard Times is fantastic.

Why don't we ever read Dickens in school? Asked my favourite genius teacher, Ms Corman, about this today. She said she'd see if she could get some Dickens on the curriculum.

'Who's sucking up to teacher?' said Tracey Hardwick on the way out, but I don't care. Some people have no ambition. If I can't be a singer, I am definitely going to be a writer.

They've cleaned the loos at KFC – for the first time ever they are graffiti-free! That will last about a week. Sad to think that Kenneth Frances Comprehensive was named so hopefully after some mayor from about a million years ago who had a dream of Education For All – hope he didn't live long enough to see how the place turned out.

Go for après-school coffee with the band, i.e., that is, Lottie, Debbie and Mad Alice.

Debbie, who's the glammest of all of us and was voted Best Bum in the school by the boys and girls together (which is pretty unusual), plays e-bass and screams, and Mad Alice tries to copy Jimi Hendrix solos off her dad's old records and breaks strings a lot. I think it's partly a way of trying to stay close to her dad's memory – he bunked off six years ago without a backward look. Lottie is my absolute BF – she plays drums and she's the best musician. People are always trying to nick her for their own bands. She doesn't look like a drummer – more like a thin owl (given her round owly specs), unless in a feather boa, when she's more like a flamingo – but she makes an amazing amount of noise considering you'd think she couldn't strike a match without breaking a bone. Me, of course, I sing.

'Listen,' I say firmly. 'We can't call ourselves Black Hole. It just sets us up for too many daft jokes – and anyway only Debs is black.'

'Let's call ourselves The Undead,' growls Mad Alice. (She's a goth: she's as thin as a music stand with a black shroud draped over it.)

'Or Jelly Babies,' smirks Lottie, with what I consider an insulting look at my boobs.

'How about the Final Insult,' I suggest haughtily, with my best haughty look.

But none of them is listening, they are all away with the fairies because hunky Horst has brought the coffees.

'Oenly twoe coffeeees for treee such beeautiful gurrrrls?' he whinnies.

'Shame he can't count,' Debs murmurs, her eyes glued to his receding derrière.

It's embarrassing sharing two lattes. But none of

us has a job yet, as Mum is always reminding me. Oh well, Black Hole it is then, for now . . .

BLACK HOLE
Live!

Elsie's VALENTINE'S BASHMENT
BOOGIE BONANZA
FRI FEB 14th
8 till late
Invitation only so don't even try it!

Lottie and I amble home in silence for a bit. A van coming up behind us starts hooting, then the guy hanging out of the passenger window starts making boob-cupping gestures at what I assume can only be me, since Lottie's boobs are invisible even under high-powered magnification, which makes her unhappy. The guy in the van has a face like a hamburger.

'Ulp,' says Lottie. 'D'you think anyone fancies those sort of guys?'

'Oh, sure, if they like hamburgers. Why not?'

Lottie is a vegetarian. She pulls a face. 'Funny, isn't it, all that shagging business?' she eventually reflects. 'I can't really imagine ever getting to that point with anyone. Or at least not anyone like those hamburgers.'

'Well, it's legal for us next year,' I say. 'Maybe you have to do it then, or it expires, like if you don't claim a Grand Prize Draw before the end of the month.'

'Don't be thick,' Lottie says, but I can see she's given this worrying possibility some thought. 'You don't have to do it if you don't want, like they say in PSE lessons. Anyway, somebody you fancy has got to fancy you, first.'

We both groan at this.

'What are *you* moaning about?' Lottie asks. 'Look at those guys in the van. Who do you think they were looking at?'

'I'd rather become a nun.'

'Graham Doodah fancies you,' Lottie says helpfully.

'Graham Doodey. And thanks very much. He makes Millhouse in *The Simpsons* look like Brad Pitt.'

'*And* Flubber,' she giggles.

I blush. Lottie *knows* I snogged Flubber two whole times before he went flubbering off with Xanthia Starr. 'It was like snogging a jelly fish,' I lie. Matter of fact Flubber scored ten out of ten in the lippy gymnastic dept – or I think he would have if I hadn't been so nervous.

'Anyway, I've got the answer for both of us,' continues Lottie, suddenly chirpy. 'Once you sing at Elsie's Valentine party all the boys will be lining up.'

'Yeah, outside the loos,' I say gloomily.

'You have to do it, you know,' Lottie insists. 'You can't let that poser Xanthia do it. I'll be right behind you. We'll have them eating out of our hands.'

I stop and grab Lottie by her tiny, narrow monster-drummer's shoulders. 'Listen to me. You've got to wise up. Most boys wouldn't care if we'd won the Brit Awards. Xanthia could saw a bagpipe in half and then blow her adorable ski-jump nose through it, and they'd still cheer their heads off. They just look at her bits moving about.'

Lottie and I are both depressed by this thought. 'Not all boys are like that though,' she says.

'Hmmmm, I know. But there are boys who are friends and then there are boys who want to get off with you. And then there are boys who you want to get off with—'

'And what you need is a boy who is all three at once,' says Lottie.

'Sounds kinda hard to find, doesn't it?' I say.

'Yes,' says Lottie. 'But it's got to be more than just liking and fancying someone, hasn't it? I don't really want to do it until I adore someone.'

'I'm like that too, really,' I said. 'Else I'd have gone all the way with Flubber.'

We continue the rest of the walk home in silence, and just shrug before we separate, like a couple of prisoners finishing a turn round the exercise yard.

'Keep looking out for the three-headed super-lad,' says Lottie over her shoulder.

6.30 p.m.

Decide if you can't beat 'em, join 'em, and try a little of the Puddings' tea of sausages and marmalade.

Go to bed early to revise for mock mocks.

11 p.m.

Puddings in my bed so I am now tucked up cosily in Pudding One's cot. Something comforting about it. Maybe it's the lullaby mobile I had when I was a baby. Maybe it's the nursery rhyme wallpaper. Whatever, it doesn't go with trying to revise science.

The solar system is alive with jumping cows and little dogs laughing . . .

CHAPTER TWO

In Which Amy Stitches Herself into a Stitch-Up

8 p.m.

'Lottie! Gandhi has eaten my maths homework.'

'Gandhi?'

Forgotten I hadn't told Lottie about the Puddings' new pet.

'The gerbil. Dad called him that because he brought Peace on Earth from the Puddings.'

'What?'

'They kept going on about a pet, so he got them a gerbil and they shut up, so he called the gerbil— Oh, never mind, it's eaten my homework.'

'Come round and copy mine.'

Great. That is what friends are for.

Lottie's house is like a second home to me. It's all cosy and untidy, like ours, but with loads of books and musical instruments wherever you look. And her parents read the *Guardian*.

'There's more books here than in the KFC

18

library,' I say, trying to clear some space to copy Lottie's maths.

'I've given up cello,' says Lottie.

Ooh. Lottie's folks were so proud of her getting grade seven distinction in cello. I think they hoped the drums was just a phase . . .

Wednesday February 5

Today's tip from *Teenacious Tips*:

> *You are not fat, you are voluptuous.*

Just six days into Looking on the Bright Side, and the Dark Side makes it impossible to see it, as usual. Things are bad, bad, baaaad.

It's all to do with Black Hole.

What has Black Hole to do with the Return of the Dark Side? you may ask. Because I got blamed for something I didn't do, but I couldn't say it wasn't me, that's what.

We (me and Debbie and Lottie and Mad Alice) are playing a game we often play in the back row of Mr Fish's PSE lesson. (Mr Fish! And I thought Amaryllis Baker was bad! He smells a bit, as well, which makes it worse.) Anyway, this game we were playing is like *Never Mind the Buzzcocks*, where you have to guess the song – only you have to do it silently of course. Debbie mimes playing

CON and DOM's
Teenwise Guide to
Safer Sex

Or whoops, there goes my condom

a bass line and mouths the words with big chewing expressions as if she's trying to eat a bowling ball. Mad Alice rolls her eyes up like somebody having a fit, sticks her tongue out and makes wild guitar loony movements with her fingers. Lottie thrashes away with a pair of pencils on the cover of *Con and Dom's Teenwise Guide to Safer Sex*.

I'm just trying to guess between *Stairway to Heaven, Hammer Time* and *My Heart Will Go On* when I hear a voice shouting, '*Amaryllis Baker!*' It's Mr Fish advancing towards us, nose twitching and fins aloft. Mad Alice stops playing the Greatest Guitar Solo in History and pretends to be counting on her fingers, which considering it's a PSE lesson is a strange and desperate choice. Debbie is stuck with her mouth open but starts feeling around inside it as if she's got toothache. Mr Fish is pretty close now. But he's not glaring at us, he's glaring at the edge of the table where I'm supposed to be working. Because balanced on it, smoking gently, is a half-finished roll-up.

'Out,' Mr Fish says, pointing at me and then at the door.

I look at him in amazement. 'But . . . but . . .' is all I can think of.

'Out,' is all he can think of, but it's a better line than mine.

I stare wildly around, as if I might see the hole in the ceiling this mysterious object fell from, or the bird with an evil sense of humour that plucked it from the fingers of somebody in the street and left it neatly where Mr Fish would get hold of the wrong end of it.

Then I catch sight of Tracey Hardwick across the row, who's looking as if she's about to give birth to the Alien. Tracey normally wears one of those expressions like the best thing the human race could do for her is give her everything it owns and then die, but she's looking sideways at me with a tortured look I've never seen before. Then I get it. Tracey is in Ruth and Van's gang. She has a criminal record in the school as long as her face, and she's up for exclusion if she gets caught for anything serious again. She wouldn't normally care, I reckon, but her dad's bunked off and her mum's in hospital with something nasty, so maybe even she's figured out she doesn't want to make things worse. What's more, she's rumoured to be up the duff – what a disaster area she is. So she's trying to get me to take the heat for the fag. And for some reason, I'm going to oblige. I can see that Debbie and Mad Alice, who'd both be happy to push Tracey H under a bus at any time, are about to say something in my defence. But I know I won't get anything near as bad as Tracey H, and she knows it too. So I stand up, pick up the cigarette and say:

'Care for a drag, Mr Fish?'

'Out,' he says, a lot louder, while the class shouts with laughter. So I get out. As I give the roll-up to Mr Fish and leave the room, I look back to see Lottie and Debbie and Mad Alice shaking their heads tragically, and Tracey H staring straight at me with her eyes wide, as if a spell's been put on her.

'Straight to Mrs Craven,' Old Fishy shouts after me, waving the offending roll-up like a flag.

Crazy Craven, the demon headteacher, takes cigarette-smoking more seriously than murder.

'Can't I go to Mrs Moon?' I stutter. Moony is our cuddly form tutor.

'Craven!' thunders Fish.

So I totter off.

Craven says Mrs Moon is going to be very very disappointed because she has always stood up for me and said I was a nice girl underneath. Oh, good. Then she puts me in detention after school for the rest of the week, and says she's going to write to my parents. I offer to take the letter home there and then.

'Because it will save the school valuable postage which could be spent on special needs, Ms Craven,' I say in my helpful voice. She is not impressed. I consider telling her about Tracey Hardwick. But I don't.

And to think it was Crazy Craven who scrawled on the end of my report: 'Amaryllis has a bubbly personality which she needs to curb from occasionally bubbling over on the wrong occasions.' What kind of English is that? Using occasion on two occasions?

Lottie is waiting for me outside when I'm finally let out.

'Did you wait specially?' I ask, touched.

'Not exactly. Got a detention.'

Lottie never gets detentions.

'What for?'

'Changing the front of my history textbook to "herstory".'

'Fascists,' I say.

Lottie has always been a campaigner. It was her who got up the petition in Year Seven for girls to be allowed to wear trousers to school. KFC has a theory that if the underclass are in uniform they'll somehow behave better. Black shoes instead of trainers and other bonkers ideas. The petition was a great idea, but the girls' trousers are so disgusting no one ever wears them. They look as if they might be made of Lycra mixed with pulped hedgehog.

Lottie peers at me anxiously through her owl glasses and smiles. 'That was a fantastic thing you did. Tracey hasn't got the face muscles for saying thanks, but you can see even she's knocked out. Maybe you've saved a Lost Cause.'

'I don't care if she liked it or not,' I say, half to Lottie and half to myself. 'She's too much of a fool to stay out of bother for long, anyway. But you should have heard the way Craven went on at me. It was only the fact that I hadn't done it before that saved my life, otherwise you'd find me lying out

23

here now with flies crawling over me and rats eating me and stuff.'

Lottie shivers. 'Shut up,' she says, with feeling. 'Old Craven will write to your parents now. What are you going to do then?'

'I think they'll be OK about it. I'll tell them it was a moment of madness. They know I can't stand cigarettes anyway.'

But I was feeling a bit shaky on this one. Mum has been nagging me recently about fooling around at school and rehearsing with the band too much. Maybe this cigarette thing might be a step too far.

'Do you reckon Tracey's really pregnant?' Lottie eventually asks.

'She's supposed to have told Fatima she's really really worried about it. Periods stopped and all that. She must have done that test by now. But she doesn't look any different, 'cept she's madder than ever, which might be a sign, I suppose. She's been seeing that Gareth Foreshaw. You know, that pin-headed guy – massive bum, wears a red and white sweatshirt – looks like a traffic cone. He's got a car and everything.'

'What do you mean, everything?' Lottie asks, just to be difficult.

'Well I've heard he's got . . .' I start, and we both get the giggles at this point. 'Humungous masculine underbits.' Actually, I never found this piece of information surprising. Gareth Foreskin is such a prat that all the millions of living cells that weren't needed inside his head probably just decided to get together and build something useful somewhere else. 'You mean you didn't know that?' I ask Lottie.

'How would I know?' Lottie says, still giggling. 'I've never seen it, have I?'

'Have you ever seen anybody's?' I ask her, pretty unfairly. I know for a fact she hasn't.

'Cheeky cow,' Lottie says. 'I've seen hundreds of them. All on the same guy, and all.'

We go down the street cackling about the man with a thousand willies.

I get home. The Puddings are apparently out with the childminder, who learned her discipline techniques from the Anti-Terrorist Squad and is the only person who keeps them quiet. If I ever have kids and somebody has to look after them while I'm on stage before an audience of roaring millions, I'll make sure it's somebody really nice.

I go into the kitchen, where I can hear Radio Four. Mum looks up from moving kitchen stuff pointlessly about.

'Where have you been?' she says. 'Some boy was ringing up about you.'

'Really? Who?' I ask her, amazed.

'I don't know. I tried to make conversation with him and he made a noise like a fish eating a sausage.'

That was no help. All the boys I know sound like that when they're talking to adults on the phone.

There is a crashing noise and Dad comes in from the shed carrying a chair. 'Mended it,' he says, looking round for applause that doesn't come. He sits triumphantly on the chair and a leg falls off, leaving him clutching the table for support. 'Still a bit to do, of course,' he says, getting up.

'Got a detention,' I tell Mum. 'Not my fault.'

'Oh, not another one! You shouldn't be getting detentions any more,' she says. 'What was it? Chatting in class again?'

The phone goes and I grab it. Maybe it's fish sausage. But no. It is the horrendous squawk of Craven.

''Allo, sorree, everybody out, all gone, I know nerthing, goorabye,' I say desperately, trying to sound like a childminder from somewhere a long way off.

'Who was that?' asks Mum.

'Just one of my friends taking the piss,' I say, laughing manically.

The phone goes again. I make a grab for it, wondering why on earth Craven is phoning rather than writing, but this time Mum gets there first.

She picks it up, puts on her daft how-nice-to-talk-to-you smile (what she'll be like if she ever gets one of these videophones doesn't bear thinking about), then switches the smile off like a light bulb and glares at me while a fearsome squawking sound comes out of the handset. Eventually the squawking stops, and Mum puts the phone down. She looks pale, and starts to sit down.

'*Don't sit on that!*' Dad and I yell in panic, catching her millimetres from disaster. We move her to another chair while she just stares at me.

'It's not that bad,' I say. 'It was just a joke. My mates were pratting around with a fag in class and I just happened to be nearest when old Fish spotted it, that's all.'

But Mum is still staring at me with a *Night of the Living Dead* expression.

Dad puts the kettle on.

'I'm afraid this is serious,' Mum says to Dad, as if she's reading the railway timetable. What in the name of Tharg's Imperial Underpants can she mean? She chain-smoked herself until last year—

'NEE NAW-NEE NAW-NEE NAW-NEE NAW!' comes a terrible siren sound from the hall. It jerks Dad and me out of the trance that Mum's strange behaviour has sent us into. It's the Puddings, who hurtle into the kitchen in their nurses' outfits bearing a stuffed dog laid out on a stretcher.

'*Not now, girls!*' Mum yells. The anti-terrorist childminder is hot on their heels, looking shaken for once – maybe the Puddings have become immune to the medication.

'NEE NAW-NEE NAW-NEE NAW,' they go in terrible unison, tipping the surprised-looking stuffed dog onto the kitchen table and setting about it with the bread knife.

'*Amy!*' Mum shouts over the din. '*Cigarettes are bad enough but this is just stupid!*'

'Look, Mrs Baker,' the anti-terrorist puts in.

'I wonder if you'd mind paying me – only I've done three extra hours this week and I've got to go now. I've just heard my mother has fallen out of a tree.' I think that's what she said – it was a bit hard to hear.

'*What are you talking about?*' I howl across the room at Mum.

Dad hands the squeaking Puddings a corkscrew and the garlic press.

'There there, puss,' go the Puddings.

'Ngggn mwrds,' says Mum, her voice dropping to an inaudible whisper as she thrusts a fistful of notes at the childminder and shoots a look at the slashing, growling Puddings that would have stopped a prowling tiger.

'*What?*' shout me and Dad together.

Mum's answer is finally understandable at a volume you could hear in the next galaxy. '*Craven says she's taken drugs!*'

The silence goes on for hours. The anti-terrorist smiles nervously, then bolts for the door. The Puddings don't know what's going on, but sense it might be wise to shut up. Dad tries to occupy himself putting his chair together so he can sit down in shock.

'What?' I say for the third time, but very quietly now.

'Mrs Craven says you were smoking cannabis in school,' Mum says. 'She's considering suspending you.'

I am gobsmacked. 'It was just a fag, that's all. She's lying.'

'She says Mr Fish didn't realize what it was,' she continues. 'But she looked in the waste bin after school. It was a joint.'

I realize to my horror that I didn't take that close a look at it, and with my cold I didn't smell it either.

'Say something, Harry,' Mum says to Dad. 'Don't just sit there.'

He's not sitting, exactly. He's crouching in the position he would be in if the chair would carry him, so as not to draw attention to himself.

'I'd be the first to say a Catholic upbringing isn't perfect, but I do feel it did some things for me that maybe I should have passed on to you . . .' He eventually begins the speech he's been making since before the dinosaurs were computer-generated. 'It does teach you some things are right and some things are wrong. And, um' – he throws me a rather desperate look – 'if this is true it's a daft thing to do, Amaryllis,' he winds up rather lamely, and from his crouching position he doesn't look all that threatening, of course.

'It isn't true,' I protest. 'I swear it.'

'So is Mrs Craven making it up?' Mum says.

'Well, no . . . I was protecting someone else.'

'Then you've got to tell her, Amy,' says Mum, softening.

'I can't, she'll be excluded.'

'Well what can we do? It's not as if it's the first time you've been in trouble. You get detentions every other week for silly behaviour, don't you? You're doing so well in English, I'm sure you could do better in everything else if you pulled your socks up.'

'Yes, but you've got to believe me, I did not smoke that joint, honest. I promise you I didn't even realize it *was* a joint. I can hardly smell a thing with this cold.'

'Well, I believe you, Amy, but Mrs Craven won't unless you say who it was.'

'I can't do that.'

'Well, then surely you can let me tell her – that way your friend won't blame you.'

'This girl is *not* my friend. But honestly, Mum, telling on her would be more or less like murder—'

'But Mrs Craven insists something has to be done about it. She says she'll suspend you! Unless—'

Faaaartttttt! comes a quiet noise from the Puddings, turning the now unstuffed dog over and beginning to operate on its rear end.

'Unless what, Mum?'

Mum suddenly looks a lot brighter. I can almost see the old light bulb of wisdom looming above her head.

'Look, I've thought of something. Suppose we say we're taking it very seriously and that we'll ground you for a month. Maybe she'll accept that—'

'But you can't do that!' I say, panicking. 'I didn't do anything except help someone out.'

'Yes, but if you don't say who it was she won't believe you. If we do nothing, she might even exclude you – you know KFC has a zero-tolerance policy on drugs . . .'

Try telling that to the kids who smoke in the loos, I thought grimly.

'It's the least we can do, don't you agree, Harry?'

'Ummphh,' goes Dad, nodding.

A horrible, cold, clammy feeling breaks out all over me.

'She was only trying to save someone else,' says Dad.

'Yes, but on top of all those other detentions and doing band practice instead of homework . . . We do have to do something, Amy, to help you see sense and get your exams—'

'You . . . you . . . can't,' I say. 'I have to sing at the Valentine's party. It's my one chance to make something of my miserable insignificant life.'

'You should have thought of that before,' Mum says, as if it's final. Which it obviously is.

Thursday February 6

So now I am grounded.

I have to be back by five every night for a *month*. And that's after one hour's detention which old Craven has slapped on top.

I didn't think Mum and Dad meant it really, but I can see they have to keep it up in case a teacher spots me. I can also see Mum was trying to save me from exclusion.

The worst thing was the disappointed looks that Moony and Ms Corman threw me.

I could of course just tell Mum who really put

that spliff on my desk. But then she'd tell Crazy Craven. And stupid Tracey Hardwick would really be headfirst down the pan then.

What a moron from hell she is – fancy taking a joint into Fish's lesson.

I can't drop Tracey in it now, it's too late, and everybody thinks I'm a saint for it.

But I'm not going to miss that Valentine's party either.

CHAPTER THREE

In Which Amy's Life Is Still Over, and That's Just the Beginning . . .

Friday February 7

Lottie rang up because some brats in Year Seven have been baiting her about her name being an anagram of 'toilet'.

'It's not as if I didn't know,' she said. 'But rhyming with grotty and spotty and snotty *and* being an anagram of toilet gets you down sometimes.'

'There are worse things,' was all I can think of to say.

2 a.m.

Maniacal crack dealers over the road still screeching up and down all night. I think they are running other funny business too as guys keep going in with dodgy-looking women.

Saturday February 8

Sunday February 9

Days drag by like snails pulled by sloths powered by very small solar panels in winter.

FEELGOOD TIP

Create some 'me' time for yourself.

Oh, sure. I'm too busy, that's it. I spend too much time out with the guys and girls instead of mooching round my room 24/7.

The Valentine party is the day after tomorrow. So is Valentine's Day. Will I get any cards?

The boy who sounds like a fish eating a sausage has rung twice. I have been out *both* times, which is pathetic, given that I'm now never out. The only out I have been, apart from doomy Class Ten A 'Your mock mocks are only weeks away', is taking Gandhi to the vet ('Sorry, Mr Mammal, I think he may have been eating too much marmalade') and taking the Puddings' videos back to the video shop ('Sorry, Mrs Tape, my sisters were trying to give Mary Poppins her breakfast and they thought if they put some marmalade in the video machine she would be able to eat it').

Anyway, doesn't fish sausage know about mobiles? (Who can possibly be ringing me who doesn't know my mobile number???)

I asked Mum to do 1471 if anyone rings me, but she says she is above all that and if people can't be polite enough to leave their name then she is not going to scurry around all hours after them. Scurry around? All hours? Was she ever young?

Lottie and Debbie and Mad Alice don't believe I'm going to get to the party, but they've been practising like loonies in case I do. Elsie has given up on me though, and booked stupid tone-deaf because-I'm-worth-it Xanthia, the Atomic Moron. Good old Lottie has got an old T-shirt and painted TOILET on it in dripping green and brown letters, just to show she's risen above it.

11 p.m.

Crazy Craven should be put in a ducking stool like witches of old.

How would she like being in poor old Tracey H's shoes?

But she has probably always been a teachery person. I bet she would have gone off and told on a starving crippled orphan nicking Smarties from a millionaire.

She should realize I am a noble person defending the innocent.

But of course she doesn't know I am defending loony Hardwick. I will have to tell her.

But if I tell, then I will not be noble any more.

Thursday February 13

Fluttery feeling in bottom of stomach. I don't catch any cute boys winking at me on the way home from school and carrying large envelopes or big gold boxes with bows on to the post box.

Our own letter box at home is a very small, pathetic, weedy one. Plead with Dad to DIY a new big one before post comes in the morning. 'Why?' is all he says. Tell him why. Look of awful panic comes over him, and he looks frantically at his watch. 'Woolworths!' he shouts, and hurtles out the door. No wonder my parents' relationship is not what it was.

> ## FAMILY CAN BE FRIENDS TOO TIP
> ### If you want to get round your parents, schmooze up to them.
>
> Have been schmoozing all week, but it cuts no ice.

Hatch Plan B with Lottie, which will involve me pretending to be ill, going to bed early and locking bedroom door. Then I climb out the window. Only problem is no lock on my door. So much for privacy.

Midnight

I am sure fish sausage will send me one. Am pretty sure fish sausage is Flubber, in fact. He will be sending me a card to say Xanthia is like a sparse Twiglet compared to the *voluptuous* chocolate cake that is me.

Friday February 14

Valentine's Day!

Leap up at crack of eight o'clock. Race downstairs. Mum is in kitchen, actually singing – a strange, mad sound, like a piano being tuned. There are flowers on the kitchen table, hooray! Curses – on closer inspection there's a note in very badly disguised Dad writing, saying,

To darling Puffball, from yr secret admirer.

It's just undignified, parents doing this kind of thing – they'll be having sex next. The flowers look a bit sad, as if Dad might have found them in a skip, but Mum seems happy enough. Lucky for some.

'Any post?' I ask casually.

'Afraid not, dear,' Mum says, only half there. 'Sorry you haven't got any cards – they'll all realize what they're missing one of these years.'

She can be so comforting, unfeeling daft old loony.

'They're saving them for the Valentine's party tonight,' I say defiantly. 'Dear nice wonderful kindly Mum, let me go, please. Surely one night won't matter?'

'You must be joking,' Mum says. 'I happen to know that party's at Elsie Crabtree's house. Her older brother's been done by the police for possession and the parents don't even mind. It would be like sending an alcoholic to a pub. Certainly not.'

I'd forgotten about that. Elsie's parents are old hippies. Well, there's nothing for it but Plan B. I call Lottie while Mum and Dad are giggling over their Valentine messages in the kitchen – yuksville, pukerama and so on – and tell her I'm getting out whatever happens.

Lottie promises to do everything she can to help. I've hardly put the phone down when Mum and Dad come out hand in hand and tell me I'm look-ing after the Puddings tonight because they're now going out for a candlelit dinner, staring into each other's eyes by the 20W electric candlelight of the Crudsville Tandoori. Aaaargh! How can Life do things like this?

4.30

Plotted with Black Hole all day and hope Plan C –
getting a babysitter – will work. Try Kath, who
works as a cleaner at KFC, and used to be my
favourite babysitter when I was little. But she's
going out for a Valentine's Night supper.
Surely Valentine's Night is for the Young?

Haha! Something has come – delivered by hand.
A card! A humungous pink envelope to Ms A.
Baker! Race upstairs with the wings of thingy and
rip it open.

    Tharg's Underpants!

    Pudding Two has a boyfriend. And I don't. How
sad is that?

6.30

I have been ringing babysitters every spare moment
and guess what? They are all going out for
Valentine's Night.

> ## COOL DUDE TIP
> Are you a chilled-out, blue-jeans type girl? Try leaving dark blue polish on your nails for three minutes, then take a damp cloth and press it over the polish. Boyakasha! Denim-look nails!
>
> Do not use crap fuzzy cloth for this, your nails will look like Sylvanian families.

Lottie, Debbie and Mad Alice are bobbing about in the garden, trying to see through the windows if Dad and Mum have gone out yet. I'm amazed they're not spotted – it's like having a female *Wayne's World* being performed under your nose without noticing it. The Puddings are watching a video of *Little Red Riding Hood* but switching over to *Casualty* every time calamitous parents go out of the room. At last they're in the hall, putting on coats.

'Don't wait up, Amy,' says Mum. 'We might get a bit tied up.' They wink at each other again. I make mental note to get in big consignment of sick bags if this sort of thing is going to go on. At last the front door slams shut, exactly coinciding with the sound of the back door bursting open and Lottie, Debbie and Mad Alice hurtling in, singing at the tops of their lungs.

'*Shut up!*' I hiss at them. 'They may be mad, but they're not deaf.'

'What are you going to do about those two?' Lottie asks, looking at the Puddings, who have *Casualty* back on and their noses pressed against the screen, trying to get the full details of a parent's head being transplanted onto their baby to save its life or something.

'We'll have to take them with us,' I say, surprised at how quickly this horrific option comes to me. 'There's no other way.'

'That's going to be great for the element of surprise, innit?' says Debbie, examining herself sideways in the hall mirror and nodding approvingly at the silhouette of her bum. 'The party's been going for an hour already and the Atomic Moron is probably wiggling her way to the microphone at this minute.'

'Where's the kit?' I ask Lottie, attempting to gather up the wriggling Puddings. 'Shut up moaning, will you?' I tell them. 'They've got a much bigger telly where we're going – you can see all the blood and insides as if it was a real hospital.'

'It *is* real oppital!' they both squeak reproachfully.

'We left it with Elsie's brother Greg and his

41

mates – Xanthia was there polishing her belly-stud so we didn't want to hang around looking suspicious,' Lottie says. 'They were a bit stoned, but they said they'd set it up somehow without giving the game away. Elsie knows, but she reckons the Atomic Moron will flounce off with the agg if she finds out, then if we don't make it she'll be left with nothing.'

'Can you catch that one?' I shout at Mad Alice. Pudding Two is attempting to make an escape upstairs. Mad Alice, who has painted her face completely white except for a scarlet gash of a mouth and blood-red rings around her eyes, gathers up Pudding Two and gives her a smile that would freeze hell over. Pudding Two wails and screws her knuckles into her eyes. I hoist Pudding One onto my shoulders and we rocket out the back door and over the garden fence under the apple tree, which unfortunately lifts Pudding One from my shoulders and leaves her flapping and revolving on a branch, like a screaming mobile.

'Leave her,' pants Mad Alice, grimacing at the now punching, biting Pudding Two.

'Are you mad?' I wail, running back to the tree.

'Course,' says Mad Alice, smiling insanely.

With Pudding One back on my shoulders, we run chaotically down the road. Lottie has by now brilliantly silenced the furious Puddings by narrating her idea of what happens next in *Casualty*, which I reckon is much better than the original, even if half incomprehensible through her gasps. In Lottie's

version, there has been a ghastly mistake, somebody has had two brains grafted onto where their
kidneys should be, so when they go for a wee,
nothing comes out but the noise of a lot of swearing in Kazakhstani and Glaswegian. Meanwhile the
original kidneys have found their way onto the
menu of hospital kitchens, and it's a race against
time to track them down before dinner. The
Puddings are completely silent by the time we get
to the back of Elsie's house. More than can be said
for the inside of it, which is heaving with the roars
of rampant male voices and the whining, Essex-
American Britney twang of the dreaded Xanthia,
obviously in full unmusical drone.

Elsie's older brother Greg and his mate Elf are at
the back door, both of them almost invisible in a
cloud of ganja smoke.

'Hello, girls,' Greg says with a where-are-we?
smile. 'Now for some real music. Come upstairs.'

'Upstairs?' we all say at once. 'But the party's
downstairs.'

'That's exactly right,' Greg says, as if it's obvious.
'But we had to set your stuff up so the Queen of
Pop didn't notice.'

'Don't you like her?' I ask Greg, running up the
back staircase and wincing as Pudding One,
screaming at Lottie to keep up the story, digs her
sharp fingernails into my skull. I suddenly realize
Greg looks rather cool in his tight jeans, and there
seems to be more of him in his T-shirt than I
remember.

'Nah,' Greg says. 'It's all poncing about, it's not music. And now – *viola*!'

Viola? I think he must mean *voilà*!

We arrive panting on the landing and he whips a sheet off a mysterious object the size of a sofa. It's Lottie's drum kit and all our instruments, wires trailing around like spaghetti.

'Climb aboard,' says Greg.

The party is deafening now, but all eyes are on the Atomic Moron downstairs, and nobody's seen us yet – except for Elsie, who turns and waves with a huge smile of relief.

'Now read on!' Lottie shouts at the Puddings, pointing to a wide-screen telly in Elsie's parents' bedroom. With a delighted squeal, the Puddings scuttle towards it.

'Boyakasha!' shout Greg and Elf together as we take our positions. We haven't even had a chance to find out if we're in tune. Not that it usually bothers Mad Alice. Anyway, what are we doing up—

HEEEEEEERE!!!!!!!!!!!!!!!!!

Greg and Elf have given us a push – which is when we find out we're standing on a decorators' table that's been strapped to four skateboards and we're now hurtling downstairs, drum kit and all, towards the party, like a pod-racer with no brakes. We arrive at the bottom with an awesome crash, followed by a spooky silence while we try to work out if we're alive, and then a huge cheer from the party when the euro finally drops. Mad Alice gets her wits together first (there are fewer to collect, and

44

anyway things like this just seem normal to her) and wheels her arms in a huge power-chord, which just comes out as a feeble twanging sound. But at the other end of the room the Atomic Moron is just in the middle of going, 'Hit me, sweetie, one more ti—' when the sound cuts out, to be replaced by the last blood-curdling howl of Mad Alice's power-chord. Somebody has pulled the plugs on the Moron and plugged us in instead. Reeling a bit from concussion but sensing it's now or never, we blast into our opening number, *Corpses Can Be Lonely Too*.

We've been better prepared for gigs – there's now a jagged hole in the front of Lottie's bass drum, and Debbie's bass keeps untuning so it sounds like a tape playing very slowly – but the excitement has given us all a buzz, and I find myself singing as if I don't care what happens or what anybody thinks. As we finish one number, they all cheer for another, and after six we've run out and have to start again. I also realize quite a few of the boys have got very close to us, and some of them are looking at me in a way I haven't seen before.

Finally, they let us off. Greg puts his arms round me and gives me a big kiss. I feel dizzy as soon as he breathes out – where does he get that stuff from? People get us drinks, ask us if we're going to make an album, go on about how long it must have taken to plan that entrance, ahem. Lottie is surrounded by wannabe drummers, girls and boys. Debbie is soon in a corner with somebody – all I can see of him is a pair of hands on her bum: they always home straight in on it. Mad Alice is whacking back the alco-pops and cackling.

'Amy! Didn't know you could sing like that.' I turn round and it is Flubber, looking smouldery.

Just about to smoulder back when the Atomic Moron oozes her way through the group of chattering boys around me, lazily pulling her top over her head and smooching to herself, 'My Gaaad, it's so hot in here.' She gives me as much of a smile as hatred and make-up allow. 'That was really cool, *Amyryllis*,' she croons. 'But somebody should ring the social services about your poor sisters.'

My God! The Puddings! I race upstairs to the bedrooms. They're in each other's arms in front of a blank telly screen, weeping buckets.

'Couldn't turn it on!' they howl, turning dementedly towards me. 'Nobody listen to us! Hobble music too loud!'

I can hear the noise of the party in full swing downstairs. This is my moment. I could be somebody. But this is all my fault too. I'm their big sister. I dragged them here. It's just not right.

'All right, babes,' I whisper to them, gathering one under each arm. 'I'll tell you a story.'

I'm not sure how long the story went on. It seemed like hours. I even started to drift off, overwhelmed by the cloud of Greg's ganja, which seemed to be everywhere, and all the emotion of the night. But then I suddenly realized somebody was in the room.

'That's a nice sight,' said a voice. 'Babes in the wood.'

Tom Carpenter.

The Easter Bunny picnic thingy. The years rolled away. I felt eleven.

He was silhouetted in the doorway against the light on the landing, but I felt as though I would have recognized him in twenty, or even fifty years' time.

He came and sat down beside us. My heart was somersaulting. I got two cushions for the Puddings' heads, and extricated myself.

'Don't do that for me,' he said. I flinched like a nervous kitten.

'Don't worry, I'm house-trained . . . almost.' He smiled. Yikes. 'You're Amy, aren't you? I bet you don't remember me. Are you feeling OK?' he asked me, almost as if it might have mattered to him. 'Your band was fantastic. I'd heard you were in one, but I didn't know you were that good.'

Heard I was in one? Had he been asking about me? I think I must have left my mouth open so long I started dribbling. I could feel myself staring at him as though he was a Being from an Alternative Zone in the dream world of my head. Say something, I thought.

Hmmm. Hmm. Something like 'Hem hem nyaaaf weasel' is what came out, I think.

What I meant to say was, Yep, I'm fine, thanks. Great night. Marvellous party. Just came up here to chill out and catch up on a bit of Tolstoy. Of course,

I do this kind of thing a lot, in between studying to be a brain surgeon. But 'Hem hem nyaaaf weasel' was what came out.

And the Being from an Alternative Zone laughed. Which is when I fell in love.

They say it does happen like that, sometimes. It was his dimple, I think. Or had it really happened four years before, when he gave me the egg? Whatever, I wanted him to like me more than I've ever wanted anything else and I felt suddenly horribly vulnerable.

'You think I'm a no-brain because I sing in a band,' I said, gathering the Puddings closer.

'No I don't,' he said. 'I think it's probably just the stress of early motherhood.'

'Well, they are a bit of a flex,' I said to him. 'What with staying up all night crying over *The Lion King*, keeping the cement mixer going that does their meals, going on at the social services to get me a bigger flat, table-dancing in the evenings so as to be able to buy them bootees . . .'

'How old were you when you had them – thirteen?' Tom asks, examining the Puddings with a critical eye.

'Six,' I say. 'They're older than they look.'

'OK,' he says. 'Still, I imagine they're a great comfort to you.'

'Oh yes,' I say. 'When I'm in the old people's

home I'll be able to know they're just down the corridor.'

'Gerble gerbil blurble,' I thought he said. But it was just the Puddings, murmuring in their sleep.

We spent the next half hour going on like that. It's surprising how much meaning you can pack into thirty minutes of solid gibberish. Then I noticed the time.

'Oh no!' I squawked. 'I'm supposed to be at home! My folks'll get back and think we've all been abducted by perverts!'

'You have,' he says, leaning over and giving me a very gentle kiss on the cheek. I nearly died on the spot. Feelings flooded through me that I'd never felt before. Panic and passion are a weird mixture though. I suddenly found myself crying and giggling at the same time.

'You don't understand!' I wailed. 'How am I supposed to get these two home – teleport them?'

'We'll manage,' Tom says, getting up. I couldn't help noticing, even in the flap I was in, and before he hurriedly turned his back, that the front of his jeans looked, um, alert. My God, why? I was just the same me as usual, maybe even dumber- and madder-looking. I couldn't imagine what had happened to my make-up in the sweatbox downstairs. I wasn't even showing any cleavage. Aaaargh! Why did I have to be stuck with this Cinderella routine and two snuffling baby seals to take care of? Why couldn't love run free?

But Tom scooped up Pudding One while I

collected Pudding Two, both of them still out like lights. We edged out onto the landing.

'I don't want to see anybody,' I hissed to Tom. 'I feel such a loonologist like this.'

Nobody would have noticed us anyway. The sound system was deafening and I just spotted Lottie, with what looked like one lens of her glasses broken, hammering away on the drums along with it, yelling drunks stumbling around her and waving their arms in the air. Elsie's hippy parents were back and doing some kind of terrible *Saturday Night Fever* dance. A couple of boys were trying to give what looked like the kiss of life to the Atomic Moron, who was crashed out on the sofa. Mad Alice and a throng of guys were watching *Match of the Day* in a corner and waving beer bottles. We crept along the landing. I spotted Debbie entangled with somebody in a bedroom and wondered stupidly for a second why I could see a bare leg when she'd come in jeans. *Caramba!* Had she passed her GCSEs in willy aerobics after all?

'Hey, it's Danny!' Tom exclaimed. 'Hi, Danny . . .'

I pulled him away. We staggered down the back stairs, trying more or less successfully not to bang the Puddings' heads on the banisters. Then we got outside, hoisted them onto our shoulders and ran for it.

'Werwerwerwerwerwerwer,' went the Puddings rhythmically in their sleep, bumping up and down unconsciously.

Two streets from my house I realized there was a

car dawdling along the kerb beside us. Oh no! The cops!

'Evenin',' came a voice from the car. 'Where you off to with them, then?'

I was dumbstruck. My mouth flapped open and shut. 'Eeeargh. Errghhh. Ummmmm . . .' was what came out.

'Hello, Mr Crawley,' Tom said. 'It's Tom, Dr Carpenter's son. How are you?'

Bandidos Yanquis! Why was he telling a policeman who he was? I wanted to get the Puddings home safely, not be arrested!

'Oh, hello, lad. Didn't recognize you at first,' the policeman said. The car stopped. 'Does your dad know about your family?' he asked Tom, laughing. Tom laughed too – usual boys' stuff.

'This is my friend Amy,' he said. 'She was babysitting her sisters but they escaped. They're very adventurous. I helped her round them up.'

'Bring 'em down the nick next time you're babysitting,' the policeman said to me. 'We'll make sure they don't get out.' He and Tom laughed a lot again and I tried joining it but I don't think it sounded as good.

'We'll give you a lift home,' the policeman said. 'Hop in the back.'

'Oh no, I . . . I mean . . .' I spluttered. But it was too late, the policeman was firmly ushering us in. We scrambled the Puddings in on our laps and Pudding One woke up, looking around in amazement.

'Neenaw-neenaw-neenaw,' she said.

'Oh, you live *here*, do you?' said the policeman as we turned into our estate. 'Don't worry, love, we're chucking that lot out tomorrow. Guy in our traffic department has just moved into this street, says he can't get a wink of sleep.'

Is this what community policing means?

The crack house wasn't looking at its best. A woman in a bra seemed to be trying to swallow a guy in a baseball cap in an upstairs window ('What they doing?' Pudding One asked, to complete silence) and a group by the open front door were pushing and shoving and shouting at each other. When they saw us, the woman upstairs wrapped a curtain round herself and the group at the door started slapping each other on the back and laughing as if they hadn't a care in the world.

But our timing couldn't have been worse. Mum and Dad were turning in at the front gate, arm in arm, when we pulled up outside. They looked round at us, stunned.

'Amaryllish!' Mum finally squealed, originally. 'What on earthsh happened?'

'Amaryllis?' said Tom, crinkling his crinkly mouth in a crinkly smile and dimpling his dimply dimple.

Curses. Even aged eleven, I only ever admitted to Amy.

'It's OK, it's OK,' I gabbled. Fortunately some small smart part of my brain realized mouth-flapping time had to stop. 'The girls ran away but they're fine now, it's all fine!'

'No we dint,' began Pudding One indignantly, 'we—'

I pulled her hoodie around her face protectively. 'Ssssh now,' I hissed at her, 'you'll get pneumonia if you're not careful.'

Tom extended a hand to Dad and smiled a big dazzling smile at Mum. 'Hello, I'm Tom, Dr Carpenter's son.'

'Oh. Hellooo,' simpered Mum, pukeanimously, winking at me in a very obvious way.

'I found the girls in our guinea-pig hutch,' Tom told her. Oh, perleeease. 'But Amy was right on their tail. She's been a real star. Officer Crawley kindly gave us a lift back.'

'Glad to have been of service,' the policeman said, getting back in the car. 'You've got a couple of little explorers there. Probably win the round-the-world yacht race or something one day. Goodnight.'

He drove off. Dad and Mum seemed in an oddly good mood despite all this fuss. Amazingly, they asked Tom in.

'Thanks, but I'd better go,' he said, handing over the sleeping Pudding Two to Dad. 'Got to be up for church in the morning.'

Don't push it, I thought to myself.

'On Saturday?' said Dad.

'Family wedding,' he said.

'Do come round and shee ush on Shunday, then,' Mum slurred. Lordy, she was pissed as a fruit-fly.

'That would be nice,' Tom said, and smiled a knee-watering smile at me as he went.

'I don't believe a word of it about the girlsh,' Mum hiccupped as we went inside. 'But Dad and I

were only shaying tonight what a wonderful thing
Valentine'sh Day can be – it makesh you think
about the more important thingsh in life. Maybe
we've been a bit hard on you lately. You didn't
take them anywhere nashty, did you?'

'No, of course not,' I lied. 'We just went to
Tom's house and played Twister.'

'Shweet,' said Mrs Mum.

I breathed a big sigh of relief.

Saturday February 15

'That would be nice.'

Does that mean he thinks it would be nice? To
come round?

What does he mean by *nice*?

Dictionary definition of *Nice*: 'Fastidious,
dainty, hard to please'. Or: 'Agreeable, attractive,
delightful . . .'

Or did he mean, 'Yeah, sure, we'll meet up again
sometime maybe. Nice if we do, nice if we don't.'

Or maybe, 'That would be nice if your daughter
looked like Xanthia Starr, Mrs Baker, but in the
circumstances she finds herself, that is, if you'll
forgive my saying so, somewhat vertically and
horizontally challenged and with Van Gogh's ear
for music, I'm afraid I should decline your kind
invitation.'

Tharg. We didn't even swap mobile numbers.

CHAPTER FOUR

In Which Days Fly By Like Violaceous Euphonias (Don't Ask)

<u>**Sunday February 16**</u>

He came round, he came round. He came roundetty round.

'Amaryllis!' screamed Dad. 'Your boyfriend's here.'

Time to go through floor without a paddle.

I had not spent that long getting ready, as it happens – only about an hour.

Before I could grab Tom to go out for a walk (anything rather than hang round the marmalade hell that is our house) the ancients had ushered him into the kitchen for 'a nice cup of tea'.

To my horror, I noticed Mum was wearing lippy.

'How was the wedding?' asked Dad.

'Good,' said Tom, with the merest hint of a blush suffusing his manly wotsits.

'And how is your father? Such a wonderful GP,' simpered Mum, her eyelashes flapping like bat's wings.

'Good,' smiled Tom. 'Have you got something in your eye, Mrs Baker?'

Half Term

The crack dealers are gone!

There are teams of council workers fumigating the place!

Everyone in our street has been out looting the skips.

Mum is over the moon. And not only because she got a pair of red brocade curtains and an MFI coffee table.

'They'll clean up lovely,' she hummed. 'I do hope someone respectable moves in . . .'

Midnight

Just back from moonlit walk with Tom.

He is like my handsomer, cleverer twin.

Text from Lottie: WHERE WERE YOU?

Oops, forgotten we were going to see Johnny Depp's latest.

Days fly by like Violaceous Euphonias. (That is an actual real bird. Tom told me. That is the kind of person he is. He knows about a bird called a Violaceous Euphonia.)

I have seen Tom *every day* this week. What is great about being with him is I don't have to play it cool, pretend to be out or washing my hair or any of that stuff you're supposed to do to keep your man interested, like it says in *Teenacious Tips*. Really, that book is for the emotionally-challenged.

Violaceous Euphonia: The female is inconspicuously coloured green (JEALOUSY)

We don't need snogging lessons. All that stuff I used to worry about with Flubber – how you decide which way to turn your head, whether to flutter your tongue like a harp-string or stick it in and hope he doesn't bite, when to throw your head back and look ecstatic – it all just seems to take care of itself. Once you're in the middle of it with somebody who feels like a part of you you'd lost a long time ago and suddenly found again – well, nothing could be easier.

'But perhaps the difference is just to do with the way you feel about someone,' I said to Lottie.

'But you really fancied Flubber, don't pretend you didn't.'

'Hmmmm. But that was just lust. I think.'

'So you don't really fancy Tom then?' She sounded rather eager.

'Fancying is too weak a word, Lottie. I have to think of a new one.'

Have been thinking. I think it is 'crave'. I crave Tom.

Its song is a rapid warble (humpf!)

Friday February 21

11 p.m.

Just when things are as good as they can be, they get better.

Tom is really the handsomest boy I have ever seen. This is not just the eyes of love and rose-tinted specs. I said to him, I always thought great-looking boys had to have great-looking girlfriends, the kind with legs like giraffes, eyes like oceans peeping mysteriously through luxuriant rainforests of hair and all that.

And he said that wasn't true.

Thanks a lot, said I. (Did he mean it wasn't true that he was great looking? Or did he mean that I was a dog?)

Then he said the following, and I am going to write it down so I never forget it ever.

'There's something else that makes you . . . that makes you . . . love someone sometimes. I think it's the soul.'

He said the L word.

The female lays three or four eggs and broods alone . . .

Midnight

But I've had a bit too much talk about the soul in my life to be sure about this, what with my dad being a lapsed Catholic. I sometimes think he still believes in it all really, or at least believes they'll get him if he doesn't.

He has been trying to talk to me all week about Tom and 'being careful' and 'not rushing into anything', and reminding me I am only fifteen.

'I'm not a fool, Dad,' I said. 'I didn't do anything silly with Flubber and I won't do anything silly with Tom.'

But I am thinking, even as I say it, What is 'silly'? And wasn't Shakespeare's Juliet only thirteen?

And maybe it is true about the Soul. I don't

know how else to describe that feeling that you're
on exactly the same wavelength as someone else.

Finally gave in and told Debs and Alice about
Tom. I wasn't going to at first, I don't know
why. I would have thought before this happened
that I'd want to put it on the national news, but
somehow it seemed private now. We were in the
middle of a rehearsal at Simon the Stockbroker's
house. Poor old Mad Alice lives there now, since
her mum married Simon, and it's very posh
and tidy and un-Mad Alice. Her black-painted
bedroom with Hendrix, the stoned parrot, is a
haven of insanity in a swamp of bourgeois bore-
dom. I wasn't going to say a word until Alice,
who is a lot sharper than she lets on sometimes,
suddenly said:

'Whashappenintoyou? Are you on something?'
'Love.'
That shut them up for about a minute and a half.
Then it was the usual – who where what how far?
I had to swear them all to secrecy on our mothers'
lives, though in Mad Alice's case that means less
than it might to some people. If this kind of news
gets round at KFC your life isn't worth living.

'I *know* him,' Debbie said. 'He was at that party.
Phwoar.'

'How do you know who was there?' Lottie asked
her. 'You had your entire head inside that guy's

60

mouth all night.' Lottie was looking distinctly grumpy.

'Piss off,' Debbie said, smiling to herself.

'Piss off!' instructed Hendrix.

'We need more than six tunes,' Lottie said snappishly. 'I reckon we should appoint Amy the songwriter. She's got to sing them, and these days she's going round singing every minute of the day. Of course, that's if she's got *time* to write a song.'

I was only too happy to agree.

'Nothing lovey-dovey, mind,' she added, as if I didn't know. Black Hole is not one of those droopy girly bands with a row of blondes gyrating to a harpist.

Lottie was grumperoony times ten on the way home. She skulked along kicking a pebble, like she used to in primary school.

'What's up, Lotts?' I asked, in my nicest BF tones, after about a century of silent pebble-kicking.

'Nothing,' she grumped. 'What makes you think something's up?'

'Your mop,' I said tactfully. I mean, it wasn't looking like a depressed mouse exactly, more like a homicidal shrew.

'My *mop*?' she screeched.

'Oh come on, Lottiekins,' I wheedled. 'Not boy trouble?'

'Oh no, not *boy* trouble – oh no. Nothing like that for me,' she huffed.

Whoops.

I haven't been paying enough attention to my BF.
And I am too happy to care.

*It can sing for minutes – a sweet,
high-pitched song (that's more like it)*

Sunday February 23

Why is it you think someone is absolutely amazingly
beautiful, when they're probably not? Or not in the
way that film stars are.

Tom really is beautiful. Handsome. Scrumptious.
But the weirdest thing is that I am beautiful to
Tom.

He likes my freckles!

He even likes my giant's feet.

'Who needs little feet?' he said. 'Little feet are
not useful. They are more likely to get stuck in
drains, for instance. Anyway, yours are not giant's
feet. They are more like ugly sister's feet. With
Cinderella on top, of course.'

Well, he had to add that bit.

I have a zit the size of a ping-pong ball on my
chin and instead of recoiling as if a pulsating red
insect was flying towards him, he kissed it!

He kissed my spot.

I had to phone Lottie about the spot-kissing event.

'Lottie,' I said, 'you won't believe this, but he has kissed my spot.'

There was one of those phone silences that are a lot more silent than face-to-face silences. I listened to it, trying to work out the meaning. I did not have to be a rocket scientist to know that I was getting boring about Tom. And that the person I was boring most was Lottie. But surely she would like the spot-kissing story, wouldn't she?

'Look, Lottie,' I said, 'I'm sorry if this is making you jealous. I know it doesn't happen to everyone, but it's happened to me. And it's . . . it's making me so happy.'

The silence got louder and then this little ant voice came on the line.

'Mmmmm. Good. Got to go.'

Oooh dear.

Monday February 24

Kenneth Frances Comprehensive is no place for young love.

Ms Corman, my absolute favourite teacher, shamed me by asking why I had written Tom instead of Romeo in three places in my English essay.

Nombre del perro! I didn't even know I had. I told Ms Corman I was experimenting to see if Spokeshave's famous saying, 'What's in a name?' was actually *cojones* or not. My conclusion from this research was that *Romeo and Juliet* wouldn't lose too much from being called *Tom and Amy* but *Eric and Barbara* might be pushing it. Ms Corman wasn't fooled, of course, but she wasn't cross either.

 She is so completely brilliant, she reads Chaucer aloud as easily as if it was Humpty Dumpty and speaks five languages as well as Latin and Greek. I sometimes think, if I don't make it as a musician, or a writer, I will try to be a teacher like her. She is one of those rare teachers who make you feel like working hard.

PE is no place for young love.

I need a note to say my hair is a bunch of glossy black grapes (thank you, Tom) that does not need to drown in the local baths. But Mum will only write notes for 'women's troubles'.

'*Cut* the pizza, put it in your pocket. *Cut* the pizza, put it in your pocket,' goes old Beelzebub. She is trying to get us to improve our crawl technique, I think, but we are too busy laughing.

I think it is very dangerous how schools always get loonies to teach PE. You could drown by laughing.

10 p.m.

The new neighbour and her ridiculous small dog have been moving into the Cracked House today.

Bleached hair and a crop-top, and she's a crone of at least forty – where do they find these people?

Dad wandered over during the afternoon to see if he could help the two knackered-looking slaves in overalls who were humping her stuff around while she flashed what looked like an expensively whitened smile at them and examined her fingernails. He came back what seemed like hours later, saying he'd just stopped 'for a cup of tea and a chat'.

'She's an actress,' he said at tea. 'Such a hard life. She's got the sweetest little dog.'

I thought Dad hated dogs.

Have spent three hours washing up and tidying kitchen.

Why can I never get any time for myself?

Mum told me I do not lift a finger to help and I said I have my mock mocks to do, which is what I always say and it usually works.

'Of course, Carpenters are intelligent and may not need so much revision time as Bakers. But that doesn't mean they should lead them astray,' she said. Has she gone mad? Oh. Tom Carpenter. Very funny. Funny. Very.

'And there's my song-writing,' I said.

'Oh yes. That's in the family, you know. Ruined Great-Auntie Bea's life.'

'What?'

Turns out Mum's great-uncle Bob was a Cockney pearly king who used to pen songs instead of earning a living and broke his pearly queeny wife's heart.

Good heavens, I knew I had royal blood.

It is almost impossible to get encrusted marmalade off the back of taps. Why did Mum leave it there so long?

7.30

Have only been out with Tom *once this week*.

Well, there have only been two days this week, I suppose.

But his parents say he isn't allowed out much now he's studying so hard for his five (yes, five) AS levels.

His folks sound like slave drivers to me.

But it is very unfair to have to do homework and tidying up when you are in love.

Have been tidying up all evening again.

'Why doesn't Dad help?'

'Oh, he's helping the new woman over the road install her washing machine,' says Mum.

11.30

Dad has just come in singing.

Midnight

At weekends, Tom and I are now like a pair of gloves – no, a wetsuit. A hot wetsuit. We are Olympic kissing champions. Last night Mum was at WeightWatchers and Dad was working late, so we snogged while we babysat the Puddings ('Millis superglued to Tom-tom – why you kicking us, Millis?' they chanted over breakfast the next morning). We have canoodled in every caff for miles around. No couple can ever have made one latte last longer. We have snogged in parks and cinemas and buses and alleyways and ice rinks and pizza parlours. Sometimes we come up for air and just look at each other, hardly able to speak.

Funny thing is I'm not just learning more and more about him, but more and more about *me* – it's like meeting myself all over again. I talk to him about books and characters I feel I know. I told him about my rewrite of Tolstoy's *Anna Karenina*. And guess what? He hadn't read it.

'It's a wicked book,' I told him, 'but it has the usual doomy I-told-you-so ending for any woman who likes fun – poor old Anna hurls herself in front of a train because her jealous hubby won't let her have it off with Vronski, the love of her life.'

'Ooooh. Sad. So you rescued her?'

'Naturally. I rewrote it as an episode of *The Simpsons*, in which Anna discovers she and Vronski have won the lottery with a ticket she thought he'd torn up in a fit of dark despair . . .'

'So they open a chain of fast-food restaurants, and win the undying gratitude and forgiveness of the local community?' said Tom.

'Hmmm, I had them turning the nuclear power

plant into a doughnut factory and making Homer the boss, but I like yours better. I think I might show it to Ms Corman, the only teacher who has a sense of humour.'

And there's my singing. Tom is grade eight piano and flute, and all his family ever listen to is classical, but he says I've turned him on to reggae and soul and he thinks I'm going to be a star.

'I'm so lucky you picked me,' he says. 'But I just need to test your tongue for flexibility, which is very important for your singing career, so could we take a short snogging break of, say, three hours?'

Lucky I picked him!

Tharg's Imperial Boxers!

Wednesday March 5

'Tom stops me being embarrassed about all the daft things that keep popping in and out of my head,' I said to Lottie as we were huddled freezing by the changing rooms, hoping not to be chosen to play Ruth'n'Van at doubles. Tennis in the spring term is unheard of at KFC, but Crazy Craven is angling for some loony wodge of gifted and talented sports money so KFC can become an athletics and needlework academy or something, and is forcing us to do it this term. 'And he's such a good listener.'

'Better than me?' she said.

'Oh, Lottie,' I said. 'Not better. Different.' The next thing I said was 'EEEEEEEEEEEAAAAAAAAAAAAAA OOOOOOOOOWWWWWW!'

'Godfathers, it looks like a cricket ball,' said Lottie.

'Felt like one, too,' I said. Sure enough, Ruth'n'Van had been practising serves with an old cricket ball and whacked one at me, 'by mistake on purpose'.

And so now I've got a bruise the size of a melon on my derrière. And my body is a love machine that should not have to risk its life on a tennis court.

Lottie linked with me on the way home, and I needed it.

'The thing is, Lottie, it's different with Tom. It's not like when you fancy the sixth formers from afar, and it's not like Flubber – you know, I mean that was just, erm, physical. And it's not just hero-worship, like when we had a crush on Johnny Depp and you had that crush on Stanley Maul—'

'What do you mean, *had*?'

'Oh Lottie, you can't still like him, surely? He may be clever, but he thinks brains are for boys and that girls should stay home doing the washing up.'

'Not Stanley, Johnny Depp,' she said, laughing. 'But listen, getting off with a boy isn't a reason to stop having fun with your mates, is it?'

'Look, Lottie, I don't think you want to hear the L word, do you?'

'Oh, the L word – so it is just pure Lust with

Tom then?' she said, fake innocently.

I looked at her closely and she examined her feet.

'No, you're right,' she said. 'It was OK when you were with Flubber, because it was exciting and fun to giggle about how far you'd gone and I suppose I just knew it wasn't serious. But I don't want to hear the L word because – well, because it makes me feel . . . lonely.'

'Lottie, you are my absolute BF in all the world, you know that,' I said, but she knew and I knew that something bigger was happening.

11.30 p.m.

Something bigger is happening all right. And it's scaring me slightly. And because it's so big I can't really explain it, even to Lottie. The truth is, Tom is a better listener even than her. In fact, he was so busy listening to me that it took a whole week before he let slip what a high-flyer he is – GCSE results you could practically reserve a Nobel Prize with, his parents' and his teachers' wildest dreams made flesh – and when I say *made flesh* I mean it.

And that's what's bothering me.

The flesh bit.

I want to sleep with Tom more than I have ever wanted anything – but when I'm at home with the Puddings and all, I still feel like I don't want to grow up too fast.

As if sex will somehow be a magic wand that will end my childhood . . . for good.

Midnight

Well, there is a small particle of the Dark Side to Tom. I'm scared of his folks.

We babysat his kid sister Tania at his house tonight.

It's one of those big houses with rooms either side of the front door in a posh suburb a couple of bus rides away from me. You could have built our house twice over on the garage forecourt, where they've got a people-carrier like an overnight coach. I didn't like the house, really. There was something about all its framed prints and polish and catalogue kitchen and digital telly and mysterious little antique objects that made things I thought funny not seem funny any more.

His sister was OK though, if a bit of a boffin.

I asked her what her favourite book was and she piped up, 'I think the one I'm reading just now, *Pride and Prejudice*.' She's *seven*, for Tharg's sake.

But she wanted me to read *The Twits* at bed time, so she's probably just pretending to like Jane Austen.

The minute I'd got her well settled, Tom and me headed for the sofa and hurled ourselves at each other. It'd been two *whole days* and we might have done the full monty there and then if we hadn't heard the old four-wheel-drive thrumming across the gravel.

I cantered off to the loo like a frightened vole and threw a few handfuls of water over my flaming cheeks. Whoops – just made me look like a wet tomato fresh from an orgy.

Do they have orgies in vegetable beds?

I had my jacket half on and was heading for the door when Dr and Mrs Carpenter swooped into the hall. They were perfectly nice to me but you could see they were surprised. I suppose it looked as if my jacket was half off, for one thing. Then they did that thing that scary adults do, which is to find out loads about you even though you're heading for the door like a bat out of hell.

So they got my age. 'Fifteen?' (*Raised eyebrows*.) My school. 'KFC?' (*Eyebrows through ceiling*.) And my name! 'Tom, do introduce us *properly*.'

And when he said, 'Amaryllis Baker,' they did not even smile. That is a bad sign.

Then Mrs C said they'd just been to this fabulous opera and did I like opera at all? And I said I liked cappuccino. I have no idea why I said that, as I meant to say Puccini, but by now her eyebrows were doing a funny little dance like wrestling earwigs right up on the top of her forehead and I couldn't take my eyes off them.

Tom tried to cover for me and waffled on about how I was a great singer in an all-girl band and Dr C smiled quite kindly and said he'd been in a band when he was my age, playing a double bass made out of an old broom and a piece of string and a box. I was so grateful to him I blurted something about my dad doing something called 'skiffle', which was invented before the dawn of time.

'Yes, it was skiffle,' said Dr Carpenter stiffly as I backed out of the front door, grinning like a mad thing. I felt I had not exactly shone.

I suppose I do look a bit of a scruffy plump slag who sings in a band, not exactly the streamlined lawyer type they have in mind for Tom.

'Don't mind them,' said Tom as he walked me to the bus stop. 'They're OK really.' He told me they want him to be a doctor, like them.

'You mean your mum's a doctor too?' I gawped. I didn't like to think of those earwigs running free in a surgery.

But Tom doesn't want to be a doctor, he wants to be a teacher, and the way he tells stories to his kid sister and helps her with her schoolwork, I think he's born for it. He said his parents thought teaching was something anybody who could read a book and write on a whiteboard could do, and that he was too good for it. That's how much they know.

I was glad to get out of there, back to the calamitous ancients and Puddings and marmalade hell. But not before we had missed two buses, snogging.

1 a.m.

Snogging isn't what it's cracked up to be.

It is insanely better.

A lot of people go on about sex as if it's all very well in its place but needs to be curbed, or tamed, like a horse.

What do they know?

73

Maybe most adults can't remember it.

Tom has just texted me to say he can get hold of the Pill! His folks have loads of packs lying around the house!

Monday March 10

I cannot wait to dive into the luxuriant throbbing whirlpool of life, i.e., that is, full-blown Passion.

I more or less told Tom so today.

It was very romantic. We were cuddling in a downpour at the bus stop.

'Hmmm, never thought I'd enjoy wet kissing quite so much,' he murmured, nuzzling my neck. 'Shame we can't find a dry safe house, with a dry safe bed.'

'Mmmmmmm, with us in it?'

'What else?' he groaned, as we missed another bus.

Midnight

Should I sleep with Tom?

I think so.

I don't think I can stop myself.

Tuesday March 11

Have started the Pill! Tom says you have to take it

for two weeks, but what is two weeks? We can wait that long, I think.

We have just got to find a safe house to do it in.

It can't be his, as I would feel the gimlet eyes of his mum boring gimlet-like into me from under her earwig eyebrows, even if she was miles away on an Icicled Planet, where maybe she is actually from.

And it can't be mine, because it is always full of Puddings, and anti-terrorist childminders.

'Simon the Stockbroker's away this week, so I suppose you could do it in Mad Alice's black bedroom, if she takes her mum out for an evening,' said Lottie gloomily, as though we were discussing the funeral arrangements of her best mate. Which, on reflection, I suppose we were.

'What, and have stupid squawking Hendrix repeat the whole thing, noises and all, to the post-man next morning? No, ta,' I said.

She was quite like the old Lottie for a few mins after that, as we improvised what Hendrix might say – a bit like *Match of the Day*.

'What about Elsie's?' said Lottie. 'Her parents are cool.'

'They're old hippies,' I said. 'They'd probably jump out from behind a curtain with a camcorder and start joining in.' This sent us into further giggles. The Crabtrees are paunchy and bearded (both of them) and wear beads.

'Are you sure you know what you're doing?' said Lottie.

'As sure as I've ever been,' I said.

'Like when you knew for sure you were going to be a vet?'

Just at this moment I got a text from Tom. 'He needs to see me urgently,' I said. 'Maybe he's found a safe house!'

'I thought we were going to the Johnny Depp film,' said Lottie.

'Tomorrow. OK?' I said, running off on the wings of love without listening to the answer.

I hared off to the coffee bar, just as the skies opened. Tom was standing outside, drenched, looking white as a sheet.

'What's wrong? Come inside, you wombat! You're soaked,' I cried.

'Nothing,' he said. 'Everything,' he said.

Then he started to cry. Not real sobbing, but a tear escaped and trickled into the rain running down his cheek. I'd never seen a boy older than twelve cry.

'What's *up*?'

'I don't know how to tell you.'

But he did.

'We're leaving the country,' Tom finally managed to say.

'For a holiday?' I asked him, snuggling up. 'That's not so bad. We can text each other.'

Long silence.

'For good. Well, years, anyway,' he said, looking at me with big brimming eyes.

'Where are you going?' I asked him, eyes feeling

as if they were getting pretty big and brimming too.

Longer silence.

'Well, where?' I said, beginning to feel the nearest to cross I'd ever got with Tom. 'Birmingham? Wales? Amsterdam? Disneyland?'

'Japan.'

'*Whaaat?*'

'Japan.'

Then it all started to come out.

It was for two whole years. His high-powered mum was being paid an awful lot of money to set up and run a new medical research thingummy out there, and his dad was going along to help. Tom would go to school there, learn Japanese, do some A-level equivalent and come back to medical school. At least, that was their plan for him. He said they hadn't even told him about it until they'd fixed it all up! They were treating him like a child!

'That *can't* be true!'

'Well . . . it was a *possibility*.' He blushed. 'But I never thought it would happen.'

'But you could just say no!'

But he couldn't – or rather, he didn't. His mum, he said. His kid sister, he said.

'They mean more to you than I do,' I wept.

'They don't. But they mean a lot.'

Then he dropped the biggest bombshell of all. They were going in less than three weeks.

I said I'd wait for Tom for ever. He said two years would go in a flash and that we could e-mail

77

and text and speak every day.

I am going to take the Pill just in case. Maybe the Carpenter ancients will get eaten by a white rhino or something, like in Roald Dahl stories, leaving us wild and free.

CHAPTER FIVE

In Which Something Happens That Has Never Happened Before . . .

<u>**Wednesday March 12**</u>

'Lottie, he's going to Japan.'

'Who?' She knows perfectly well who.

'Tom.'

'Goody, that means we can go to Swanage.'
Lottie has been coming to my gran's in Swanage
every summer since we were both dots.

'Not for a holiday. His family are *moving* to
Japan.'

'*For ever?*'

'Two years. It might as well be for ever.'

'Oh, don't fret, kiddo, it'll go in a flash.'

Maybe she's trying to be kind, but I don't like
her tone. It's definitely on the verge of cheerful.

7 p.m.

I cannot believe that Tom could do this to me.

He said the L word, and now he is going to
Japan. I have texted him eight times saying I never

want to see him again.
And he hasn't even
replied.
I do want to see him again.
I think I might have to see him now.
Right. Time for a text.

C ME NOW OR I DIE.

Thaarg! I pressed send. I shouldn't have.

7.10 p.m.
Doorbell. Tom.
'That was quick.'
But he hadn't got any of my texts. Battery down.
We walked in the rain.
'It will go in a flash. It's worse for me, anyhow.
You've still got all your friends.'
I suppose it is worse for him.
'I've found a safe house.'
What? What? Is he suggesting a meeting of the
pube tubes?
A full-blown groin-join?
Only to leave me pining and wailing, or whining
and paleing?
Yes, he is.
Compañeros calientes!
'I know we shouldn't,' he said.
'We'd better not,' I said.
'You're right,' he said. 'It would be unbearable
to leave you, after that.'

'It's unbearable anyway,' I said.

'So?' he said, his lips brushing my eyelid.

'Definitely not,' I said.

Red Nose Day

Lottie has raised eighty-six quid doing red nose hair-dos, which is a kind of bun on top sprayed puce. The whole class have been wearing them, boys and all. Mikey even let her do his dreads. She said Flubber said she had magic hairdo fingers. Why is she doing Flubber's hair? He is in Year Twelve.

'I told him that, about your magic hairdo fingers,' I said. I didn't like to add I had said it to defend her when he was saying she looked like a neurotic owl.

She giggled in an annoying way.

4.30

'What's up? You're looking like last Friday's fish supper,' said Mum kindly after school.

It has been three whole days and she has only just noticed that I am plummeting into the abyss of terminal despair.

'Tom's going to Japan.'

'Oh! How exciting!' She looked at me a bit closer. 'Maybe we could push the boat out and take two weeks in Swanage this year as a special treat. The Puddings will just love it now.'

First prize one week in Swanage. Second prize two weeks.

I thought of the Puddings last year in Swanage, complaining about the sea being wet and the sand being sandy. I felt a strange pressure in my head, as though my brain was twice its usual size and trying to get out through my ears.

'I'm not five years old any more! I *hate* Swanage! He's going for two whole years!' I shouted, hurtling up the stairs and slamming the door.

6.10 p.m.

Mum has just come up with a plate of sandwiches. She said she is very sorry, but that it will go in a flash and that at my age two years is nothing.

Who does she think I am?

Everybody knows that when you are ancient like Mum two years flash by and at my age every day is like a year, a year whose days are long. Oscar Wilde said that.

He was in jail at the time. Well, so am I. The sandwiches look like cardboard.

Watched Red Nose Day on telly.

Everyone is having fun raising money for the poor and abandoned.

I will always think of this day from now on as Red Eyes Day.

11 p.m.

Have just got home. It's Tom's last day in England.
We have spent the afternoon in the bedroom of a
friend of his.

In bed.

To begin with we did everything you can do without Actually Doing It. And that was only because
he said we shouldn't – Suppose there was a mistake,
suppose I got pregnant, he said, he'd feel so awful.
But what I was thinking was, I love you, if we
don't do it now I may never get a chance to sleep
with someone I love.

'I will be old and grey and lonely and never love
any but you,' I heard myself saying aloud. He
groaned and looked at me meltingly.

'And it's really unlikely I'll get pregnant, because
I've still got my period,' I said. 'And I've been taking
that pill you gave me every day.'

'And you're only fifteen,' he said, tracing my lips
with his finger. 'You're not even legal.'

'Oooh, you big seventeen-year-old thing you.'

'How can I resist you?' he said. 'I know, I will
practise iron willpower.'

But we went further, just the same.

I saw his big seventeen-year-old thing too. Well,
I didn't know whether it was big or not of course,
not having anything to compare it with. Mad Alice
says she's seen stuff on the Internet where men's
willies look like baseball bats, but Tom's wasn't

like that and it seemed to me just fine the way it was.

I found I wasn't embarrassed, even when we took all our clothes off, though I got cross for about a millisecond when I remembered my cricket-ball bruise, which has spread in little blue ripples all down my thighs, making them look like a tabby cat, only fatter. And less furry, of course. Great, I thought, first true love has to happen when you have your period and your legs look like something out of *Tom and Jerry*.

'You got it playing *tennis*?' Tom traced the bruise with a finger. I shivered.

'Hmmm,' he murmured. 'Love, fifteen. I'll have to kiss it better.'

He was embarrassed, a bit, and he slipped under the duvet without letting me see him at first.

'Look,' he said. 'This is my first time too, you know.'

'Of course it is,' I said. 'You were waiting for me.'

Then the duvet stood up like the Post Office Tower.

'Help!' I shouted. 'There's a six-inch midget in the bed!'

Tom looked at me critically. 'Looks a lot bigger than that to me,' he said, giggling.

I really wanted to know what it would feel like inside, and I was really scared of finding out at the same time. But because it was Tom I wanted to more than I didn't. He was very close and I could feel myself forgetting about being afraid, forgetting about KFC, and Mum and Dad, forgetting about the Law, forgetting even about what could happen to me if we did it.

He touched me, then I really did forget everything and when I touched him I think he forgot about most other things too, if the look on his face meant anything.

I know exactly how I felt then – it's as if I'm feeling it still – and yet I don't know the words for it. The short words you hear in the loos or the long ones they use in the PSE books don't get anywhere near it. It felt like I weighed nothing, and Tom's wiry body on top of me weighed nothing either. Boys I'd fancied from a distance, or on the telly, seemed like gods, giants who could make you feel tiny and pointless. But here was Tom, who really was a god, and he seemed to be morphing into me and me into him, and so lost in it I was amazed to find I felt protective of him, as if I had to make sure somehow that he wouldn't disappear into this dream completely.

And then he did. I was drifting away, melting, silky, floating off in clouds . . .

'Aaaah, bollocks!' came a shout, and I could feel the daft smile was still spread over my face even as I realized he wasn't there.

'Darling,' I whispered anxiously, and I thought for a moment that I'd never said that word that way before. 'What's the matter?'

'Condoms,' came a muffled snort. 'Need condoms.'

I realized then he'd started leaning out to feel

around in the pocket of his jeans on the floor, and fallen out of bed.

I screamed and fell out of my side of the bed. I glanced underneath and spotted a pile of his mate's dirty mags.

'God, look at this,' I said to Tom, hauling myself back onto the pillows. He was struggling to open a little packet, and cursing to himself. 'How many of them are there in this picture?' I said, amazed. I was trying to be cool about it – I didn't want to show Tom I was uncomfortable looking at what seemed private to me; it was like finding a window open on a medical examination.

Tom took the magazine out of my hands and dropped it on the floor. 'God, that Damon's a wanker,' he said.

I briefly glimpsed him taking something out of the wrapper before he slid it under the duvet and wriggled his body a little. I suddenly felt strange and clammy and awkward. I shouldn't have looked at that magazine.

'Maybe we should use two, to be on the safe side?' I squeaked.

'Isn't mine enough for you, you naughty thing?' Tom laughed, but he got out another packet anyway. 'I've got spermicide as well, so it's safe,' he whispered.

He started to move his thigh across mine, but I found myself not letting him, and nestled my head into his chest instead.

'I feel weird,' I whispered to him. He didn't say

anything, but just stroked my neck very gently. Slowly the ripply tide came in again and started to take my weight. My bones were silk. I hardly noticed that it was Tom's hand that was moving, it all seemed to be part of the same quiver all over my skin. And what happened next was not quite what I'd thought it would be – breathless and sudden – and then Tom pulling back from me with a strange look that seemed to be happy and sad and worried about me and himself all at once.

But I wasn't worried about me, or him. I hugged him and we lay there for what seemed like hours. I'd never felt so peaceful in my whole life. It was as if life had gone backwards all afternoon and I'd ended up as a baby floating safe inside Mum again. And then he was gone.

Midnight

Tharg's knickerbockers!

Floating inside Mum!

Today was Mother's Day!

When I got home everyone was all tucked up in bed and the kitchen table was littered with cards made by the Puddings out of old pasta and loo rolls.

I wrote a little note:

Love you, Mum. Sorry I forgot Mother's Day!

and propped it against the teapot.

Tom is in the air.

And I am on the ground.

But weightless.

At break, Lottie emptied an entire boob wallet of tissues to stop me blubbing.

'Lottie, I never knew you padded your boob wallet,' I said.

'Them as needs to, does, and if you tell anyone I will break every bone in your body.'

But can you break bones that have been turned to silk?

First thing this morning the Puddings come belting into my room saying the car has been stolen. Well, I think that's what they're saying.

'Car gone! Buggler!'

What do I care? We never go anywhere in it, except Swanage, to see Granny Meg.

But I know what's going to happen when Dad hears. He loves that car. Well, he must do, considering the amount of time he spends lying underneath it –

probably a lot more time than he spends lying underneath Mum, but it's too early in the morning to think about going there, and so is any other time of the day for that matter. Anyway, to most people I know, it's an old Renault Espace with the bumpers hanging off. To Dad it's a Porsche that just dresses down to avoid being recognized in the street.

With the Puddings pulling my arms out of their sockets, I get up groaning and go out onto the landing just in time to see Dad hurtling downstairs two at a time. I'm also just in time to see he's wearing his string vest and what appears to be a pair of Mum's knickers, which he must have pulled on in the dark on hearing the Pudding alarm. I don't think it's a sign of any change in his sexual orientation, but you never know. The Puddings also spot this and roll downstairs in a ball together, chortling deafeningly.

We all go downstairs after Dad at varying tempos, slug-with-hangover in my case. He flings open the front door and hurtles out onto the front path, connecting at collision speed with our wheelie bin, which has just been propelled up the path in the opposite direction with the usual scowling fury by the departing dustmen. I speed up my arrival in the hall slightly, in time to spot the following: down goes wheelie bin with Dad spread flat on it like milk-white surfing porpoise. Both go skidding out onto pavement and run over small ridiculous dog belonging to blonde out-of-work-actress-over-the-road, who happens to be jogging by in a huggy sort of Lycra number. Dog disappears under wheelie bin with squelchy whine. Blonde actress-over-the-road lets out anguished shriek. Dad is unconcerned about either small ridiculous dog or looking like wet fish on slab and is just shouting, 'Did anyone see who took our car?' at the top of his lungs. Curtains start opening up and down the road. Holy wombats! Why do I have to live with a houseful of loonies?

Small ridiculous dog unfortunately emerges unscathed from other side of wheelie bin, so blonde actress-over-the-road stops squeaking and clocks Dad's unconventional nightwear with carefully made-up raised eyebrow. Dog discovers remains of various Baker family takeaways that have escaped the wheelie bin, and buries its snuffly, spotless white face in a grey cheeseburger.

'Giselle, honey!' screams actress-over-the-road, appalled. 'Don't eat that, it's poison!'

'No it's not, it's made out of one of her relatives,' I say to the Puddings. Actress-over-the-road shoots me look of withering hatred that would blacken flowers. Meanwhile, Dad has thought he probably ought to scramble to his feet to be polite, then wishes he hadn't. He stands blushing like a post box and trying to cover his paunch, his bald spot, his vest and Mum's lace-front underwear all with the same pair of hands. 'I'm really sorry, Emma,' he says.

I'd forgotten she was called Emma. She would be.

'Kids, you know, they'll eat any old rubbish,' Dad says lamely.

'That was your cheeseburger, Daddy,' the Puddings reliably pipe up with one voice, and Dad just simpers at actress-over-the-road, his mouth flapping open like a fish.

'Do you know what time it is?' comes a grumpy voice from a bedroom window next door. I look at my watch. *Zut alors!* 5.45! I haven't been up this early since . . . wait a minute . . . since last April the First . . .

'Sorry about crashing into you,' Dad is muttering, trying to edge behind the hedge. 'My car's been stolen.' There is a silence for a second or two, as we all stand there staring at Dad's car, parked where it always is, looking smug.

'*Apple fool!*' shout the Puddings hilariously.

'I must get on,' says actress-over-the-road, beginning to jog on the spot, but flashing her expensively-whitened smile at Dad, now pressed in agony into the hedge and visible only from the neck up. 'I've come to love the early mornings ever since there's been nobody to stay in bed for.'

Aaargh, cheeseville. She's not as young or as firm around the assets as she'd like everybody to think she is any more, and nobody can remember actually seeing her in anything except our street – but the qualities that once got her clothes-shedding parts in such GCSE EngLit texts as *Whoops, Wrong Bedroom, It's All Right, I'm a Gynaecologist* and *Pole-Vaulting Vicars* are still definitely noticeable to middle-aged men, and it's pathetically obvious Dad has noticed them too, impaled by thorns and underwear embarrassment though he is. Why don't ancients have some sense of decency?

Actress-over-the-road jogs off with impressively undulating buttocks, followed by gaze of Dad and voice of yapping ridiculous dog, which, following the wheelie-bin encounter, is now hobbling on only three good legs.

'I'm going to wash my hair,' I say rather irritably to nobody in particular.

'No, you're not,' says Dad. 'I'm going back to bed. I'm not having you crashing about in the bathroom for the next two hours.' He stomps off back inside, with the Puddings following cackling and pointing at his lacy bum. I trail after them, go up to the bathroom, and lock myself in.

And I howl.

The biggest thing that ever happened to me has just happened. And Tom is in Japan.

And I have somehow got to keep going to school as though I am the same person as normal.

CHAPTER SIX

In Which Amy Falls into a Bottomless Ditch...

One Week Later

It is a whole week and I am still crying every day.

My mock mocks are a mockery.

We have had only sixteen e-mails and fourteen phone calls.

Oh, and eighty-four texts.

Have just e-mailed the following:

Tom Carpenter,
A day without you is like six months without string.
How will I cope? (As two whole years will be like
365 years and I will be dead and never have
wrapped any parcels.)
Sincerely,
Ms Baker

Got this by return:

Ms Baker,
I am sending you two years' supply of sellotape.

Please wear it in your knickers till I am home.
Missing you unspeakably.
Affectionately,
TC

How can I live without him?

Lottie has come up trumps though. In fact she seems quite jolly since Tom went away.

She came over with a man-size box of Kleenex. She had second thoughts and kept half.

'Bosom padding,' she reminded me.

Oh yes. Well, I may not have a boyfriend but at least I've got bosoms. But what good are they without a bosom fondler?

I started snuffling again – anything seems to set me off. I said to Lottie, 'The weeks go by like snails' snails.'

'What do you mean, snails' snails?'

'Well, if snails were us, and they had snails eating *their* gardens then those snails would be as slow to them as a snail is to us. Geddit?'

'Oh. Yeah. So snails' snails' *snails* would be even slower,' she said, with the piercing intelligence of a person seeing the old light bulb of wisdom.

'Yeah, that's it,' I said.

Mum popped her head round the door with a mad smile and asked if we'd like to take the Puddings to the park. She pops her head round my door every five minutes these days to check if I'm 'moping'.

We went to the park. I am filling my lonely days pushing Puddings on swings.

I wonder how Tom is filling his?

I haven't spoken to him for two days and he hasn't replied to my last six texts . . .

What is he thinking?

Well, now I know.

Tom phoned this evening.

It was so amazing to hear him, I didn't take in what he was saying to me at first. I just squeaked and sighed and cooed and made noises like Marge Simpson makes when Homer finally gets back from the bar.

But gradually what he'd called to say finally started to sink in.

He said some of the following, but I can't remember in which order.

'We're too young.'

'So were they in *Eric and Barbara*,' I said to him brightly.

'We have to forget each other.'

'How can we? Every brain cell in our hearts sings our song,' I said, testing my lyric-writer's talents to destruction.

'Two years is too long to expect you to be tied to me.'

'It will pass in a moment,' I lied.

'You're too good for me.'

'True, but I'm prepared to overlook it just this once.'

'We hardly know each other, really.'

I can't remember what I said about that.

'It's better for both of us to end it now. I'll never forget you.'

Not too sure what I said about that either. I was running out of fake bouncy ideas by now, so it might have been 'Fnnrrrrmph' or 'Ayeeeurrrrrghh'.

'You won't forget me, will you?'

Forget him? I've *slept* with him, for Tharg's sake. I *love* him.

What does he think I am?

I can't believe it. It was Dr Earwig-eyebrows, I suppose, telling him that a girl who texted every hour was unbalanced. Telling him there were plenty of other fish in the sea. Ones that would look a lot better swimming by his side in the great Ocean of Life.

Or has he met someone else already?

This thought is too horrible to think.

Mum took one look at me as I came off the phone and said, 'Ooooooh,' with such a look of heartbroken sympathy that I burst into floods.

Of course it wasn't too long before she and Dad and the whole underpanting neighbourhood (Mum has a bush telegraph about my affairs) were dropping in with words of wisdom from Clichés Anonymous: *Other fish in the sea, plenty of them . . . Doesn't know how lucky he is . . . Wasn't worth it anyway . . . Couldn't hold a candle to you . . . Never saw what you saw in him – you could do much better*, were just a few of them.

The last one really hurt. As though I'd waste my time on anyone who wasn't worth it . . .

Grown-ups always dismiss young love. Adults just don't believe in it. They call it a crush. Or puppy love. It's insulting. I know all about crushes. I've had loads, ever since I was about eight. I thought Flubber was love for about a week, but what did I know?

Love is quite different, I realize now. Love is mutual and beautiful and tender and playful and passionate and overwhelming, like thunder, like music. Music with an orchestra of two. But Tom and I made our music for just six short weeks.

This cannot be happening.

Can it?

Midnight

Have been going over and over and over the appalling conversation with Tom. Cannot even remember what I said, except for the sound of a long low wail like a lone wolf at the end of the world, when Mrs Wolf and all the little wolves have died one by one, leaving him lonely on an ice floe hurtling to his doom.

He is not replying to my e-mails or texts and he is not answering his phone.

Why? He hasn't even given me a proper explanation!

Tuesday April 8

In bed.
Off school.

It is either flu, or a broken heart.

Or both.

It is both. My temperature is 103.

Tom is still not responding to e-mails, or texts. I have even tried phoning him from Lottie's mobile so he couldn't tell it was my phone, but when he heard it was me he just hung up.

How could he?

Mum pops in and out, nervously patting the duvet.

Ragged bales of tumbleweed blow miserably across the derelict and abandoned town that was my brain.

Decide the only thing for it is an old-fashioned letter. Spend three feverish hours writing twenty-six pages, when all I want to ask him is why? And all I want to tell him is I can't live without him.

Wednesday April 9

Still have high fever and delirious dreams where I am fighting a Japanese mermaid for Tom. The dream always ends with me drowning.

Dad came in and sat awkwardly on the bed, patting my hand. 'First love is always the worst love,' he said.

It meant a lot to me that he said 'love'.

I liked having him there. He hadn't sat on my bed since I was little and he used to read to me. I was the apple of his eye then and I think I used to love him more than Mum. But he drifted towards the Puddings the minute they were born, and recently he's seemed to be drifting away from us all.

'You haven't come and sat on my bed like this for years, Dad,' I said.

'It's all gone too fast, Amy,' he said. 'I blinked and you'd grown up.'

Thursday April 10

Lottie comes by in a Red Nose.

'Lottie, it's very sweet of you to try to cheer me up but Red Nose Day was last month.'

Lottie says, trying to be kind, 'You mustn't think Tom's dumped you because you let him sleep with you, you know.'

'What are you saying? That Flubber dumped me because I wouldn't sleep with him and that Tom dumped me because I did?'

'No, I didn't mean that . . . But Tom hasn't given you a reason, has he, really?'

'No. And I know what that means, don't think I don't. It means he's found someone else.'

'Yeah,' said Lottie, looking relieved. 'My mum said that when people leave it always means that. But they're never brave enough to say.'

'Thanks a lot, Lottie,' I said, and burst into tears.
Poor Lottie was mortified.
But not as mortified as me.
What a bastard.
But is he a bastard? My heavenly Tom?

BROKEN-HEARTED TIP

Be grateful that you aren't going to be dating a boy who doesn't want to date you any more. Go out with your girlfriends! Treat yourself to a new You! Remember, the best divorce is the one you get before you are married!

That's a relief then. Who needs Tom? I can be a blue-jeans type chick with a face full of honey and furry fingernails instead.

Stagger back to Broadmoor, which is what KFC seems like these days. Don't want to, but my temperature is back down and I have to get some work done sometime.

It is strange to be at school again. You see all the people you know in a different way, as if by magic they ought to understand exactly what you've been through and it just seems selfish that they don't. The boys say nice encouraging things like 'Wossa matter, got the painters in?' The girls take an arm each and sweep you into a corner, chattering questions at you so fast your head spins. I'm not sure I've ever been that sort of girl.

But two things have changed since I collapsed in a heap.

We have a new boy in the class, who never stops reading and jumps out of his skin if you speak to him. He is a refugee and Moony gave everyone a little pep talk before he came about how he is from a war zone and is scared of loud noises. Poor Iqbal, KFC is the last place he should be. We've also got a new Spanish teacher, Señor Mondragon.

I suppose he is quite handsome in a boring Spanish way. Lottie and Debs are besotted. They are just like silly teenagers.

'You are behaving like silly teenagers,' I say.

'We *are* silly teenagers,' they shriek. 'Have you noticed his bum? It is *soo* perky.'

'*It is the bum of a matador, It is the bum that I adore,*' trills Lottie, then goes triple puce as Flubber walks by with a gang of rudes.

'Hello, sunshine,' he says to her and gives me a very ignoring look. As if I care.

'Iqbal's not half bad either,' says Debs. 'Big soulful

eyes. And I bet he's got big soulful masculine underbits too.'

'God, all you two think about is sex,' I say.

'That's a bit rich, since you have done nothing but moon over a boy for—'

'That's not about sex,' I say furiously. 'You've never been in love, obviously.'

Debs pats my shoulder. 'Ames, you don't want to go losing your sense of humour, you know. Life must go on.'

Tracey Hardwick gives me some of her packed lunch.

Her packed lunch is sugared almonds and Slim-kwik.

My life is better than Tracey Hardwick's, isn't it?

But then Gareth Foreskin drives by the playground waving and her face lights up like a traffic light at the sight of his cuddly traffic coneiness.

I am jealous of Tracey Hardwick.

I am jealous of my carefree friends and their carefree matador bum adoring.

I am jealous of the pigeons in the playground, all billy and cooey.

I am jealous of Moony because she has a pic of her hubby and grown-up kids on her desk and she is all wise and sorted.

'All right, Amy?' she asks as I droop out after registration. Moony has sixth sense, I swear it.

I want to tell her that my life is over before it's begun but all I say is, 'Fine.'

Why?

'Time to get your life back,' says Lottie firmly on the way home. 'Band rehearsal tomorrow.'

1 a.m.

Stayed up writing song based on my letter to Tom. Not to boast, but rather fine, I think.

Saturday April 12

Easter Hols

7 p.m.

The band liked my song.

I think they liked it.

They more or less said they did.

Debbie said she thought seven minutes was maybe a little bit long, but I started to cry.

So then I let Debbie and Mad Alice persuade me to go to the pub 'to cheer me up'. Have decided to make an occasion of it. I put on some lippy, lashings of mascara (as they say in the mags), a skirt and a loose white shirt of Tom's I liked that he gave me before he left. It feels good to be wearing his shirt.

I know now it must all be a mistake.

When he gets my letter, he'll change his mind. Course he will.

Dad and Mum look quite pleased – they think I must be getting better.

2 a.m.

Just when you think things are really bad . . .

At the pub, Debbie and Mad Alice bought me a shandy and then got roped into a gang with Ruth'n'Van and a couple of lads from the next estate. Looking back on it, what I can remember, I think they probably reckoned that if they got me completely smashed I'd forget about Tom by the time it wore off, like that memory-blasting thing they do in *Men in Black*. The bar staff might have stopped it if they'd noticed me, but Debbie and Mad Alice and the Ruth'n'Van crowd look old enough to be running a bar, never mind drinking in one. I wished Lottie was there – we could have moaned in a corner and then mooched home together, singing, '*If it wasn't for bad men, we wouldn't have no men at all.*'

But then Stanley Maul came in.

Stanley Maul is the school boffin. KFC doesn't have many boffins, but there are two famous ones, Lavinia in my year and Stanley, who is in Year Twelve and doing six AS levels. Lavinia is the real thing, a genuine brainiac who is also dead kind and sweet, but I've always thought Stanley was a bit of an oik. Clever all right, but arrogant with it. Whatever you've done he knows someone who's done it better, or he's done it better himself. Or worse, he's done it better but he tells you he thinks he screwed it up really, or wasn't trying. It drives you up the wall.

Stanley doesn't usually take any notice of me, and for that I was pretty grateful. I don't go for guys who think they are God's Gift. Anyway, his laugh sounds like he has frogs for relations. But tonight he was a lot friendlier. I suddenly remembered Lottie had had a crush on Stanley in Year Seven. Now that I looked at him closely, I could begin to see why.

He is, in fact, quite hunky in an oiky way.

He's very tall. He has quite nice eyes, I was beginning

to think, as I poured something fiery he gave me down my throat. I think it may have been vodka, but whatever it was, it made me feel the world was a kindly sort of world, after all.

He said Ms Corman had told him I was the most promising English student in Year Ten – it made me feel good even if he did spoil it by saying I shouldn't waste my time singing in a band. 'You're made for higher things,' he said.

He bought me another drink and started patting me gently – for him – on the thigh.

Then he went over to the juke box and put on *You Can't Deal Me All the Aces and Expect Me Not to Play* and came back with two more drinks. 'Maybe this is our song?' he asked, and I felt vaguely alarmed, thinking perhaps I'd seemed a bit too friendly.

I got up. 'I'm jusht leaving,' I shaid.

'The night is young! And you're so beautiful!' Stanley recited. I sensed the others were drifting away into their own night out, probably relieved somebody was taking me over. 'But you don't look happy. What is it, a guy? If he's giving you the runaround, he must be a fool.'

Stanley was getting closer now. I would have edged away, but I was losing my bearings altogether – I was almost incapable of standing up. I managed to signal to Debbie and she came charging over, looking agitated.

'What's up, Ames? You OK?'

'She's fine, just a bit weepy. I'll see she's all right,'

said Stanley, and I suddenly realized he
sounded not so much froggy, more
like a fish eating a sausage.
My heart suddenly
warmed to him.

'Have you been ringing
me up?' I asked him.

He blushed. It made him look almost sweet.

It felt suddenly incredibly nice having a boy taking
an interest in me.

'Yeah, I'm fine,' I said to Debs, who was hovering
around looking anxious.

'Are you sure?' she asked. 'Shall I take you
home? You look like you might have had a bit too
much . . .'

'Honest, I'm fine. I'm feeling the best I've felt for
weeks,' I said. And it was true.

'Well, me and Alice are going off to Mikey's
party – come with us.'

'I'll come later, honest. It's only round the corner.
I'll be fine.'

'OK, if you're sure?' she said.

'Sure I'm sure.'

And Debs gave me a wink.

'Y'know,' Stanley said as Alice and Debs left, 'I
used to think you were a bit of a dog, but you've
got much nicer lately. Kevin says you remind him
of the sexy one in *What Are Friends For?*'

I didn't know whether to laugh or cry, and for
some strange reason laughing won.

'But you've got much bigger . . . eyes,' he said.

COCKTAIL MENU

Axe Murderer
Bionic Beaver
Down Home wet dream
Electric Camel Basher
Extremely Drunk
Flaming Asshole
Frog in a blender
Hawaiian Hard on
King Willy
Pan Galactic Pussy
Sex with the bartender
Spooky Hedgehog
Tequila mockingbird
Turbo Shaglauncher
Vodka Virgin Vixen
Wild Squirrel Sex
Zombie Urine Sample

'And perhaps a better understanding of Chaucer?'
He bought me a cocktail, what the pub subtly calls
a Turbo Shaglauncher. He could have chosen a
Tequila Mockingbird, a Pan Galactic Pussy or a
Bionic Beaver, but he chose a Turbo Shaglauncher.
It tasted very nice, but it took away the use of my
legs altogether.

'I don't think I can face Mikey's party – you go
without me,' I said, feeling suddenly a lot drunker
than I'd ever felt. 'I'm ready for bed.'

'Are you indeed?' he said, steering me to the
door. 'Me too.'

Stanley said he'd see me home, of course. Well, he carried me home, virtually. Through the park. Halfway through it I realized I was desperate for a pee.

'Don't leave me here,' I wailed at him as he left me behind a tree and turned his back.

'I won't, I'm just being a gentleman. Whoaa! Careful!'

I hadn't realized the tree was on a steep slope, and I rolled down it. By the time I hit the bottom I was soaking wet and whether it was with wee or rain I was past caring. I started laughing hysterically.

'Are you all right?' Stanley called out anxiously from the top. I think he was finding me a lot more trouble than I was worth.

'Nothing a bit of emergency surgency . . . I mean emergery surgery . . . won't cure . . . I mean . . . have you got a crane? Hang on, don't look.' I struggled out of my mud-spattered tights, finished weeing and scrambled back up, my head whirling. For some reason, it seemed almost fun.

Stanley took my arm and helped me on. I was longing for some human warmth, even from him.

'It's a boy, isn't it?' he asked me as he struggled to stop me steering us both into another ditch.

'Yesh. None of your business.'

'Do I know him?'

'No.'

'Has he dumped you?'

'*No!*' I tried to pull away from Stanley, but what I could see of the world in the dark was spinning round. 'No. He had to go away. It wasn't his fault.' I stumbled and nearly fell again, but Stanley had an arm around my back. He pulled me nearer to him. This time I didn't resist, I don't know why. He brushed a hand against my cheek. It was clumsy, but it seemed to say he wanted to be nice.

'I'm sorry.'

'S'all right. Maybe it wouldn't have worked out. He was cleverer than me, and posher, and thinner, and his parents didn't like me, and—'

Stanley kissed me. I was so surprised, I let him go on doing it.

'I think you're just great,' was all he said when he stopped.

I burst into tears. Stanley held me very close – I could feel his thigh against my leg. I turned my face up and let him kiss my neck, just like I had with Tom. It made me feel really weird, disloyal and guilty and grateful and wanted all at once. I put my arms round him and kissed him back, pretending he was Tom. He started undoing my shirt and slipped his hand inside. I felt myself responding, warming, as his hand moved down – and we slid in a heap onto the wet grass. 'Tom,' I whispered, pulling him to me. Then everything started spinning.

I don't know how long I was out for. But when I came to, for a magic moment I thought Tom was in my arms, and his voice was murmuring my name. Then I remembered it was Stanley. But now it didn't seem like a gentle Stanley any more. It was a drunk, selfish, oiky, horrible Stanley, and his rain-soaked head was in my open shirt front. I could feel the wet grass on my legs, my skirt was up, and all I wanted was for this never to have happened. I pushed him off with strength I didn't know I had.

'You bastard!' I yelled at him. Suddenly I didn't feel drunk any more. I started hitting and kicking as hard as I could.

'Oi! Leave it out! I thought you wanted to!' Stanley was trying to scramble to his feet. I thought somebody must hear us, but there was no one around. I tried to aim a kick at where his fingers were struggling with his zip, but missed.

'Don't touch me, don't touch me. Leave me alone!' I shouted – and then I ran for it. I have honestly no idea how I got home.

But here I am.

Godfathers. How could I?

CHAPTER SEVEN

In Which Amy Tries to Put Herself Down to Experience

That must have been a bad dream last night.

I am not telling anyone about it, no way.

It's better just to forget it. Put it down to experience.

Noon

I am in the bath.

I have been in here for two hours now and no one has come to see if I am dead.

I had to wash all of Stanley off and pretend nothing had happened.

Well, nothing did happen really.

I just feel like I have had slugs crawling all over me.

I have washed my hair four times.

It's weird, writing a diary in the bath, and it's not just the steam that's making it soggy.

I am dead angry with Maul.

I hate him.

6 p.m.

Have spent day in bed. Told Mum I had bad period.

She is looking all anxiety-strewn again and I can't stand it.

Had to wash hair again.

Tharg, am I turning into Lady Macbeth? She used to stumble around at night trying to wash imaginary blood off herself. But of course she put Macbeth up to murdering people, so if she imagined stuff like that she couldn't blame anybody but herself. Why am I feeling so tainted by something that wasn't even my fault?

I have snogged another! I did snog him, I can't deny it. I kissed him back and let him feel me up. I just hope it didn't go any further than I can remember . . . it's all a bit of a blur.

But I haven't really betrayed Tom. He is still all I think about – the horrible contrast with Stanley is just a reminder of how rare and fantastic Tom is.

Wednesday April 16

Thank Tharg it's the holidays. I don't feel like going back to Broadmoor ever again. Everyone will know about me and Maul. He's the kind of boy who will post it on the Internet.

Anyway, everyone saw him pouring Shaglaunchers down me in the pub and they will have put two and two together and made number ten. And I need to wash my hair.

Have convinced Mum I am having worst period in world. This always works with old Mum. You can be stumbling around the house blasting the windows out with sneezing and she calls it 'just a sniffle'. But she's like a mother hen about 'women's troubles'. Her mum, Granny Meg, still calls it 'the curse', so perhaps it's not surprising she's sensitive about it.

Teenacious Tips, subtly subtitled 'It's Tuff to Be a Teen', is hopeless. It has bum-all about the Stanley Mauls of this world, though if anything makes it Tuff to Be a Teen it's people like him. It has bum-all about Turbo Shaglaunchers being marketed to rampant young boys to soften up impressionable young girls. It has zero minus nothing about mad hair-washing either. I think I will burn the clothes I was wearing.

But I was wearing Tom's shirt.

I let another boy undo the buttons!

I hope I'm not turning into a mad person.

Thursday April 17

Lottie came by today.

'Oh. Nice of you to drop by, so soon,' I said, with more than a hint of sarc.

'But you're going to have periods for the next forty years,' Lottie said, shrugging. 'What are you going to do – say "Sorry, I don't feel like being a brain surgeon today – time of the month, you know"? Anyway, it isn't due again yet, is it? What are you doing, having them weekly so you can just claim you're More Woman than everybody else?'

'Oh, shut up, I can't help it,' I groaned.

'Come on, what is it really?' Lottie asked, a bit more softly.

So I told her about Maul and the Mauling.

'Oooooooooooooooh,' she wailed, and pulled a whole handful of man-size tissues from her bra. I was touched. I blew my nose for about an hour.

'I should have been round before,' Lottie finally said over the alpine-horn noise of me blowing. 'I'll kill that dickhead Maul.'

'If you kill him,' I told her urgently, 'don't tell him why. If you tell anyone, even Mad Alice and Debs, I'll never even look at you again.'

'Course not, but, well, erm, they did say you seemed to be getting on rather well with him in the pub,' she said. Then, 'But it was only a snog, wasn't it? I mean, he tried it on, he took advantage of you being legless, but—'

'Yeah. It was just a snog,' I said. And I believed it too.

And I felt a whole lot better.

Friday April 18

Just a snog. Everyone does it.

Just when the albatross of doom has nested in your psyche, the bluebird of happiness flies by and drops its egg in your puccini.

'*Phone!*' shouts Mum. 'Sounds like a midget who's swallowed a helium balloon.'

It was Mad Alice with a voice that had risen about five octaves.

She was telling me something so good I couldn't take it in at first. She has got us all tickets for Glastonbury. Some guy in a band got free tickets and gave her four. Well, that's her story. This is quite the most amazing thingy that has ever happened to Yrs Truly.

'We're playing at Glastonbury,' I lied to Mum, more to find out if she'd take it in than anything else. She did. She sat down very suddenly on Dad's wonky chair and from there slithered to the floor. I helped her up.

'We're not really,' I said, dusting her off. 'But we're going though. Mad Alice has got tickets. I don't know how she's done it. Must have sold her organs for medical research or something.'

'You can't go, you're too young,' Mum said, sitting down gingerly on another chair. 'You'll get given terrible drugs, and go deaf from all that noise. Anyway, what about Swanage?'

'Glastonbury's at the end of June, you dafty. I'll be fine. All the rest of the band'll be there. We can look after each other – help build the tent, dig a nice big hole in the ground for a loo . . .'

Mum nearly slid off the good chair onto the floor again. Maybe our family should just live on the floor. It would be easier really, if it wasn't for the marmalade.

'It's all right,' I said, patting her. 'They've got loos, really.'

'Have they?' she said, cheering up. This gave Mum the bright idea of all the families going too and making a little camping holiday out of it.

'Yeah, that would be great,' I say, to give her confidence.

But I know the tickets sold out just four hours after going on sale, so she has no hope.

Saturday April 19

Have thrown *Teenacious Tips* into the bin about twenty times, but Mum keeps pulling it out again and putting it by my bed. However, she has put a pink Post-It note in the bit about Positive Thinking and Forward Planning, and even I have to admit there's some sense in it.

For a start, it says,

> ### STUDYING IS COOL TOO TIP
> *Make your work space a
> pleasure to inhabit.*

So I make a wall chart. Draw images on stickers that separate different activities from each other.

Decide on pic of bright-red head exploding with brains hurtling in all directions for Revision, yellow smiley face with hair standing on end and lightning bolts flying out of open mouth for Band Practice,

 sleeping face with ZZZZZZZZZs coming out of nose for Helping Out in the House, two stick persons leaping in air together for Social Life – some chance.

Armed with these Little Helpers, draw up big mock-mock revision/chillaxing/rock star/sex goddess plan.

Will do two hours' revision every a.m., starting at nine.

Aiming for excellent results in music and English.

And OK results in, erm, geography, Spanish and food tech.

Can I maybe even scrape Cs in science and maths? Course I can.

Then two hours chillaxing.

A snackette, then two more hours' revision.

Then band practice.

I am turning over a new leaf.

And when Tom sees the error of his ways, as of course he will, I will be a shiny new leaf.

Except of course I am doing it for *me*.

YOU'RE WORTH IT TIP!

Respect yourself. You're all you've got!

---

as it says in groovy hip *Teenacious Tips*.

Have got a big pile of books from the library and am going to forget myself in literature.

Lottie tells me I should re-read *Lord of the Rings*. I think she fancies herself as an elf. But I am definitely Hobbit, or possibly Orc, and I think one trip to Middle Earth will last me a lifetime.

Dad is very jolly, I can't help noticing. He has taken to early morning jogging to lose a few pounds. It's nice when your parents decide to make a bit of an effort.

_____ **Sunday April 20**

Easter Day

2 p.m.

Ever since the Puddings were born, Easter has been my chance to be a Holy Roman Chocoholic while pretending to be a Nice Big Sister.

Mum and Dad stage an Easter Egg Hunt for the Puddings in the garden, so they can find about five million tiny eggs hidden in very obvious places, retire under a bush together to eat them all, go completely raving sugar-rush bonkers for about an hour, and then throw up in all directions. Mum tells me I did the same thing when I was their age. Maybe that's why I sometimes wake up screaming that I'm being eaten by a giant truffle.

But now the thought of eating an Easter egg has quite unexpectedly become totally unappealing.

'Amy!' Mum's voice interrupts my daydreams.

'Are you coming out to help the girls find their eggs?'

Groan. Lurch towards garden. Doorbell rings. Groan again and lurch in other direction. Groan thrice. It's actress-over-the-road.

Doesn't she know only teens can get away with crop-tops, especially ones that aren't much wider than a boob-wallet, and extra-especially worn with shrink-wrapped denims? Gaaaad.

'Hi,' she says, turning on that gleaming white smile like a light bulb, though she's obviously pissed off it's me. 'Is your dad in? I seem to have a little domestic crisis.'

'Dad!' I yell towards the back of the house like a stadium PA system. She looks puzzled and deafened at the same time. After a couple more window-rattling yells, Dad comes in pursued by two giggling, chocolate-encrusted Puddings, and is about to pick a diss with me for interrupting when he spots actress-over-the-road, who's now actress-over-the-top-in-our-front-door.

'Sorry to bust in,' she trills.

Har har har.

Dad didn't exactly lie on the ground wagging his tail and waving his legs in the air, but he might as well have done.

'Come in, come in,' he splutters. 'Come and have a choccy.'

'Better not – have to watch my figure, you know,' she gurgles.

'Right,' says Dad, watching her figure.

'Look, I know this is a terrible pain, but my

washing machine's flooding and I don't know how to stop it. You couldn't be a real lovey and see if you can fix it, could you? I'm sure it wouldn't take a minute.'

'Why don't you look in the Yellow Pages?' I ask her, smiling the best version I can make of my own gleaming white smile.

Dad hastily interrupts. 'Just take the girls back outside for a minute, Amy,' he says, smiling his own patent yellowy-grey broken-fang smile. 'I'll just go over and see what I can do. Tell your mum I won't be long.' He gets his toolbox out of the hall cupboard and off they go.

'Byeeeee,' says actress-over-the-road, giving me a little wave like the Queen from the window of a limo.

I go outside with the Puddings and tell Mum what's happened.

'That's nice, dear . . .' she says, trying to stop Pudding One from using her skirt to wipe her face with.

'Don't you think he ought to have a chaperone or something?' I ask Mum. 'She's looking like something out of a very low-rent lap-dancing club.'

'Oh, don't be silly, darling,' says Mum. 'Women like that stopped looking at Dad about twenty years ago. Anyway, she seems quite nice. She can't help what she looks like. Have an egg.'

Innocence, thy name is Mum.

'No thanks,' I say. 'I've gone off eggs.'

Mum looks at me with interest for the first time

that day. 'Really? It's always been impossible to prise them out of your sweaty hand at Easter.'

'Thanks very much. Trying to watch my figure these days.' I strike actress-over-the-road pose which makes Mum and the Puddings laugh.

Mum and I put our arms around each other and wander down the garden in the sunshine. The Puddings squeak because they've seen more eggs in the gutter of Dad's garden shed. Mum takes no notice as they struggle precariously with the ladder.

'You seem a bit preoccupied lately,' Mum says to me.

'Yeah . . . well . . .' I say. 'Maybe we should have a chat about it—'

My mobile rings. It's Lottie. 'Hi, Britney,' she says. 'Fancy a blow? Alice says Elsie's folks have gone to some sheep-sacrificing alternative-Easter lunacy at Stonehenge or somewhere and we can use her house. She thought we could have a blast of high-quality grunge.'

'OK, you're on.' I look imploringly at Mum. The Puddings choose that moment to fall off the ladder. Terrible shrieking rends the peaceful Easter air.

'What's happening?' crackles Lottie at the other end. 'Is it a terrorist outrage?'

'More or less,' I say, trying to pull splinters out of Pudding Two with my free hand. 'I think I might be a bit delayed.'

'That's all right, sweetheart,' says Mum, cradling

one wailing Pudding in each arm. 'You go out and have some fun. I think it's time these two had a little afternoon nap.'

5.30 p.m.

'I've got us a gig,' Mad Alice is saying. We're taking a break after a couple of hours of solid funkaliciousness and blue-flash soul that makes your hair stand on end, and it must have been pretty good because after a bit even Elsie's neighbours came round to complain, and they've heard everything. 'It's that pub down World's End Lane, where Elsie's brother works,' Mad Alice goes on. 'I know it looks just like a local for ancients at the front and hardly anybody goes there, but there's a club round the back that apparently has them queuing down the street. The guy who runs it heard us at the party. He thought you were destined for really big things,' she says to me. 'Like playing every week at his place, stuff like that.'

'Does he know how old we are?' Lottie asks.

'Well, I trailed off a bit answering that one,' Mad Alice chuckles. 'But I was wearing me bikers' leathers with the suspenders on the outside at the time, which looks kind of . . . mature, I guess.'

'When does he want us?' the rest of us ask in one breath.

'This Thursday,' Alice says. 'And – who knows? – maybe every Thursday? Unless you're, um, too busy dating Stanley, that is.'

'I wouldn't date him if he was the last boy on earth,' I say.

Of course Alice and Debs raise their eyebrows to the ceiling, but Lottie shoots them a look to freeze hell over and says, 'Leave it out,' so they do.

Wednesday April 23

'A pub?' Mum says, her voice going into dog-whistle range. 'Your dad'll never let you sing in a pub in a million years.'

'Look, Mum,' I say desperately. 'The others are depending on me. I can't let them down. And it might be the start of my career as a superstar. I'm not doing anything illegal by just being there. It's not as if I'm going to be ordering gin and tonics all night. I'm just going to sing, it's a job. They're going to pay me and everything.'

'Really?' asks Mum, interested. 'How much?'

'I don't know yet. Maybe quite a lot. And I might get noticed by somebody from a record label or something. Look, it's a hell of a lot safer being there than at Elsie's party, where everybody was mad as a cut snake and the only licensing law was to get totally off your face.'

Whoops. Mum doesn't know I was at that party. 'Er, according to Lottie,' I add.

But all Mum says is, 'Can I come? We could tell Dad we're off to the cinema for a girls' night out.'

'Hmmm, maybe,' I say dubiously. 'Not sure you'll like it.'

'Try me,' says Mum.

The pub is called the Ferret and Flugelhorn. It's all polished wood and engraved mirrors in the front, but the room out the back is another story.

'Nice, innit?' says Duane, the guy with an Ibiza tan and one earring who runs it. 'Used to be the pub's outside khazi.'

The red bulbs and black walls don't quite get rid of that impression, or the smell. But it's exciting, like being a real band. Duane shows us into a tiny little back room with peeling walls. 'You're on at half eight,' says his voice outside. 'Better stay in there until then. I'll bring you out some Cokes. Don't ask for anything else, you'll get me in trouble.'

It seems an age until half past eight. Mad Alice tunes her guitar about a hundred times, then untunes it and looks happier. Lottie practises para-diddles on a couple of paint tins until our teeth chatter. Debbie doesn't touch her bass at all but keeps adding and subtracting bits of her make-up, and trying to decide if her top looks better off the shoulder than on. Finally, the door bursts open and Duane beams in.

'All right, my little darlings,' he says. 'You're on.'

The gig is terrifying at first. Elsie's party was one thing – we knew most of the people there. But in this place we can hardly see anything from the stage except a sea of shadowy strangers. Duane has plugged our instruments into a sound system that looks like something out of air-traffic control. We look at each other blankly for what seems like minutes. Then Mad Alice takes the bull by the horns and swings her arm into an anticipated guitar *kerraaang* we all flinch at. It should flatten most of the surrounding buildings coming out of Duane's brain-melting loudspeakers. Not a batsqueak. Duane's cheery mug pops up at the front of the stage.

'Sorry, folks,' he says, completely unembarrassable. 'Would 'elp to plug it in.'

A friendly ironic cheer goes up from the audience, which makes me feel strangely better. Obviously, not being plugged in at first is going to be Our Thing, a bit like Spinal Tap. Duane goes off to switch the power on, gives a thumbs-up to Mad Alice, who lets out a metal-splintering ripper that makes our knees wobble. Lottie whacks the crash cymbals with both fists in a big Welcome-to-Hell explosion, and catches her glasses with the upswing on the follow-up; they fly out into the darkness, never to be seen again. Closing my eyes tight shut,

I growl the first few bars of *I'm Missing You, Honey, But My Aim's Getting Better* and realize it sounds OK over our drama-queen opening shots – then I open my eyes just in time to see a familiar figure in

the front row collapse backwards into the crowd, which is so tightly packed no harm seems to be done.

Even in this light, I can see it's Mum. *Quel fromage!* What have I done? I leap into the audience, still clutching the microphone, and still wailing, like a stuck disc. A big roar goes up from the audience, which parts like the Red Sea. I come face to face with Mum, who has been stood upright by an assortment of concerned goths, skins, rudes, and people held together by tattoos. She lets out a terrifying scream, which I find myself repeating like an echo. Then she smiles a big ear-to-ear smile. There is a pause for a moment. The band behind me thunders into our version of The Doors' *Light My Fire* – Mad Alice is a killer on the fancy baroque bits. Mum starts a kind of strange, hopping dance, which I've never seen her do before. On an impulse, I decide it's safe to take a flying leap back on stage, and somewhere in mid-air my multi-coloured, ethnic, worldbeat sarong comes unpinned, revealing my grey-coloured XXL underwear. An even bigger roar goes up, and I can see Mum hysterical with laughter.

The gig is a triumph. We get swept off to the bar in the Ferret and Flugelhorn, but though Duane and his mates offer to get us anything we want, I'm not falling for that one twice. I look out for Mum, who's on the edge of the crowd in the bar. She catches my eye, and waves. Duane introduces Jack, a very handsome mate of his who has a pro band of his own. Debbie tries even more of the top-off-the-shoulder on Jack, but – *incroyable!* – he only seems to be interested in me.

'A star is born,' he says, taking care not to blow smoke in my face and blowing it over Debbie by accident. 'I've been looking for somebody like you all my life.'

'Really?' I say, originally. 'How long's that then?'

'Well, I don't come out with that kind of information for just anybody,' he says.

'But I'm not just anybody,' I tell him.

'Look,' says Jack, pulling me away from the others. 'You need some experience in a real band. They're all right but' – gesturing at the others – 'you could do a lot better.'

'That's my band,' I say, raising an eyebrow at him. 'They're who I work with.'

'Join mine,' Jack says urgently. 'I've got two backing singers – one's leaving to have a sprog. You'd be just perfect.'

'I'm not a backing singer,' I say, but Jack *is* very good-looking and very close. 'I'm a singer . . .' I say, tailing off a bit.

'Everybody has to start somewhere,' Jack says, smiling a heart-fluttering smile. His hand is resting on my hip. 'This business is ruthless – you need to know your way around, get a bit professional. Clothes, for instance: somebody like you needs something a bit more sophisticated – no offence. We can sort all that. Good repertoire, you get to know what the people want when you've been on the road for a bit. Microphone technique . . .'

I can see Mum trying to make her way towards me through the crowd. Debbie and Mad Alice are throwing me such looks of envy, contempt, surprise and betrayal all together – Lottie can't see further than her nose, so she has no idea what's going on – that they make me explode into laughter. Jack takes his hand off my hip, stops smiling and turns back to Duane at the bar.

'Suit yourself,' he says, his face not half as nice now. 'Your funeral.'

Mum finally reaches us, and gives me a big hug. 'That was wonderful,' she says. 'Not quite—'

'Your thing,' I say.

'– my thing, but I was really proud of you. I wish Dad had stayed.'

'What do you mean?' I asked her. 'You didn't tell him, did you?'

'Nearly. I met him in the bar just before you came on. Extraordinary coincidence. He'd come to meet somebody about a possible job, but it didn't work out. Poor old Dad. Do you want to come home with me, or would that be too big a blow for the cred?'

'No, I'll come,' I say, winking at the others. 'My manager's here,' I tell them. 'Sorry, Mum, but I have to go to the loo first.'

'That's OK,' Mum says, 'I'll wait outside.'

I head for the door marked CHICKS. Heavens, must check if the men's is COCKS . . .

But *horrendous lavabos!* Actress-over-the-road is in there, preening her eyelashes.

'Well done, Amy,' she says to me. 'Dark horse, eh?'

'Thanks,' I say grumpily, hopping from foot to foot. Somebody else goes in the cubicle while this is going on, which makes me grumpier and hoppier still. 'Didn't know this sort of thing was . . . your sort of thing . . .'

'Well, I was . . . kind of at a loose end,' she says, staring critically at the mirror. 'God, the smoke in there plays havoc with your eyes. Are your parents here?'

'My mum is. My dad's gone.'

'Oh,' is all she says. 'Well, see you around.'

'Right,' I say, as somebody else jumps the queue for the cubicle. 'See you around.'

CHAPTER EIGHT

In Which Amy Hits the Malls and Gets on a Song-writing Roll

<u>**Monday April 28**</u>

Back to Broadmoor!

Lottie called for me and told me to smile all day. I gave her my best pitying look.

'Suppose Maul's been bragging about me to his horrible mates?'

'He probably has,' said Lottie, 'but what do you care about them? They're probably all saddos who paper their walls with pictures out of *Loaded*. Anyway, they make up most of the stuff they go on about. Gary Sprocket was telling people who saw him in the street with those two blondes that he'd done it with both of them at once. They turned out to be his cousins from Wigan, and all they did together was watch *What Are Friends For?* and play Monopoly.'

Great.

'But it's just unfair,' I moaned to Lottie. 'It's one law for boys and another for girls. Boys who do it

with loads of girls are heroes, like it's just part of
learning to be a Regular Guy. But girls still get
called slags and skets and hos.'

'Ruth'n'Van don't mind being called slags,' says
Lottie, hooting. 'They *like* it. They spend most of
their days in the loos putting on eye shadow and
most of the nights getting the boys to lick it off.'

'Yeah,' I said, 'but I don't think many of the
boys like them all that much . . .'

'Well,' said Lottie, 'they probably like each other.'

'True,' I said. 'I suppose we're all the same when
it comes down to it. I think I was really mean
about Tracey now – I mean, she probably loves
Gareth Foreskin.'

'You weren't mean about Tracey! You saved her
neck!'

'I know, but I sort of looked down on her at the
same time.'

'Hmmmm,' said Lottie.

6 p.m.

School was OK, as it happens.

Stanley shied like a frightened horse when he
saw me in the lunch queue. He didn't make any
horrible remarks and I don't think anyone except
Lottie noticed.

Ruth'n'Van didn't make anything of it at all –
I suppose it was all in a night's work to them.

Got sent out of food tech for eating half Mikey's
ingredients. He is doing a fantastic thingy involving
sweet potatoes and spinach and I have got a thing

about spinach just now, so I couldn't help it.'

Mikey didn't mind, he thought it was flattering. He is going to be a chef, doing Caribbean and Olde Englishe. He says he wants a restaurant for ordinary people: 'No rudes, dudes, chiefs or riff-raff, you get me?'

I think he was hoping for a lot of old West Indian gents in trilbies and guys in flat caps who stand in holes in the road, but I told him these were dying breeds. 'They will come back flocking to my ristorante,' he insisted.

I asked him if Black Hole could sing at his opening night, but he said he was going to have a string quartet playing Bob Marley tunes. This could be worth hearing.

Tuesday April 29

Gloom, doom, mock mocks. How can you take something called 'mock mocks' seriously? It sounds like a chicken. Only thing I can do is English anyway.

I've been put down to the bottom group for maths, which means I can only get a C now, at best.

'That is crap,' says Lottie, who is in the top group, where I used to be before the power of love sapped my powers of concentration and I got put in with mad old Dr Tangent. 'You should get your folks to complain. Tangent can only teach people who already know how to build spaceships.'

'True. He's got PhDs and doctorates coming out

of his ears but he can't control the class and he can't speak English.'

'What? He's from Cambridge, isn't he?'

'Exactly,' I say.

Cannot face telling Mum about this – she still thinks I am a late-starting genius who will get going when the going gets tough.

Bright side is Stanley completely ignores me. Or rather, I sometimes catch him looking at me, a sort of frightened look. Whatever he's thinking, it's much better than him boasting about it in front of all his mates. Maybe he's ashamed. Some chance.

I wish he would just vanish off the planet though. What happened always makes me think of Tom, and what he would have thought if he knew. Or if he'd seen! The thought makes my knees go watery.

Midnight

Wrote another very short letter to Tom. Just twenty-eight pages. In case the other one got lost in the post. They often do.

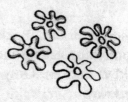

Wednesday April 30

7 a.m.

Gandhi has shredded my letter.

7.30

Maybe the letter looks more heartfelt now, all

sellotaped back together and wet with tears.

Tom won't know it's Gandhi's wee, will he?

5 p.m.

Calamitousness. Tracey Hardwick thinks she is my friend! I was getting my stuff together at the end of English – and she tagged along with me while we walked to food tech, which is a lesson wasted on most of us but Tracey H in particular.

'It's all a bit over the top, that Shakespeare, innit?' she says, making conversation. 'Imagine if your husband choked you every time he thought you'd snogged somebody else, the school'd be nearly empty.'

'And all because some other guy had her handkerchief,' I say. 'If she'd used Kleenex like normal people, none of this need've happened.'

'Yeah, right,' says Tracey, perfectly seriously. 'It's dead unrealistic.'

Tracey's noticeably pregnant now.

'What're you going to do about that?' I ask, pointing at her middle. 'You leaving?'

'Yeah, can't wait,' Tracey says. 'Look.' She waves her left hand under my nose. There's a ring on it. 'I'm engaged to Gareth now.'

'Bad luck – I mean, congratulations,' I say.

'I know people think he's a dickhead,' Tracey says, as if she doesn't mind. 'He is, a bit, but he likes me, I think. He's going to work in his dad's garage, so we'll be rolling, get our own place and everything. Would you come to the wedding?'

I think about saying I have to go to an important budgerigar's funeral on the day, but what finally comes out is: 'If you'd like me to.'

'It'd be nice,' Tracey goes. 'I haven't forgotten what you did about that spliff. Well, see you.'

She's just about to bunk off when she stops, as if there's something else on her mind. 'Sing, don't you?' she says, looking in the other direction.

'Um,' I say.

'Everybody says you're fantastic.' Tracey's looking at me now. 'Will you sing at my wedding do? It's just going to be in a boozer, there won't be any dosh – but the booze is free, you can get as pissed as you like. It'll be a laugh.'

'OK.'

'Nice one,' Tracey says.

I want to sing at Tracey's wedding about as much as I want to sit on Cliff Richard's knee. Which is not at all. Not one tiny little bit.

Why am I so nice? What I need is Nastiness lessons.

Tuesday May 13

Two weeks later

Everything reminds me of Tom. I keep seeing him in parks, turning into shops, jumping on buses. I even jumped on one after him last night, I was so convinced.

I pulled at his arm. 'Tom . . .'

A man turned round. He looked like he'd just

136

escaped from an undertaker's. He smiled at me and his teeth looked like a fence a car had just driven through. 'Well, helloooo,' he said.

'Sorry, thought you were my dad,' I said. Bit mean really – he was probably only about twenty-five.

Wednesday May 14

Couldn't get in the bathroom for hours. Dad was in there. When he finally came out his hair had gone black, he'd just had his annual shave, rubbed some stuff on his face that made him glow like a traffic light, and he was smiling all over. It was like seeing your doddery old dad go into the bathroom and Terry Wogan come out, singing as well.

'Thanks, Terry,' I said, pushing past him. 'Some of us have to get somewhere in the mornings.'

Dad's glow went dim for a minute. 'Trouble with this household,' he says, 'is that nobody appreciates what a gift life is.' He went off down to breakfast, singing again.

Saturday May 17

Have become a shopaholic. Me and Lottie hit the malls with the money from Duane's gig. We felt really proud of ourselves, grown up and spending our wages any way we wanted. Well, not exactly wages. We got a tenner each and Duane said that was generous.

We got hats today.

I think hats are going to be big this year at
Glastonbury. We are thinking
of putting flowers and
twinkly doo-dahs on them
and wearing them with
long gowns – maybe a
stuffed parrot on top: Hendrix
is due for his come-uppance.

'D'you remember when we were six and
watched the *My Fair Lady* video every day for a
month? We'll look just like Audrey Hepburn at the
races,' trilled Lottie.

Well, that would definitely require leaving out
the parrot. And Audrey Hepburn vanished if
she stood sideways, but these days I'm bigger
sideways than facing the right way round. There's
lots of flash low-cut tops made for girls like me,
but I don't quite feel ready for them somehow. I
haven't quite got used to this new shape yet, and
I've still got mixed feelings about it. I can't work
out if it's because I'm not a virgin any more, or
because I really have slimmed down in the right
places and filled out in the other right places,
but I definitely notice boys looking at me a lot
these days.

I just wish they were Tom.

5 p.m.

Lottie and I chatter on about Glastonbury on the
bus back. It'll be great to be free – no parents, no
teachers, no don't-do-this-or-that. I like that hippy

thing they have there, love and peace and all that. They probably wouldn't even let somebody like Stanley Maul in: they'd have a prat-detector at the gate that would pick up his vibe.

Sunday May 18

Up at crack of 11 a.m. to measure my boobs. They are definitely growing.

I am going to have to save up now, for a boob reduction. Lucky about my giant's feet, otherwise I would just topple over.

COOL CHICK TIP
Just be yourself and the world — as well as the boys — will be at your feet!

Oh good. Then They can all laugh TogeTher at my size nines.

Noon

Actress-over-the-road is at the door again, saying her car won't start. Bloody hell, why doesn't she just get a part in a do-it-yourself programme? I've come racing down from boob-measuring to open the door because Lottie's coming round with a new song she wants to show me, but it's just stupid lip-gloss-on-a-Sunday-morning Emma Dearest. Anyway, I'm pleased to see that the inflating balcony of Yrs Truly is now overtaking the one she's so proud of pouting around, and I've got youth on my side too – yah. We're eyeing each other up suspiciously when Dad rockets to the door as if he was pulled to Emma Dearest on knicker-elastic, which I'm beginning to wonder if he is.

'Tell your mum I won't be a minute,' Dad says over his shoulder. 'Probably just need to get a spark going.'

Emma Dearest giggles, and pushes him. *Possibili Dad pornografia!* Are all males except Tom like Stanley Maul underneath? Even my dad?

'Do your shirt up,' Dad calls over his shoulder to me. Grrrr!

Lottie's coming up the path just as actress-over-the-road goes off with Dad to take a look at the crankshaft or whatever. Yeech. Lottie gives me her best owly look as she comes in.

'Off to church, are they?' she says.

'Don't ask,' I say. 'Have you got the song?'

Lottie has a scruffy bit of paper in her hand, and we go off to my room arm in arm to look at it. I don't like to tell her it's just like everything you hear on the radio though: '*Give me your love and I'll never cheat on you, Give me your love, it's for always just we two*' – that kind of crapola. The tune's not bad though.

'How about this?' I go. 'Something more like:

'Once my troubles seemed a long,
long way away,
Now you've gone and left me,
I cannot make you stay . . .'

Lottie frowns. 'Think I've heard something like it before somewhere,' she finally says.

'I think I have too,' I conclude gloomily. 'Maybe all the songs have been written already. All right, how about:

'If we'd known there was an ending,
we'd have given it more care;
It's just a cry in space I'm sending,
maybe somewhere you're out there.'

We stop and look at each other.
'From the heart, eh?' Lottie says. 'It's not bad.'
'I'll work on it,' I tell her.

Saturday May 31

Two weeks later

Have just finished *Captain Corelli's Mandolin.* Which is proof that even the most unlikely things can happen in love. Maybe. I texted Tom that he should read it, but I might as well text thin air . . .

6 p.m.

This boob thing is getting out of hand. I have had
to buy two new boob wallets – well, boob ruck-
sacks, really. And my new groovy hip chinos which
cost a whole month's pocket money are too tight!

I only bought them
two weeks
ago.

My
period is
overdue,
I expect
that's why.

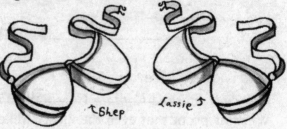

Shep
Lassie

I am always bloated when my period's overdue.
Actually, it's *nine days* overdue!

I didn't really have a proper period last month,

142

just a trickle for a day.

My periods are crap, anyway. Sometimes they are like Niagara Falls for a week, sometimes I miss one. They are often a week late.

Am going to begin diet today. Well, tomorrow. I can smell sausages and you can't begin a diet when you can smell sausages. I will have to tell Mum to get low-fat ice cream.

FIGHT-THE-FLAB TIP
Eating too fast? Slow yourself down by eating with chopsticks!

Good heavens, why didn't I think of This before?

Midnight

I will never look like Xanthia Starr of course, but then Xanthia Starr will never sing like me. Or write songs like me either. I've finished the one I started with Lottie, and the band are over the moon about it. It's just called *Love, Fifteen* of course. I've started four others now.

Tuesday June 3

9 p.m.

Daft to worry about periods at my age. They're always all over the place. I missed one altogether last year. So obviously I'm just missing another one. I'll get one this month, no worries.

Am feeling jolly for first time since Tom went – as long as I don't think about him, that is. When I think about him I start to get mad. It is shaming that he hasn't replied to any of my messages but I can't bring myself to hate him.

Why?

Because I still feel there's some explanation that is going to make it all OK, that's why.

Because my instinct is that he still loves me.

Maybe there's some other girl from way back who's turned up in Japan and is making him feel guilty.

Maybe he's just breaking it to her gently that he loves only me?

Maybe something like me and Stanley happened to him and he felt our pure love was besmirched?

When I think of this I ache with jealousy, and yet what happened with Stanley has shown me that you can get carried away and feel sexy without it meaning a thing.

That could have happened to Tom too . . .

I've shown him I can be faithful, in my heart and soul at least, by e-mailing every day.

I know I'll hear from him soon, I just know I will.

It's what keeps me going.

But love does seem to have unleashed my creativity, I can really hear something happening to me musically. I'm writing songs like a maniac. At this rate, we'll have enough for an album soon. I think of poncey old Jack at Duane's pub gig – maybe he can give me a break as a backing singer; perhaps I'll get a chance to hold his microphone for him, nudge-nudge. Who needs it?

I will be a free independent woman, since I will never love another but Tom. Completely gone off the idea of sex, which is a big relief.

Two kids of about fourteen were snogging on the bus today. Why can't they do it somewhere private?

Now that I've decided to be a celibate virgin, I can eat as much as I like.

Well, celibate, anyway.

Wednesday June 4

But perhaps I have missed two periods, not just one. That one in April was just a trickle . . .

Thursday June 5

What a nightmare, there's a gig at the Ferret and Flugelhorn tonight. Just to prove how down I am, I picked up *Teenacious Tips*, which I grew out of weeks ago.

I threw the book across the room.
'Life choices'. Pah!
Picked it up again after having joyful thought
that period would gush in any moment, and read
the following:

This was more like it.

4 p.m.
Raided freezer and cooked whole boxful of
chopped spinach that Mum usually used for
trying pathetically to shovel down Puddings,

between ladles of marmalade.

Yum yum! Funny how much of my life has passed without understanding the joy of spinach.

Topped up with a doughnut and six marshmallows.

Midnight

Ended up fighting fit for the gig, and it went great. Well, except for the fact that there was some European Cup football match on telly, Duane had mixed up the dates and in the end he wasn't even there himself, and we had to set all our own kit up. A few people did drift in from the bar but they insisted on having the telly on full volume while we played. We got big cheers when we hadn't done anything special, and groans when we were great, so I don't think the noises were anything to do with us really. But we had a nice play, and the new material is really coming on. I'd forgotten my worries by the end.

But I hadn't counted on Dr Lottie.

'Are you OK?' she shouted through the smoke as we were packing up.

'Bright as a button. Why?'

'Well, your mum's worried. Said you'd been looking really peaky. And—'

'Yeah. Something I ate,' I said. 'What else?'

'Nothing. Only . . .' Then she said in a fake jolly voice, 'Got your period yet?'

'Oh yes, been and gone,' I lied.

Well, I was worried enough. I didn't want her worrying too.

I can't let on. I can't even think about it.

What will I do?

I'll get a pregnancy test.

That's what I'll do.

CHAPTER NINE

In Which Amy Goes to the Chemist and Gets Cold Feet

Friday June 6

You learn a lot about KFC hanging round in the loos.

Today I heard the following:

'Debbie's got the hots for Mikey. She says her mum'll kill her if she finds out she's seeing a rasta.'

'What you mean? Her mum's Jamaican, why wouldn't she like rastas?'

'Nah, but she's a Holy Roller. Thinks rastas just chill all day and never get a job.'

'Mikey's not like that.'

I couldn't even work out who was talking – I was weeing for England and by the time I'd finished they'd gone.

Why hasn't Debs told *me*?

Saturday June 7

Shop shop shoppetty shop. Bought two fluffy

elephants for Puddings. They are four in two months!

I always like buying presents for them – they're grateful in a way you never get from anybody older.

On way home, spot our car parked two streets round the corner from the house. Well, it's always breaking down, maybe it passed out on Dad just before he got home.

A missed period or two is no big deal.

I really don't see why I need to take a preggers test.

Course I don't, my next period will be along on June 19th, sure as eggs is eggs.

Eggs.

Ooooooooooooooooooh.

Only four more days till my period. Can hardly wait. Mum is thrilled because she thinks the anti-terrorist childminder has persuaded the Puddings to eat spinach. 'There's none left!' she said.

'They probably just binned it,' I said, unable to reveal the terrible truth, which is that I have snaffled the whole lot.

Just three teeny days till my period . . .

We did ogling Señor Mondragon today.

You have to take turns. It was Lottie's turn today and I could tell she had been practising. You go, ogle ogle ogle, until he notices, then you say, 'Sorry, got something in my eye.'

Then you wait for *Brief Encounter*-type moment when he says he'll have a look. Only Señor M is wise to that. He is obviously tragically not one of those teachers who are going to get caught in a trousers-down situation with a Year Ten.

'Maybe things will improve when we're in Year Twelve,' I say to Lottie, who is looking a bit droopy after his lack of interest in her eye probs. 'We'll all be legal by then.'

Tuesday 17 June

Only two days to go . . . yippeeee.

Am reading *Catch 22* – best book I've ever read.

Mentioned it to Ms Corman and she waxed lyrical about it being a classic. 'Not just an anti-war book, but a timeless satire on the fine line between sanity and madness. I'm so glad you appreciate Heller's genius, Amy,' she said.

'Teacher's pet,' sniggered Ruth after English.

But Iqbal asked me if he could borrow it! Said he wanted to read about Americans who hated war.

'You might like *Stupid White Men* or *Dude, Where's My Country?*' I said. 'Americans are not all baddies, you know, because those books sell very well over there.'

'I know that,' said Iqbal. 'Don't take me for a fool, because my English is stringy.'

'Not stringy, Iqbal, *ropey*.'

In fact, his English is better than most of my mates', which is a bit shaming.

Asked how he'd learned so much so fast and he said: 'Necessity is the Mother of Invention.'

I think I must have given him my goldfish look, because he gave me a sweet, pitying smile. 'You are a serious girl, Amy Baker,' he said. 'Not like these other noodles.'

'I'm not serious,' I said, laughing. 'I am . . . bubbly. And don't you dare impugn my friends.'

'Bubbly? Impewn?'

'Er. Bubbly, um, means, sparkly – bouncy – jolly. And impugn is, like, to diss – be rude about.'

'You are right, madam, of course. I must be kind to British noodles. Do you know who said, "Do unto another what you would have him do unto you"?'

'Er . . . Jesus?'

'No – well, sort of, but a different version and centuries later.'

'Mohammed?'

'No.'

'Gandhi?' I thought of our gerbil.

'No.'

'I give up.'

'Confucius. So the Chinese invented peace and gunpowder. And you know what they did with the gunpowder? They made fireworks, not bombs.'

Goodness.

Midnight

Am I a serious person who hides behind jokes?

Wednesday June 18

Just one day until my lovely period! Hooray!

Stanley Maul and I ended up next to each other in the lunch queue at school today. After a bit, it seemed impossible not to say something.

'Y'aright?' he asked, not looking at me.

'Never better,' I said, helping myself to the spinach.

'Started your exams yet?' he asked. 'I've got double maths AS level next Tuesday. Should be no problem – my parents have been getting me loads of revision books.'

'So've mine,' I said. Some chance.

'I hear you're singing tonight,' Stanley said, trying to bag a double helping of chicken curry and getting yelled at by the dinner lady. It's true, we're booked opposite Jack's band at a much bigger pub, the Weasel's Trousers. 'Can I come?'

'I'd prefer it if you didn't, but I can't stop you, can I?' I said, shrugging. I didn't want to think of him out there, watching me. But I knew I couldn't drag this memory around with me for ever – then he really would have won.

He went red and moved on with his tray. It was

strange he asked me if he could come, rather than just showing up with his leering mates. Maybe that's his way of saying sorry. Pah.

And it didn't get to me, I sang like a bird. The place was too big to see him in the crowd, anyway. Every gig I do seems to get easier. It's like I become a different person when I'm singing. We got a big reception for our set, and funnily enough the new songs went over better than our old stuff and the hits everybody knew. 'You blew them away,' the manager came and told us afterwards. 'I would've put you top of the bill if I'd known. They've heard all Jack's stuff before, it's like Golden Oldies time. But you've got something different.'

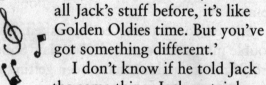

I don't know if he told Jack the same thing. Jack certainly made a big point of ignoring us all evening. He's one of those guys who think teenage babes are impressed by guys in bands. And I am one big teenage babe who is not.

12.10 a.m.

No period yet, but of course my period will be thinking this is still Wednesday, because I haven't been asleep yet. It will be here tomorrow, of course it will. Will put winged superplus towel on and wake up happy. Oh lovely lovely period, I just can't wait to see you.

I promise, dear goddess of tampons or patron

saint of panty-liners, or Mrs Tharg or whoever you are, that I will never complain about my periods ever ever again. Only please please please let it come.

Period Due

Today's the day! I know it will be OK.

Gave Iqbal my old copy of *Slaughterhouse Five* by Kurt Vonnegut and explained to him about the local library. Cannot believe no one has told him that yet.

He was amazed. 'You can take books away for no money? Like in school?'

'Yes, only better, because there's more choice. You can order books too, if they don't have them.'

'Order? Like tidy? Or boss?'

I explained exactly how the libraries work.

Perhaps I will have career being a noble person helping the poor and disadvantaged.

Mad shopping after school with Lottie.

Can't understand why I am such a balloon.

'How's the diet going?' Lottie raises her eyebrows as I try to lever my rear cleavage into some hipster flares.

'Brilliant, I've lost four pounds,' I say.

'Amy, cut it out,' she says. 'It's me, Lottie, remember?'

'Oh, so it is,' I gabble. 'Let's get some more hats.'

11 p.m.

I know it will come. I will wake up tomorrow and it will be here.

Friday June 20

My period has not come.

Ring Lottie.

'Lottie, come over.'

'Shut up.' She rang off.

How could she? I rang again. She has turned off her mobile. How *could* she?

Then I looked at the clock. 3 a.m. Tharg.

7.30 a.m.

Lottie phoned.

'I dreamt you rang me at three a.m.,' she said.

'I did.'

'Gaaaaaaaad, what's wrong?'

'My period hasn't come.'

Long silence.

'When was it due?'

'Yesterday.'

Laugh of hyena.

'If you don't count last month,' I added, when the laughter died away.

'You mean you've missed a period already?'

'Er . . .'

'I'll be right over.'

But she didn't come. She rang back to say she

had double science and if she missed it she'd never be a vet.

What is more important, me or a hamster?

Dragged myself to school and caught up with Lottie on the way home.

We went to the park.

'Remember when we used to push the Puddings on these swings?' I said.

'That was only April,' she said.

'Things were so easy then.'

'Tom had just left and you were blubbing all the time,' she said.

But she was helpful though. 'Look at it this way – you've only missed one period and you missed one last year.'

'But I only had a teeny trickle in April.'

'How teeny?'

'About a drip, for half a day, really.'

'Oh.'

Long pause. Then she said in that strangely jolly voice that she has taken to using with me recently as if I am a mad person, 'Still, that probably counts, so this one's not late yet, it's only due today. Um, get a test.'

'I can't. I can't go to the GP. Suppose they talk to Tom's dad.'

'Er . . . wouldn't he be in Japan, you pretzel? Anyway, doctors are forbidden to talk about your case, unless you say they can.'

'Oh. Yes.'

'Anyway, you get them at the chemist's.'

'Yes.'

'I'll get it for you if you like.'

'But I can't be pregnant. I only did it once, with Tom – loads of contraceptives and it was during my period! It's not possible, is it?'

'I guess not,' said Lottie. 'But, erm, you didn't, erm, go a bit too far with Stanley Maul, did you? I notice you giving him the evil eye whenever he comes near—'

'Oh God, Lottie, I'm not sure . . . No, of course not,' I add firmly.

Well, of course, that's not what happened. I'm not even going to think about it.

Lottie didn't want to think about it either, so we went to ogle Horst and I had two doughnuts and a puccini.

It has not come.

It has not come. But as Lottie has pointed out, it is only five days late. I will run round block and have a hot bath – that should bring it on. OK.

9.30 p.m.

Watched telly programme about women taking fertility treatment. One old dear went on and on about how she was a week late and virtually ordering the cot and the babygro and then her period came and she was insane, as though someone had died! How weird – all over the country half the women are wetting themselves because their period hasn't come and the other half are going up the wall because it has. It's no wonder men run the country.

7 a.m.

It has come! *Bandidas hurratas!*

Just a weeny drop, so far, but it will be flooding by noon. Huzzah!

Thank you, goddess of tampons. Thank you, patron saint of sanitary towels, who has chosen to smile on an ancient forty-something desperate for her last go at motherhood, and to spare me to live my young, buoyant life with my bubbly personality intact.

With my rucksack bursting with sanitary-ware, I hurtle to KFC on wings of panty-liner.

'Lottie! It has come!' I cry, to guffaws from Ruth'n'Van, who are lurking behind the loo doors.

'I mean *the letter promoting my dad*,' I say very loudly.

'What, is he allowed to clean loos with a brush now, instead of his mitts?' they chortle.

'Oh great. That means he's got the contract for Catherine Zeta Jones's jacuzzi then?' said Lottie. 'And you're all invited to the opening?'

Which shut up even Ruth'n'Van.

I felt really bad later, when Iqbal said he was pleased my father had a great new job.

5 p.m.

One drop. That's all it was.

Lottie says I must get preggers test.

She says she threw the runes, or matchsticks, or whatever it is she does the *I Ching* with, and it said:

If one is sincere when confronted with difficulties, the heart can penetrate the meaning of the situation. And once we have gained inner mastery of the problem, it will come about naturally that the action we take will succeed.

'See?' she said, looking wise.

Frankly I have not the foggiest idea what these words of wisdom mean.

6 p.m.

Teenacious Tips on periods:

> ## HEALTH TIP
>
> *Stoppages lasting two to twelve months in the first two years after periods started are normal.*

Two to twelve months! Huzzah! Why didn't I consult this teen bible earlier? I bet there is nothing so useful in the real Bible. Or the Koran. Or the I Ching Chong Chang.

Phone Lottie. 'Yah boo, Lottie,' I say, in a sophisticated way.

'Yes, but . . .'

'But what?'

'Get one anyway, just to be on the safe side.'

Thursday June 26

I was out the house at 6 a.m. and into the middle of town. I wasn't going to the local chemist where anyone might see me.

I chose a big posh one. I thought there'd be

more shelves to hide behind if I saw anyone I knew, and you can tell them what you've come for without everybody else in the place learning your entire medical and sexual history (in my case, not a big memory test for anybody).

But having got there so early, had to hang about outside before they opened up of course. The fact that God definitely has a sense of humour was proved when Ruth'n'Van staggered by looking as if they hadn't slept all night (which they most likely hadn't). Ruth got a manky-looking packet of condoms out of her bag and offered me one – 'Save you waiting till they open,' she said, taking a drag on her fag and choking with a mixture of smoke and hysterics.

'No thanks,' I said, 'I'm trying to give them up.'

'Well, that'll be the other reason you're here then,' said Van, winking. Gaaaad! Why can't people mind their own business?

I decided I would ask for a diet sheet and something for conjunctivitis and then slip in a casual 'And do you have a pregnancy test, by the way?' as though I'd just thought of it. But I couldn't face going up to the pharmacy. I wandered insanely about, looking at shampoo. A plukey security guy in a hat too big for him started following me. I started scratching my bum and it scared him off, in case I was going to ask him where the itchy women's bums stuff was.

People started coming in and queuing up at the pharmacy. *Pescado y fritas!* Maybe I'll have to stay in here all day . . .

Feeling I had to look as if I was buying something I grabbed some spot-witherer (*he kissed my
spot*) and some freckle-blaster (*he licked my freckles*)
and then started staring, in a must-have sort of way,
at a section that included hot-water bottles, things
for putting in shoes to stop them smelling, men's
shaving stuff, verruca nukers etc. Finally! The queue
at the pharmacy disappeared and I took a deep
breath and shot over to the smiling Asian woman,
who looked rather startled at my hurtling advance.

Instantly a queue formed behind me before I
could speak. I was stood in front of a nervy forty-
something, probably one of those women off the
telly film, who would kill for a baby. Probably her
period was a day late and she'd come in for a test.
And I would take the last one and she would top
herself. Or maybe me. I was just about to bunk off
when the assistant asked if she could help me.

'Er, just these please.' I threw the zit-eraser and
freckle-blaster at her. She looked alarmed, but
whipped out a bag. It was now or never. I leant
closer and whispered, 'Have you got, um, a thingy
for you know . . . um . . . if you're . . . um . . .
missing a period . . . ?' I whispered.

'A pregnancy test?' she asked, very sweetly and
not very loudly, but in the sort of crystal-clear, five-
hundred-A-star, Oxford voice that you can hear all
round a room.

'It's for a friend,' I squeaked.

'You know the doctor will do it for nothing,' the

pharmacist fluted, looking at me with a smile they could have used to advertise their own teeth-whitening products.

'My *friend* wants to do it herself.'

The chemist nodded knowingly. I wondered if they had lie detectors as well as video cameras in big posh chemists. Maybe they listened to the tapes with cackling Special Branch officers every evening: 'Just a normal day, officer – twenty-eight people fiddling free prescriptions, fourteen teenage boys asking for Lucozade when they want condoms, and eighty-two teenage girls saying their pregnancy test is for a friend.'

But I suppose the chemist was trying to be helpful, not nosy.

She said there were a lot of places you could go to for advice if you were pregnant and perhaps my *friend* would like some leaflets?

I stuffed the leaflets in my pocket, blushing like a post box. 'My friend and her *husband* will be *very happy* if she is having a baby,' I blurted.

It's lucky I had a twenty on me.

It was £8.25p!

4 p.m.

My bedroom.

The pregnancy test is called Herald. Great! Blow the trumpets! Hang out the flags! Hold the front page! The chicken has come home to roost! A Little Bundle of Joy is on the way!

164

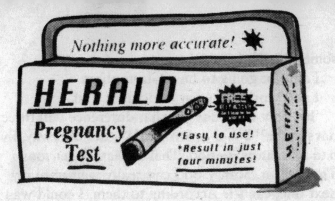

Nothing more accurate! ✹

HERALD

Pregnancy
Test

• Easy to use!
• Result in just
  four minutes!

They should call it Tenterhooks. Or Tough
Luck. Or You Are Not Alone.

I will wait till Mum's hauled the Puddings off to
the park.

7.30

I have read the instructions fifty-six times, but I
can't face doing it. I'll wait till after Glastonbury.

8.30

Rang Lottie.

'I don't care if you are engaged in willy aerobics
with Johnny Depp himself,' I said. 'Come over
right now.'

'Oh Johnny, right on the spot, as always. But it's
my best friend in the world, I've got to go,' she
panted. '*Eueergh*, sorry, I forgot your wife was
eating an éclair underneath.'

I couldn't help giggling, despite everything.
Lottie agreed to come straight away.

She'll be here in a minute. I'll just make us

some spinach fritters.

I am not going to miss Glastonbury.

I will work out what to do after that.

'It's only three days – what difference will three days make?' I said to scolding Lottie. 'Anyway, I've had a "scanty" period. That's what *Teenacious Tips* calls it. Scanty. So I can really wait until my next one, can't I? According to them, I could wait twelve months!'

'But the baby would be three months old by then. I mean, you'd know . . .' said Lottie, while I got those snuffly giggles the Puddings get. 'Anyway, that sort of advice is aimed at virgins, I think,' she added bravely.

'Lottiekins, I have done it once in my life, during my period, worse luck, and it was a multi-contraceptive experience.'

'But what about—?'

'Stanley? I don't think anything happened. He doesn't act like it did. It was just a snog, I'm sure. But I will do the test, after Glasters, honest.'

'Fine.'

'Fine.'

CHAPTER TEN

In Which Black Hole Meet the Earth Mothers

Friday June 27

Glastonbury

Mum had a bit of a wobbly when the Day of Glasters dawned. Luckily the god of music has made today an inset day, so she couldn't moan on about me missing school. But she had enough other worries.

'You will be careful?' she wailed. 'Don't take anything silly, Amy, will you? Or, you know, go off with a boy you don't know . . .'

'Don't be ridiculous,' I said. 'Glastonbury's probably about the one place in the world where nobody means any harm to anybody else.'

'That's just naive,' she moaned. 'There's nowhere in the world like that.'

'That's the trouble with getting old,' I said, rather unsympathetically. 'You lose faith in human nature.'

The Puddings crashed in at this point, whacking the daylights out of each other.

'*My* packetta crips!' Pudding One yelled.

'*Mine!*' Pudding Two responded, unwisely thumping Pudding One with a clenched fist also holding an already crushed crisp packet. Very small flakes of crisp burst all over the floor. Both Puddings howled dementedly and began wrestling on the carpet amid the mess.

'I'm going to miss my train,' I said to Mum, before she could say anything about Human Nature.

'You will eat properly, won't you?' she flapped, as I struggled to stand upright having heaved my rucksack on. 'Have you got some loo rolls?'

'Yeah, but I'm trying to give them up – the paper sticks to your teeth. Look, please stop flapping. Anyone would think I was going up the Amazon or something.'

I gave Mum a kiss. 'I'm meeting the others at the bus stop. I'll see you Sunday. You can call me if you want.'

I'm not sure Mum's attempt to look cheerful wasn't worse than her expression of desperation. She smiled weakly. 'Don't do anything I wouldn't do,' she finally said.

Poor Mum. She wouldn't do hardly anything these days. I gave her a big hug, attempted to hug the struggling Puddings without success, and finally tottered out of the door, wondering why I seemed to have packed exercise weights in my rucksack.

The others were standing at the bus stop, pretending to be asleep. Lottie had the tent-poles sticking up out of her rucksack, making her look like an owl playing the bagpipes. Debbie had the tent in a huge canvas bag, so with her rucksack as well, she looked as if she was emigrating. Just as well she's the strongest of us.

'Oh it's you,' they all yawned. 'Where have you been? We've been here for days.'

'Sorry, an old lady was strangling a cat on the way. I couldn't just walk by on the other side,' I said.

'Fair enough,' Mad Alice agreed. 'Like my hi-tech security arrangements for the tickets?'

She'd sewn them into her pink leather knickers. A couple of guys at the bus stop, who certainly didn't look like they were on their way to Glastonbury, started to get interested.

'Well, that's great, isn't it?' Lottie said, peering through her specs at Mad Alice's low-slung jeans and high-slung underwear. 'Does this mean you've got to be undressed by the door staff before we can get in?'

'Nah, it's all right, I'll just go behind a bush and dig them out when we get near the place,' Mad Alice said. The guys in the bus queue looked quite disappointed.

We got to the railway station, and I've never seen so many hippies in my life. The place looked like a dog pound full of spaniels. The train was packed and we couldn't find the seats we'd booked. All the coaches were just a jumble of ruck-sacks and guitars and people who looked like whole eco-systems were wriggling and twittering away inside their wigs.

We all piled out of the train in a woolly heap and got taken to the Glastonbury site. Mad Alice forgot to get the tickets out so it was a bit of a palaver when we had to swap them for our wrist-bands at the turnstile. But, hey, wow, this is Glasters, where everything is love and peace and like an old sixties film, baby, so Mad A stripping off and unpicking her fancy anchor stitch didn't cause the kind of argument it would have if you were queuing for your tube ticket, say. We all got given a welcome pack – a map and a spliff (not really, ha ha). Then we were through the vast impenetrable fence that no one seems to be able to tunnel under any more, and in! Wow.

It was a sea of tents, like a medieval battlefield 'cept people weren't chucking boiling oil at each other or walking around with hatchets in their heads but stumbling about with big smiles on their faces.

'It's a teen dream, innit?' Mad Alice said, nudging me. 'People living with crap and chaos and rubbish all around them and nobody shouting at them to clear it up.'

'Umm,' I said, not quite sure yet. I was glad my mum wasn't looking at this scene. I took a deep breath, and got a lungful of mingled ganja, wood smoke and hot dogs. Looking around, I saw there were stalls and shops everywhere, selling daft T-shirts, souvenirs, bongs, pipes, beads and beer.

I'd never seen so much beer in my life.

'We'd better find somewhere to put the tent up,' Lottie said sensibly.

'We should head for the Green Fields – that's where it's all "happening",' said Mad Alice knowingly. We stumbled about for a while, wading through smoke and smiles and stilt walkers and jugglers and people on springs dressed as kangaroos, and finally, what seemed like miles from anywhere, we found a spot. It wasn't surprising other people hadn't taken it: the ground was so rough mountain goats wouldn't have been able to keep upright on it. We put the groundsheet down and it looked as if it was covering a rockery. Then we tried to put the poles up and the tent over them, and the tent up and the poles under them. Debbie and Mad Alice crawled underneath and stood up under the tent with their arms out looking like ghosts ('Just stay like that all night,' said Lottie. 'That's really helpful, thanks'). I tried to bang the pegs in and succeeded only in hitting first one thumb and then the other, and then, having got the tent up to knee-high, we wriggled underneath for a well-earned rest and a chat about the next step. Having lulled us into a false sense of security, the tent then sneakily fell on top of us, muffling Lottie's initial words of wisdom on its future.

'Leffww frarnrrr,' a voice like Mad Alice's said.

We all wearily pushed the tent upwards for another listen.

'Let's party,' Alice turned out to be saying.

'It's been such a hassle getting in under here to start with,' Lottie said, 'why don't we just . . . er . . . have an evening in?'

'Yeah,' said Alice. 'We could rent a hippy-ripper video and get a lentil takeaway. I won't say it isn't tempting,' she went on, getting up as best she could, enshrouded in tent. 'But if I can ever find a way out of here, I'm going to check out some action. No point lying here with you slags. I might as well have stayed at home under the duvet. At least I'd be with someone I love.'

A chorus of raspberries greeted this, but the others did start getting to their feet – well, to their knees anyway.

'You go,' I said. 'I'm knackered.'

Like true friends, they made a big show of hopefully balancing the poles at weird angles here and there in an effort to keep the tent up, and then headed off into the night singing, *Corpses Can Be Lonely Too*, which you will recall was a smash hit for us the length and breadth of Mad Alice's bedroom.

I then fell into the deepest sleep the world has ever known since the Dark Ages, when everybody was asleep waiting for electricity to be invented.

3 a.m.

The tent was on top of me. No sign of the others. Had to find a loo . . .

I staggered out into a starry night and a thousand campfires and picked my way through an even more amazing scene than we'd seen when we first arrived. People were sitting around in the firelight, singing and playing guitars, some smoking spliffs the size of leeks, a few snogging, a couple sharing a sleeping bag – either doing a lot more than snogging or trying to catch an escaped ferret – some talking about the Meaning of the Universe.

Eventually I saw what looked like a line of portaloos and opened the first one. Phew. Come back, railway loo with single unsinkable beige floater, all is forgiven.

'Why not try over there?' said a small round woman swathed in primrose satin. She was pointing at another row of buildings.

I couldn't stop thinking how much like a melon she looked. Being still almost asleep, I even found myself saying, 'Thanks, melon . . .' as I staggered towards the other loos. They were wooden seats with a pit below them. I was past caring.

'You're psychic,' said a fluty voice as I stumbled out. 'It takes one to know one.'

'Eh?' I said intelligently.

'You knew I was called Melanie,' hummed the primrose sphere.

'Oh, no—' I began, but thought better of it.

'And I see you are with child,' she intoned.

That woke me up. 'No, no,' I squeaked.

'Oh yes, the goddess of fecundity has swooped down and left her blessings with you.'

'No, I just need to diet,' I insisted, backing away.

'The truth will come to you when you are ready. Visit us in the morning and we will bless your babe,' she said, pressing a small leaflet into my hand.

Oh my God.

The EARTH MOTHERS
+ + + + + + + + + + + +
New Age Birth
Birthing Pools
Aromatherapy
Aura Readings
Check out your
Karma!
Your Baby
Dances Within!

Wigwam Paradiso, Acacia Gdns
Stone Circle Lane, Bramblerow, WILTSHIRE

'Where have you been?' squeaked Lottie when I got back. 'We've been looking for you everywhere.'

I let this bare-faced lie go. 'I've been chatting to New Agers,' I said waftily, showing her the leaflet. 'Oh my goddess,' said Lottie. 'Have you done the test?'

'No. It's all garbage,' I laughed. 'Let's party.'

But of course I'd missed all the bands that night – the only sound came from an old Blues singer in the next tent singing something like, *I Ran Over My Old Dog in My Pickup by the Railroad Comin' Back from My Old Ma's Funeral After I Got Out of Jail, in the Hurricane.*

Saturday June 28

Glastonbury is the coolest place on earth. It's like being back in playgroup but with much more fun things to do, and nobody organizing you to do it.

We have been sneaking to the family field if we want the loo, as they are the only decent toilets, but people give you funny looks if you go in without a child, so we all shove jumpers up our front, and do our preggers walk and everyone waves us through. The jumpers look especially good under Debs's T-shirt, which reads: GOD IS BLACK AND BOY IS SHE MAD.

I was in a trance after a while, and it wasn't the low cloud of ganja smoke that was causing it either. It was the music – the sound of it all around, and what it does to people too. Music's very power-ful stuff. Everybody's known that for thousands of years. That's why they play nice quiet classical music in the dentist's to fool you the world's full of harmony and peace instead of grind-ing noises and torturers peering at you in masks; or mad governments who don't want to hear people's opinions like bossy marching music to pretend we're all going in the same direction anyway and don't need anything messy like elections; or listen to Bob Marley if they want to remind themselves the world can be a much better place.

I stopped thinking about what might be about to happen to me. I never felt so happy to be a singer. In fact I found myself singing everywhere we went.

'Shaddup,' Mad Alice said from time to time. Lottie simply stamped on my big feet occasionally.

'You want me to practise, don't you?' I asked them.

'Yeah,' said Mad Alice, 'but maybe in the same key as what they're playing in.' She was pointing at a band who were playing a strange kind of punk-Latin music in the half-empty tent we seemed to have stumbled into.

'Frog fritters! Since when have you given a monkey's about what key anything's in?' I protested.

'Sometimes it matters, sometimes it don't,' Mad Alice said mysteriously.

By midnight I was ready to drop, but Alice was raving away like a hamster on speed.

'She isn't taking anything silly, is she?' I whispered to Lottie.

'No, it's just natural adrenalin with her,' said Lotts.

The drift of Alice's loony riff was that she'd met some guys who could fix us up with a gig in one of the little bars, for Sunday morning.

'Are you mad?' Debbie asked. 'What are we going to play on – loo paper and combs? Anyway, the place is full of nang musicians. We're going to sound like total pistachios.'

'I taught this spotty guitarist a lick he didn't know,' Mad Alice carried on, unfazed as ever. 'He was so chuffed he said we could borrow his band's stuff for a blow. It'll be like Christmas – they've got a Fender bass and a drum kit without bits of elasto-plast on it and everything. All we have to do is . . .'

She trailed off, then leapt to her feet and made a big *kerrranggg* air-guitar gesture to show how much she was looking forward to it.

'All we have to do is what?' we all asked at once.

'Nothing, nothing,' Mad Alice said, cartwheeling her right arm and bending posily over one knee. 'I think they just hoped we might . . . hang out with them for a bit, that's all.'

'What do you mean, *hang out with them*?' Lottie asked suspiciously.

'Well . . . in their tent. They've got a great tent. It's better than Simon the Stockbroker's house,' said Mad Alice optimistically. I think she really hates Simon, and sometimes she hates her mum for getting tied up with him.

'You mad cow,' Lottie said, fifty per cent accurately. 'Now you've pimped us out to a bunch of spotty boy scouts just because you want to play on a Fender.'

'Oh, I don't know,' Debbie mused. 'What did the rest of them look like?'

'Worse,' Mad Alice admitted. 'But we don't have to do anything. We can just talk Old Skool rock bullshit with them for a bit and then piss off quick.'

We were split down the middle. Lottie and I didn't want to do it, Mad Alice and Debbie did.

'Do it as a duo,' Lottie suggested.

'Don't be dumb,' Mad Alice groaned. 'It's all for one and one for all. But look, this is Glastonbury. It's a world-famous thing. There might be record producers, big agents, star-makers

. . . This could be our big chance.'

In the end we were nearly ground down. I almost fell asleep in mid-argument. Lottie finally shrugged in what looked almost like agreement. A delighted Alice slapped Lottie so hard on the back that her veggie burger shot straight into the mush of a grimy kid dressed up as a rainbow.

'Oooh, sorry, darling,' gulped Lottie. Then she clocked the kid, who looked about eight. 'You're up late,' she said.

'No problem,' said the infant. 'Come and see our Rainbow Festival tomorrow,' and he pressed a grubby leaflet into Lottie's burger and passed it back to her.

'Blimey, it's the Earth Mothers again,' said Lottie. 'What do they want with us? Don't they realize we're all here to get away from mothers?'

The leaflet said:

RAINBOW FEST
WEAVE MAGIC CHARMS FROM
THE COLOURS OF LIGHT.
DISCOVER YOUR AURA AND
GET IT WORKING FOR YOU.
RELEASE YOUR INNER BEING.

'Release your inner being,' Lottie repeated to me. 'I haven't got an inner being,' I told her.

'Don't say that!' squawked Mad Alice. That thing about people getting to be like their pets really does work for her: she and Hendrix are impossible to tell apart. 'We've all got one. Mine's madder than I am. You've got a cooler inner being than all the rest of us put together.'

That's nice of her, I thought, but right now I wish she hadn't said it.

'Those guys we're borrowing the kit off are hoping to meet our inner beings,' Mad Alice cackled. 'Keep your legs crossed.'

I was suddenly filled with a terrible feeling of panic. 'Look, I can't sing at Glastonbury,' I said. 'I mean, this is Glastonbury, for God's sake, this is Coldplay and Stereophonics, and . . . and . . . Roots Maneuver.'

'It's just a little bar tent, moron,' said Alice. 'Everyone'll be at the big stages. It's just a great chance to say you've sung at Glastonbury.'

I didn't want to do this. I was feeling cross. I was also feeling sick. Nothing but hot dogs for two days didn't seem to be my thing any more. 'There's no way I'm singing here,' I said. 'We need about five years' more practice.'

'And anyway, we want to go to the Rainbow Festival,' said Lottie.

'Sad,' said Debbie as we headed for our tent.

Sunday June 29

The Tepee field

Tepees are cool, but as Grey Hawk and Little Dove told us, rainbow festivals are in the Spiritual Field.

Stone circles, love and peace . . . hey wow.

Me and Lottie were swooped on by Melon seconds after we got to the Spiritual Field. She drew us into a little tent full of joss sticks and crystal balls.

'Here she is!' she hummed to an even smaller sphere swathed in purple.

'You must be Plumella,' I said psychically.

'No. Jane,' she said. 'Your psychic balance needs adjusting: we must read your chakras and auras straight away so you can accept and welcome the budding life within.'

Lottie gaped.

'Look, if I'm pregnant, which I'm not,' I said, 'I'm definitely not having it, so you can forget the Earth Mother stuff. We wanted to see the Rainbow kids.'

'Not having it?' she said, smiling a sad wistful smile like a saint on a rock. 'Not helping its little soul into the world so it too can be a Rainbow child?'

'Per-lease,' I said.

'If you change your mind,' hummed Melon, 'just call us. You can visit our community and we will take care of you and your babe.'

I took leaflet number three and fled.

'They are nuts,' said Lottie. 'But look!'

And then we saw about a dozen kids dressed as rainbows doing acrobatics. They were like little

flashes of sunlight, leaping and bouncing and dancing and somersaulting and laughing their heads off.

'Well, their kids are all right, I guess,' I said.
And I had a lump in my throat.

'You OK?' said Lottie.

'Yeah. Think I must've swallowed a fly,' I said.

One of the Rainbows ran up to us. 'We've found
frogs,' it said. It seemed to be a little girl, though it
wasn't that easy to tell.

'Come,' said the Rainbow, in a no-is-not-an-
option voice.

They had certainly found frogs, tiny ones that
must have been tadpoles about five minutes ago.

'Sweet, aren't they?' the Rainbow said. 'They're
our friends.'

'Where do you live?' Lottie asked the Rainbows.

'Here,' they squeaked.

'But you can't do. This isn't here except for . . .
when it's here.'

'We do, we do. We live here all the time,' said
the first Rainbow. 'We play in the woods, and talk
to the birds and thquirrelth.'

'But you go to school,' I said.

'No we don't. Our parenth don't believe in it.
We stay at home and learn proper things.'

'Proper things?'

'You know. About nature . . . and . . . and . . .
music.'

'Music?'

'Yes,' said the Rainbow firmly. 'Music comes
into it somewhere.'

'Careful with those frogs,' Lottie said, getting up.

'Right,' I agreed. 'Play them some nice music.'

'Did you know frogs are called *grenouilles* in French?' enquired the first Rainbow brightly.

'Bloody hell!' I shivered. 'Where do they come from?'

'Glastonbury,' said Lottie. 'They're Rainbow children. They know about the Balance.'

'That's right,' said Melon, who out of nowhere was suddenly trotting along beside us. 'They're in harmony with life, not fighting it— Shit!'

She had fallen over a tree root at this point – and being rather round, had trouble righting herself, after a certain amount of beetle-like flailing of her legs in the air.

'Are you OK?' I said, brushing her down. 'Have you hurt yourself?'

'No, no, anyway there's plenty of arnica in the Range Ro— I mean, the log cabin. I'll leave you now, but with a thought: Your baby is singing to you, I can hear it clearly . . .'

Lottie and I cocked an ear, but all we could hear was a junkyard clatter of guitar noise and the unmistakable thrilling roar of the Mind Bandits and the opening chords of *Taking the Gloves Off.*

'Damn,' murmured Lottie. 'I'd forgotten they were on now. We'd better go.'

'Beware of Sirens,' Melon said, weaving a bit.

'Don't get drawn off The Path.'

The roar got louder. A Siren sound it definitely wasn't, except maybe a fire-siren. I clutched Melon's hand.

'Are you sure about that . . . baby singing?' I asked her.

'It couldn't be clearer,' she said.

Lottie pulled me in the direction of the Mind Bandits.

'I'll see you,' I said to Melon, who was waving feebly.

We started to quicken our pace towards the noise of the band.

'Bollocks,' I was saying, mostly to myself.

'What d'you mean bollocks?' asked Lottie, trotting now. 'The Mind Bandits are bollocks? Babies are bollocks? Frogs are bollocks?'

'Everything's bollocks,' I moaned. 'You don't believe all that stuff she says, do you?'

'I don't know,' said Lottie. 'But I'd love to have grown up like those kids, free as *grenouilles*.'

'What?'

'Doesn't it make sense, that we need to get back in tune with nature? We're musicians – who knows that better than us?'

Kraaaaaaaanggggggggggg went the Mind Bandits in the distance.

I pulled Lottie to a standstill and hugged her suddenly. 'Do you think Melon might be right about me?'

There was quite a long pause and the Mind

Bandits respectfully seemed to hold the noise for as long as it lasted.

'Yes,' Lottie said. 'I think she probably is.'

CHAPTER ELEVEN

In Which Lottie Says 'Oh My Goddess' in Very Big Letters

Monday June 30

7.30 a.m.
Mobile. Lottie.
  'Hi,' she said.
  'Hi,' I said.
  'Brilliant, wasn't it?' she said.
  'Great,' I said.
  'Have you done it yet?' she said.
  'Errr . . .' I said.

Monday July 7

A week later
'Have you done the test?' asks Lottie casually while
we are ogling Hunky Horst over our lattes.
  'No. The loo in marmalade hell is always full.'
  'I'll stand guard while you do it at school,' says
Lottie.

'Lottie, you know why no school-age child in England ever does a jobbie in the daytime, don't you? Those loos make Glasters look like Tinkerbell's bidet.'

'Don't exaggerate,' says Lottie in her snooty voice.

'Anyway, you know I had that little scanty one. If my next period's a day late, I will do it.'

'When's it due?'

'Thursday week.'

'If you get to school on Friday without doing it I'm never going to speak to you again . . . until . . . until . . .'

'When?' I say unhappily.

'Break time,' she says.

I must widen my circle. Lottie only ever goes on about one thing.

Period due!!! **Thursday July 17**

I am scared as a loony.

HEALTH TIP

Late periods can be due to anxiety.

---

it says in fabulous *Teenacious Tips*.

Good.

At lunch hid from Lottie in the library. Iqbal was in there, reading as usual. He had a thesaurus, a dictionary and Fowler's *Modern English Usage*. He was reading *War and Peace*.

I sneaked up behind him and whispered 'Boo' and he leapt out of his seat and spun round with his fists up, scattering books everywhere.

'Sorry, sorry,' I whispered. I keep forgetting how he does that.

He looked embarrassed and frightened at the same time and I felt crap.

Luckily it was the nice librarian, Ms Vellum, on duty, so she only sssshhed a bit while we rustled around picking up books and Iqbal's notes.

I sat next to him, pretending to read *Hamlet,* and for some reason I was desperate to ask him what I should do.

I wrote him a note: '*Enjoying* War and Peace?'

'*Magnificent,*' he wrote back. '*But the names are very hard. I would like to learn Russian.*'

'*Who is your favourite character?*'

'*Natasha. Tolstoy says she is "a strikingly poetic, charming girl, overflowing with life!"*' And he showed me a passage:

Natasha, half grown up and half child, was now childishly amusing, now girlishly enchanting.

Iqbal waited a few moments and then whispered, 'You see? Natasha is bubbly. And serious.'

Hormone alert. Why does it always have to be like this with me and boys?

'Are you all right? Too hot in here?' he whispered, completely innocently.

I glanced at him and I realized, partly with relief and partly not, that he didn't mean anything by it, although he had obviously remembered our bubbly serious conversation.

'It's just that I'm worried about something,' I found myself whispering.

Ms Vellum threw us a warning look.

Iqbal scribbled a note: '*Very worried?*'

I shook my head – don't ask me why – and made a small sign, as though I was just the tiniest bit worried. He scribbled again:

'*Do you want to tell me what it is, madam? I am as silent as the grave and will respect your confidence.*'

'Later.'

I tried to find Iqbal later but Mooney said he had gone off to a fast-track Russian class at the sixth-form college. 'He's part of our gifted and talented programme,' she said.

11 p.m.
In Bed

What on earth made me think I could confide in Iqbal? He is interested in ideas more than people, I think. Unless the people are in books.

Midnight

I will have to do the test tomorrow.

Last day of Term

A promise is a promise.

I left for Broadmoor for registration and picked up everything I needed for the holidays and then bunked off home when the coast was clear.

Using the preggers test was dead fiddly. It consisted of a pencil-shaped thing that you hold under your wee ('Just hold the urine absorber in your urine stream for one second, place inside the cartridge and read the result').

I had read and re-read the packet about fifty times by now and I knew what to expect.

It said: 'You are not pregnant if a dot is visible in the small window only.' And then: 'You are pregnant if a dot is visible in both windows.'

So, I peed on the stick, closed my eyes, counted to ten, opened my eyes. Only one dot in only one window!

I looked again.

One window: dot.

One window: empty.

Hosanna. Alleluia. Tharg be praised!

Life is a breeze! Happiness is a fragile and beautiful thing! My life stretches before me full of hope and joy and all the wonderful things I will do. I'd like to say there was a nano-second of dog-in-the-manger type disappointment, like when the boy you've said 'no' to gets off with somebody else. But there wasn't.

Just to make absolutely two hundred per cent sure, I double-checked the instructions again.

'Result in just four minutes.'

Four lots of sixty seconds.

I looked again. A little dot in both windows. Unmistakable.

I walked to the river.

I thought about throwing myself in.

I thought of floating peacefully down.

I thought of the inquest: 'The balance of her mind was disturbed. You do know she was pregnant, Mrs Baker?'

Pregnant.

Was I?

Could I possibly be pregnant?

Apart from my ecstatic multi-contraceptive experience with Tom I have lived like a nun.

If you don't count Flubber.

And then I let a drunken oik fall on top of me for about a millisecond with his zip undone . . . Was his zip undone? It doesn't matter how much I replay this stuff in my head, I just can't remember.

I don't deserve this, I thought. But then, who does?

I'd've done it fifty times a day with Tom if I'd had the chance . . .

But I didn't have the chance, so I might as well say, Cheerio, world.

I thought of my funeral, all flowers and tributes to a wasted young life and Crazy Craven and Mr

Fish saying what a credit I'd been to KFC. Maybe I'd get one of those white coffins covered in teddy bears.

I thought of my mum and dad, crying. Perhaps it would bring them together.

I thought of Tom, heartbroken, gaunt with devastation, a gaunt stubble on his gaunt sunken devastated cheeks, flying back from Japan, flinging himself sobbing into my grave – too late.

If this was an old movie, I'd have hurled myself into the river, been rescued by a bronzed coast-guard, Clint, and all three of us would have lived Happily Ever After.

But this isn't an old movie, it's my life, right now.

And luckily, thinking about my funeral went just a thought too far . . . I thought of Lottie and Debbie and Mad Alice blubbing at the service then going shopping to cheer themselves up. And taking Tom home for a meal to cheer *him* up. And one thing leading to another . . .

I resisted the river. I didn't fancy drinking duck-weed, specially if it was the last drink I ever had.

4 p.m.

'LOTTIE! LOTTIEEEE!'

Well, she was over and up in my room at the speed of light.

Midnight

'OH MY GODDESS' was all Lottie

could say for about half an hour. It is a bit irritating at times, her feminist side.

Then she said, crossly: 'So how? I mean it can't be Tom's, can it? Not with your period and the Pill and everything? So you *did* do it with Stanley? Why did you pretend you didn't?'

'Lottie, I thought I was being honest with you. I thought it was just a snog, I hoped it was, but . . . I did kiss him back and – you know, I wanted to feel wanted. I mean, I didn't push him away . . . and then, well . . . It's all so mixed up, to be honest I don't know if we did it or not . . . I was completely sloshed . . . I suppose we must have.'

'Bloody hell,' said Lottie. 'I see. Then you've got to tell him.'

'Lottie, no. I can't bear it.'

I made her swear on her mother's life to give me time to think. I am not telling Mum and Dad.

I am going to get an abortion and then run away. Or maybe run away and then get an abortion.

I am too tired to think.

Saturday July 19

5 a.m.

Sleepless night.

Will go for walk by the river.

There's quite a pretty bit of it with a few trees where you can  have quite romantic thoughts if the council's been round sweeping up the condoms the day before.

Ducks started floating towards me, hoping for breakfast.

It was one of those bright blue dawns. The river glittered like Christmas. The sky and the river didn't know anything about me. They just went on glittering and blueing as though it was a normal morning. I had to think – but I couldn't. I was just overcome by huge waves of emotion.

At New Year I'd been normal, carefree. Now I was up to my neck in the kind of crap I'd thought only happened to other people.

What would Tom think if he could see me now? *Why* did he go? *Why* hasn't he written? This would never have happened if he had stayed. I *hate* him!

These sophisticated reflections were interrupted by someone calling my name.

'Amy! Amy! Amy!'

I looked round to see my mum hurtling down the path towards me like a small cannonball in a nightie.

'Amy! Don't jump!'

I hardly had time to think before she cannoned straight into me.

Whoosh!

I didn't realize how near the edge of the bank I was, but into the river we plopped.

For a few seconds we did a lot of splashing and thrashing and kicking and clutching and squealing. Then we both found ourselves standing up in the mud, with the raging torrents flopping about just over our knees. The ducks sat looking at us.

'Whayoudoinyoumadoldbag?' I spluttered.

'Amy Amy Amy. My *baby*,' was all she could say. I've never heard her voice like that.

Well, I have. But it's always when she's talking to the Puddings.

We limped home.

Unfortunately we passed hunky Horst. I don't see why he had to split his sides laughing. What's so funny about two small shoeless soaking sobbing women? Even if one of them is wearing a nightie with ducks on?

Course, I didn't know I had a condom stuck in my hair until we got home.

What is it with that riverside – does dirty water turn people on or something?

Later

Tharg's knickerbockers, Mum had woken up for a wee, seen my door open and spotted the pregnancy test!

I'd been hiding it in my knicker drawer, but after I'd used it, just when I really should have destroyed the evidence, my mind had gone blank. Or maybe I wanted her to see. Who knows?

Of course the first thing she asked, when we'd got home to a blissfully chaos-free house, was who the father was.

'Mr Stork. I went into the gooseberry bushes and there was a stork in there saying he'd got a parcel for me . . .'

194

(Only the bushes weren't gooseberries and Stanley is a mangy old pigeon.)

'Darling, you haven't had a boyfriend since Tom, have you? Did something happen at Glastonbury? Oh God, I knew I shouldn't have let you go—'

'No, Mum. It was a stupid snog that went too far. I didn't mean to—'

'So he forced you, did he?'

'N-no . . . No, he didn't,' I said firmly.

'Did he drug you? Was it one of those date rapes I keep hearing about?'

'Mum, you're not helping. No, it wasn't like that—'

'Well, who is he?'

'I'm not telling. I don't want to think about it. And please, please, don't tell Dad anything, not yet.'

'I must.'

'No. Not yet. We can't. He'll go crazy. Please, Mum, please, please, please!'

Dad's always seen me as his little girl – he made that clear when Tom dumped me. I just don't know if he can handle anything as big as this. Like a lot of ex-Catholics, he has a crazed torturing voice in his head ranting on about standards that comes out at unexpected moments. He's always been keen for me to 'better myself', go to college and all that. But at the same time he's scared of me growing up.

'He'll put me out in the snow, like in a Victorian novel,' I said to Mum, trying desperately to make a joke of it. But my real fear was, maybe he'd blame Mum, or use it as an excuse to go off into the sunset with Emma Dearest.

But Mum was deep in thought. 'Maybe we could keep it from him a little while longer, while we work out what's best,' she agreed. 'He's off to Blackpool for a few days tomorrow, helping his mate Ken convert that B&B he's bought. That gives us a bit of time.'

There was a pause. 'In fact, perhaps he need never know.'

'What do you mean?'

'Nothing. Nothing. Look, I'll make you a cocoa—'

'Mum? What *do* you mean, *he need never know*?'

'Well, you wouldn't want to keep the baby, would you, darling? Not at your age?'

'What, you mean be sent away somewhere till it's born and lie to Dad for months and then just . . . just give it away?' This sounded a bit sick, some-how. It was a great idea in theory of course, but I didn't like it.

'I don't mean adoption, I mean . . . termination.' I must have looked like a zombie of horror or something, because Mum added hastily, 'It . . . it isn't such a bad thing if you do it straight away.'

'You mean abortion!' I bellowed. 'You want to kill my baby!'

I ran upstairs and locked myself in my room and howled. Mum wants to kill her own grandchild.

So here I am. I am staring at my stomach, trying to

see through it – see this thing that's started to share my life with me.

Of course I'm going to have an abortion. It's the only sensible thing to do, isn't it?

But I don't want my own mum to feel like that. Why?

9 p.m.

Mum has been sitting on my bed, talking.

It was the nearest thing to a mutual heart-to-heart we've had for years, and it even managed to survive Dad busting in about every five minutes to ask where his toothbrush was, or his spare glasses, or his best shirt.

'What do you want that for?' Mum did get around to asking him. 'You're converting a house, not a church congregation.'

'Ken's local's fussy about builders' clothes,' Dad muttered, going back to packing.

When Mum was sure he'd gone again, she took a deep breath and told me she'd thought she was pregnant herself when she was only a little older than me. 'Luckily, it was a false alarm, but at the time I think I'd have had a termination.'

I wish she hadn't said that. It could have been me.

'But Amy, you were a wanted, a longed-for baby.'

I was a longed-for baby. Nice. Very nice. And I suppose the Puddings were longed-for twins, if such a thing is possible. And my baby is not.

Oh, God.

Mum looked stricken. 'Darling, I'm just telling

you it would be OK with me if you did want a termination. Look, I'm sorry I said it, I don't know why I did, it's just that I want you to go to college, have a life . . .'

11 p.m.

I am feeling a bit weird. I wonder if Mum is trying to tell me she actually *did* have an abortion.

Twenty-seven years . . . What would my twenty-seven-year-old half brother or sister have been like?

But then, if he or she had been here, I wouldn't.

 My brain is hurting.

Also, I am going mad. All she said was, she would have considered it.

And that is perfectly reasonable.

I am considering it too.

In fact, what else can I do?

10 p.m.

Abortion or adoption?

If I get it adopted, everyone will know I'm pregnant, and I'll have to go through labour all for nothing, just to give it away. Everyone will want to know who the father is . . .

Worse, there'll be no chance of getting back with Tom. I guess abortion isn't so bad. It's what I want really. It'll be a big relief. We don't even have to tell anyone I've been pregnant. Life will get back to normal. I can do GCSEs and have a life. Tom will come back. The doctor will sort it out. It will all be all right.

A little voice in my head is telling me this is selfish. That there are loads of people who want to adopt babies . . . That I am depriving someone of a life . . .

Mum came in and sat with me. 'Let's see what the doctor says tomorrow. I'll take the day off work and get you an appointment first thing,' she said.

Monday July 21

8.30 a.m.

Can wishing make it happen?

While Mum was pressing ringback every six seconds for the doctor, I checked my e-mails, just like I do every day, pathetically hopeful.

There is an e-mail from Tom! I almost screamed.

I feel faint. It's like the pregnancy test. I can't open it.

If I do open it, I won't be able to read it.

It's now or never.

Darling Amy,
I've done my best to forget you, but I can't. I know you must have been terribly hurt by my behaviour and I don't *know* if you will ever forgive me . . . but I have been re-reading all the messages you sent me and I just know we were right. You can truly love someone from the moment you see them. And I

don't think that's going to change. I don't dare phone until you've read this, in case you've met a tanned hunk, or even decided you hate me. But if you haven't, and if I have even the smallest chance of winning you back, please sit by your mobile tonight at 6 p.m. your time. So please please answer your phone! When it rings, pick it up. Then say you love me. Please.
All the love – and sorrow – in the Universe,
Tom

I knew it. I knew he loved me.

9 a.m.

'*Amy!!*' Mum'd been on the phone for hours pressing redial. Our doctor's is like something out of *Casualty* on a Saturday night usually, with people sitting around with hatchets and stuff sticking into them, and you have to wait two weeks for an appointment unless you're dead. Or a preggers teenager!

'They say you can see Dr Sahidi at noon. Lucky girl,' said Mum. 'Well, I didn't expect you to look that happy,' she said, clocking my radiant mush.

I told her about Tom's e-mail. 'It's going to be all right. He loves me,' I say.

Mum hugged me. At that moment I didn't care about having an abortion at all – pregnancy was just a mistake I could wipe out. I was too happy to care.

'I can't have it now. I will have lots of babies with Tom, to make up.'

Mum nodded. I can see she's really relieved, but

she doesn't want it to show too much.

Mum came with me to the doctor. I decided I couldn't face it without her. Dr Sahidi was very kind. I told her about the pregnancy test and she checked my wee and nodded.

She asked if I was sure I wanted a termination. She said adoption was an option.

I kept rhyming adoption and option in my head.

'I said, Are you sure you'd like a termination?' she repeated.

'Oh yes, we've had a long talk,' said Mum, to fill the silence while I gulped.

But Dr Sahidi was looking straight at me.

I nodded.

'Well now. When was your last period?'

'Well. Um.'

'Yes?'

I gabbled like a loon about how my last proper period had been in March but I had had a little tiny bleed in April so I thought it was OK and then missed May's but I'd missed periods before and then June's had been just a drop really, and *Teenacious Tips* said that was quite normal so I didn't really worry and then July's didn't come bang on time so I did the test not really thinking and . . .

There was a stunned silence, while they counted.

'Four months!' squealed Mum. 'Four months! So the baby's Tom's!'

'*No! No!*' I wailed, and broke down.

'You can't have a termination if you're four months gone!' shouted Mum. 'What do they teach you at school? I'm so so sorry, Doctor. Only she'd only just had the test. I'd no *idea* she'd left it so late! I'd have thought she had more sense.'

'Perhaps we think teenagers these days know more than they do,' said Dr Sahidi gently to Mum, who had gone a funny purple colour.

Me, I felt enormously stupid and enormously preggers and enormously pukey.

I just got to the loo in time.

When I re-emerged, Mum looked calmer and Dr Sahidi was patience on a monument.

'Of course, a termination would still be possible, but you'd have to go through labour, I'm afraid. The foetus would be viable at twenty-four weeks so . . . The baby will be quite big already . . .'

Labour pains for a dead baby?

'I can't do that,' was all I could say. How could I have been such a fool? was all I could think.

Dr Sahidi asked me loads of questions and gave me some stuff to read on adoption. And late abortion, if I changed my mind. She also gave me lots of leaflets on contraception.

'Well, that's bolting the stable door after the horse has gone, isn't it?' said Mum primly.

'I won't be needing these anyway,' I said, trying unsuccessfully to hand them back. 'I'll never go near a boy ever again.'

Dr S smiled at me with a knowing 'they all say that' sort of look. But I meant it. It was true.

'Now you and baby need a lot of looking after,' she said. And I realized I had started the long process where 'baby' was a person too, just like me.

'I'll book you in for a proper antenatal at the hospital, as this one is a bit squeezed in,' she said, glancing at her watch, 'but I think your baby will be due around December twenty-eighth.'

'Your birthday!' squeaked Mum.

My birthday. I will be sixteen.

'Could be a week or two either way though,' said Dr Sahidi. 'I'll book you in for a scan. It doesn't hurt. You can see baby on a monitor just like a telly. It's exciting. You can see baby move.'

'Is it moving already?'

'Oh yes. You won't feel any movements for about a month. It looks something like this.' And she drew a little picture of a four-month foetus, with all its little bits and pieces. 'It'll fit in the palm of your hand.'

I had one of those inside me. I couldn't believe it. It was a little person already. Late abortion? Forget it. I would just have to have this little creature. I'll wrap it in an incy-wincy lacy white blanket and put it on Stanley's doorstep with a note:

Hi. You left This with me in The park nine monThs ago. I ThoughT you'd like iT for The nexT nineTy years.

Except that I didn't want to write to Stanley.

I didn't even want him to know. I couldn't bear to think of my baby having anything to do with him.

'Amy, do you realize what this means?' said Mum when we got outside. I realized with surprise that she was looking really happy. 'It must be Tom's.'

'Oh Mum, I wish it was!'

'But, darling, the timing's right and you haven't had another boyfriend.'

'Oh, God, do I have to say this? It was just a grope in the park with a boy from school. He took pity on me because I was miserable about Tom going away, and then . . . Well, I *hate* him now!'

'Why do you hate him?' Mum asked, looking worried. 'He didn't . . . take advantage, did he?'

I couldn't get into this. 'Well, no. I'm afraid we were both pissed and it just got out of hand . . .'

Mum gave me a big hug. I felt grateful she was so understanding.

'But whoever this boy is, he can't run away from his responsibilities. He needs to know what he's done and what it means, and he and his parents have to face it, just the same as us.'

'I can't tell you, because I don't want him to know. I don't want his girlfriend to know. They're engaged.'

God, I'm turning into a brilliant liar, but it was the only thing I could think of to stop Mum from asking more, and it certainly worked.

Poor old Mum, what could she do? I'd have

loved her to say she would take the baby and bring it up as if it was hers. But she had the Puddings, so I suppose that was wanting the moon.

It's lucky Dad is off hammering his thumbs and falling through ceilings with his mate in Blackpool. I couldn't stand having him going on at me too.

We decided we would wait for the scan before we told him.

Tom is going to phone at six.

Obviously I won't be going back to KFC.

I have to do my English and music GCSEs though. I have to.

What will I say to Tom?

9.30

I turned my mobile off, but of course Tom rang our landline. I told Mum to say I was out.

She said he sounded a bit low.

I said, 'If he rings again, tell him I don't want to talk, but I'm writing to him.'

'Are you sure?' she said.

I have no option. I can't lie to him on the phone, I know that. I'll just start crying and tell him everything. And he'll hate me. I can't stand that.

Midnight

He rang again at 10.30.

She said he sounded very low indeed.

Well, tough. Not as low as me.

I can't tell him the truth.

CHAPTER TWELVE

In Which Amy Discovers Something About Mathematics

Dreamt I was going to a party. I was happy, because Tom was going to be there. But when I arrived, all the guests were giant infants, the size of houses. They made baby noises at treble the usual volume.

Googoogoo! Ga ga ga!

Then they advanced on me with vast plastic spoons and ate me alive.

8.30 a.m.

Lottie came round.

'If you tell Stanley I will kill you and him and then myself and you will be responsible for the KFC massacre,' I told her.

'Well, he's got to face up to it. It's illegal for starters.'

'You sound like Mum. Anyway, I don't want the baby to know. Don't you understand that? I want it to think it had a decent dad.'

'You mean you're going to *keep* it?'

'No! No! I don't know! Just don't tell anyone yet, OK?'

So then she helped me write to Tom.

Lottie should be an editor on a newspaper.

We ended up cutting out everything except the basics.

Here's what it said:

Dear Tom,
Thanks for your e-mail, but you were right
the first time. We are too young, or at least
I am. Thank you for a wonderful time.
Amy

'Are you sure you want to do this?' said Lottie, as we both looked mournfully at the note, which did look a bit of a skinny thing after the usual twenty-eight pages.

'Well, you think I should tell him I'm up the duff with Stanley Maul? Look, I can't stand thinking about any of this any more. I'll e-mail it. Then it's done.'

Lottie watched mournfully as I did the deed.

Wednesday July 23

The scan's at 12.30.

I have now hardly slept for two nights and look like one of those sad girls the magazines round up to 'change their look'. Only worse.

Have decided I will ask for a late abortion after all.

OK, it'll be horrible, giving birth to a dead baby, but women have been doing stuff like that for centuries. It'll be better than this wriggling sack of responsibilities hanging round my neck.

ETERNITY

Feed Sleep Cry Change

Sleep Cry Feed Cry

Change Feed Cry

Cry Cry Cry Change

Cry Feed Cry Cry

I'll never have a gap year! I'll never have a holiday romance!

I'll never have a night out when I don't have to watch the clock like bloody Cinderella.

I've got a sodding timetable written out for the next fifteen years until my little sprog has a sprog of its own in the grand Baker family tradition.

What's the point?

11.30 a.m.

Have now said all this to Mum.

She looked horrified. 'It's sixteen weeks, Amy . . . There are so many couples dying to adopt . . .'

'Well, people often have abortions at sixteen weeks if there's something wrong with the baby,' I said. I felt cold as ice.

Abortion it is.

And in the back of my mind is a glimmer of hope. Tom still loves me, after all. If I can survive giving birth to a dead baby, I can make it up with Tom again. If.

Midnight

Well, the scan changed all that.

We went to a big Victorian hospital on the other side of the borough. Mum and I looked at it dubiously from the bus stop.

'Do you think they let you in if you're not wearing a strait-jacket?' I asked.

'I'm sure it's perfectly nice inside,' Mum said. 'Come on.'

We found the antenatal department after such a long time and so many journeys up and down corridors it probably ends up as the postnatal department for quite a lot of people.

'I don't think I need this, I've decided to have a late abortion,' I was going to tell the scanning people, just as if I was a confident woman of the world. But the man-with-the-scan was a Scottish sex grenade, and when I saw him in his tartan technician's outfit (not really, but he was like Braveheart in a white coat) I went all wobbly. I didn't want him to think I was just any old pregnant teenager, so I said I didn't come here often and he cracked a smile with a lot of eye twinkle.

What is going on with me? How can I be thinking willy aerobics at a time like this? My hormones are having a party and they have not invited my brain.

Scottish sex grenade spread cool jelly on my huge belly – I do think this is tactless; why can't they give jobs like this to very old people, or nuns? – and ran a sort of little electronic trolley over it. Then he raised an eyebrow. I was beginning to get the hang of these laid-back medical signals. Doctor types get so used to seeing people walk in with axes in their heads, chairs clamped to their bums, couples who are permanently welded together by muscle spasms etc. that they don't look surprised at anything. So a raised eyebrow is a Big Deal.

It meant something was wrong! With my baby!

I had a few mad seconds where it didn't matter about me any more – just please, please, please, let the baby be OK.

'Is the baby all right?' I forced myself to ask him.

'Babies,' he said, nodding as if it was the most natural thing in the world.

'Babies? Did you say sssssssss?'

'Um. Babies. Two babies.' He kept on watching the screen, as if my reaction was going to be hard to take, much worse than all the axes in the head. Then he finally looked at me, and saw that I wasn't going to throw something expensive at the wall.

'You're having twins, Amaryllis. They look in pretty good nick, too.'

What happened next was a bit blurred, as Mum fainted. And the room was suddenly filled with women in white coats.

The NHS is actually wonderful.

The scurry to revive Mum left me alone for a few moments with my thoughts. Twins. Two lives. Two hearts beating. I was eating for three. Well, I can't have an abortion for two babies, can I?

Mum was hilarious when they brought her round.

'Ooh. I don't know what came over me. I thought

210

the man said my daughter was having twins!'

'Your daughter *is* having twins, Mrs Baker,' said the man-with-the-scan. You could see he was thinking, Poor wee girl – twins and a mad mother. Or maybe he was thinking, What a lovely young thing, how I would love to crush her to my manly bosom and take care of her and her little offsprings.

Sex grenade winked at me and handed me a little envelope. 'Good luck,' he said, meaning, obviously, Good luck with your multiple birth and your mad alcoholic parent.

I waddled off with as much dignity as possible, a protective arm around my poor mad alcoholic parent.

We went to the pub, where I had a fizzy water and my mum knocked back two whisky macs in quick succession.

'Twins.'

'Twins.'

'Twins.'

We said, not necessarily in that order.

I opened the sex grenade's envelope and gasped. He had given me a photo of the babies, taken from the scan. It was blurred, but you could make out two little heads.

'Isn't nature bloody amazing? God blesh them – blesh them, God blesh ush all,' said Mum. And she leant forward and stretched her small plump arms round my belly – well, as far as she could; it seemed to have got bigger in the last hour, as though it could relax now its secret was out – and pressed me to her bosom.

And that's when I looked down and realized I had Eurotrash cleavage and no one to share it with. Except two little souls spinning and dreaming in a watery world.

They're in there now, floating about. What are they doing? Setting little alarm clocks ready for December? Reading video game magazines in order to be ready for childhood? Studying Chicken-U-Like home-delivery menus for the next fifty thousand meals they're going to get off me? Maybe they're talking to each other in little gurgly ET voices.

Omigod I'm pregnant.

Naaah.

I'm up the duff without a paddle,
I cannot walk without a waddle.
Who will help me?
(Maybe God'll.)

It is brilliant that my song-writing gene is still active, even if it is from a loony pearly king.

Lottie phoned the second we got in.

'It's twins!'

'Oh my goddess. I'll be right over.'

But I told her I was too knackered. I made her promise not to tell a soul until I've had a bit more time to think. She's coming over tomorrow night.

I was completely unready for Tom's
phone call. I'd thought my e-mail would
put him off, but he obviously hadn't
checked his e-mails yet.

'Amy.'

'Tom!'

'You sound wonderful.' (God,
he's so sensitive, he could tell how I
was feeling, just by the way I said his
name.)

'I am. I mean, I feel—'

'Oh Amy.'

'Oh Tom.'

'Oh Amy.'

'Oh Tom.'

'Oh Amy.'

'Oh Tom.'

'Oh Amy. Did you get my e-mail?'

'Yes. Tom . . . but . . . you didn't get mine?'

'No. What do you mean?'

213

'I mean . . . I mean . . .' (I mean, I'm having twins, Tom, by a boy I hardly know and like less. I'm a total slag, Tom. You'll have to forget me.)

'Amy, what's up?'

'It's over, Tom. I'm sorry, I can't explain.'

'Over?'

'You and me. Over.' A dream that had barely begun.

'You don't mean it! I'm so sorry. I'm so, so sorry – it's all my fault.'

'No it isn't.' (Yes it is. Without that phone call I'd never have got drunk, never have gone off with Stanley, never . . .)

'What is it then? You must tell me? Is there someone else?'

'Yes.' (Two people, actually. I'm going out with them every minute of the day and night.)

'I see.' Tom's voice was glacial.

'Tom, I'm so sorry. I'm so sorry. I can't explain.'

'You don't have to. Glad to hear you're so happy. Couldn't happen to a nicer person. Bye.'

'Tom!!'

But he'd rung off.

'Oh God, Mum.'

'Poor Amy, poor poor Amy.'

CHAPTER THIRTEEN

In Which Black Hole Make a Discovery and Amy Hunts for Crocodiles

Thursday July 24

9 p.m.

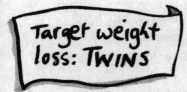

Target weight loss: TWINS

Lottie due any minute.
   Babysitting. Mum is at WeightWatchers. Maybe that's the answer for me . . .
   The phone rings.
   'Hullo, is Harry in?' a man's voice asks.
   I always have to think a bit, translating 'Harry' into 'Dad'.
   'No, he's away in Blackpool, fixing a house with Ken. Who is this?'
   There's a silence for a bit.
   'Ken,' says the voice eventually.
   'Oh,' I say, eventuallier.
   'Blackpool, eh?' says the voice, with a kind of nervous chuckle. 'Well, tell him I called, will you? Thanks a lot.'

And Ken-who's-obviously-not-with-Dad hangs up. A horrible little nag of a thought starts itching its way into my head. I go to the front door and down the path to get a look at Emma Dearest's house. The curtains are closed and her tarted-up little sports car isn't there. Oh no. I don't believe it.

Debbie and Mad Alice come up the path.

'Where you bin all my life? You've missed three rehearsals,' says Mad A, as they clatter into the kitchen. She is like a machine gun.

'You are like a machine gun,' I say. 'Hush up, I only just got the Puddings to bed.'

Debbie is looking at me with a thoughtful look. 'Whassup, Ames?'

'Nothing. What should be up?' I realize I sound like a mad hyena on liquorice allsorts, but hey.

'Oh come on, Ames. Lottie's gone all funny whenever we ask about you. We're your pals, you can tell us.'

'I can't. I mean . . . there's nothing to tell.'

'So d'you want to leave the band you gotta tell us it'll be a bummer but there's always Xanthia no offence but we've gotta know so we can teach her your songs an' that,' says Mad Alice.

It is nice to have such tactful friends when you are in a major crisis. It is comforting to know you can rely on them to stand by you through thick and thin.

I say something like this, but it comes out in a wobbly sort of angry way, as though I'm feeling wobbly and angry, which I am.

'Hey, cool it,' says Mad A.

'How can we stand by you if we don't know what's up?' says Debs.

'Sit down,' I say.

Obviously the mothering instinct is in me already: I am looking after my twin sisters and now I am telling my BFs to sit down because I think they're going to be upset by my news, which my own dad, blood of my blood, doesn't even know yet. I am Mother of the Year, certainly.

I want Lottie to be here, but it's now or never. I'm going to have to tell them.

'I'm pregnant,' I say.

I thought they were going to say they knew. After all, I've been going round in a size sixteen smock for a month and the only other person who does that at KFC is Tracey, so you'd think that might have opened their peepers, but no. My dear BFs both look at me with their eyes on stalks and say godfathers.

Then they get all mothery and start making tea.

'Aw, it's so unfair – I mean, you don't go with boys much, do you?' says Mad A.

'Once is enough,' says Debs, in a vicarish sort of tone that really got up my nose.

'If I hear that again I'll throw something, or throw up. How many times have you done it, Debs? Or have you lost count?'

'Well, I have never gone the whole hog in actual fact. My mum would kill me if I got up the duff.'

Obviously my hormones have been partying in

my eardrums and affected my hearing. I check.
'Debs, sorry, but I thought you just said you'd
never done the full willy aerobics.'

'I did,' she says.

'Not even once?'

'No, but don't tell anyone, will you? My name
would be mud,' laughs Debs.

'Why didn't you say?'

'You never asked.'

You could have bowled me over with a
feather. Debbie, who'd been chased by every
lad in the school and who we'd all assumed, at
least since Elsie's party, had got a doctorate in
underbits gymnastics, has never had sex. My world
is spinning. Maybe Lottie was right, and half
the boys who went on about it with all the fist-
and-elbow gestures and *whoaaa* noises hadn't
either?

'What, not even Mikey?' I can't help adding.

And Debs bursts into floods of tears.

Mother of the Year gets a kitchen roll and about
five hours later Debs stops blubbing and starts
hiccupping.

'He hasn't rung. I think he's seeing Lavinia,' is
all she can say.

Oh well, who can compete with Lavinia – boffin
extraordinaire and nice too? No contest, I think.

'He'll come back,' I lie. 'But are you sure he's
seeing her?'

'She told Elsie she loves him,' says Debs, making
a horrible howling whooping noise that I recog-

nize. Where have I heard that noise before? Then I remember: it's the noise I made when Tom told me it was over.

'But that's not the same as him loving her, is it?' I say.

Debs brightens. 'Oooh, do you think I should phone him?'

'Course you should,' says Alice.

Hang on a minute, I think. Isn't this supposed to be about me?

'Yeah, but what about *me*?' I wail.

'You can have a . . . you know, if you want,' suggests Debs.

'I can't. I'm four months gone. It's too late for an abortion. Practically grown up already.'

'Great! It can skip school and earn a living and you can put your feet up and chew gum,' says Alice.

'Would *you* have an abortion, Debs? If you had to go into labour and have a dead baby?' I ask.

'No-o. I don't think I'd ever have one myself. But I don't think it's wrong or anything, not if you do it early. I know your dad'd probably think it's a sin and all, because of being a Catholic – and so would my mum, but that means there's a hell of a lot of sinners walking around. Keeps the religions in business, I suppose.'

Mad Alice says, 'If men got pregnant, there'd be little abortion clinics on every high street – prob'ly part of the bogs in pubs. You'd prob'ly be able to sort it out in one trip. They'd have an attendant like those loos in posh places. They could prob'ly do it and give you a shave and a manicure at the same time—'

'Stopppit!' I shout. 'It isn't early. It's *late*.'

'I'd go for adoption,' says Mad A. 'Nice little white kid – no offence, Debs, but there'll be loads of offers. You could probably auction it in the street up Highgate . . . Er, is it white by the way?'

'Not it – *them*,' I say.

'Wha?'

'Them. It's twins.'

Mad Alice has got one of those very long thin faces like a knife. So when her jaw dropped she looked like somebody in one of those weird mirrors you get at a fair. 'Bloody hellfire,' she says. 'Tweedle-dum-di-dum-di-dum and Tweedle-deedle-deedle-dee.'

'Have you told Tom?' asks Debbie.

''Snot his. Wish it was. It was a one-night stand. Mistake. Nobody you know,' I say.

Debs and Alice both stare. I could see their brains whirring. There's a long pause.

Alice looks stricken. 'It . . . it wasn't Stanley, was it?'

I don't miss a beat. 'Stanley Maul? You must be joking!'

'But you were with him in the pub that night . . . and I left you and I knew I shouldn't,' says Debs.

'Leave it out – we just got a bit sloshed and I went home. He went on to Mikey's party, didn't he?' I'm amazed how well I'm lying. 'Anyway, he's an oik.'

'He's not!' says Alice, but she looks relieved. 'But he didn't turn up at Mikey's . . .'

'Oh, that's right, I remember now. He boasted he needed to do a bit of revision for boffins' further maths,' I say. 'Look, it was a boy I knew ages ago, from Swanage. He's got a steady girl-friend, it was a stupid mistake, I don't want him to know.'

And they believe me.

I can't face anyone knowing about Maul. I wish I hadn't even told Lottie.

Then the bell rings and it's Lottie.

'Oh my goddess, what'll you dooo?'

I suppose that more or less sums up life: from choosing lip gloss to being preggers. It's all relative.

'It'll be hard to give two away,' says Lottie.

'Oh it won't be that hard,' I say. 'As long as I don't hold them. If you hold your babies, you might get fond of them. But if you don't meet them, then it's easy.'

Lottie does not get irony. She has not got the irony gene. Maybe she is American. 'Amy, I don't know if you've noticed, but you find it hard to give away your old Barbie dolls.'

This is unkind of her. She is the only person on earth I have shown my childhood collection. And I only showed her the two teddies, three Barbies and My Little Pony Princess with the lilac mane. I only showed them to her because she used to like playing with them too. Lucky I didn't show her the Sylvanian Family house, or Mr Lemon and the Pencil Family. You can't trust anyone.

'I have kept a Barbie or two for my grand-children,' I say snappishly. 'They are hair looms.'

'Well, maybe you could keep one?' ventures Mad Alice.

'What, a Barbie?'

'A baby, stupid.'

'You mean give one baby away and keep the other? Oh. *Excellento!*'

'Yeah, then you won't have to read the local paper saying, TEENAGE MOTHER OF TWINS SHOCK HORROR. You could be BATTLING TEENAGE MUM.'

'Yes. Yes. I could keep one.'

But how would I choose?

'You're dead lucky really – five more weeks' holiday before Crazy Craven needs to know a thing.'

'But will they let me go next term?'

'You'll prob'ly have to go to one of those teen mum centres because the school won't have you for health and safety reasons. That's what Tracey was gonna do, but she's dropping out.'

Tharg. Tracey has Gareth and his cuddly traffic conieness. And I am a health and safety risk.

'You'll do the big gig in a month though? You gotta do that,' says Mad Alice, as though we've just been discussing a torn nail. She was buffing her talons, too, at the time. They are black, and about a metre long.

'I can't. Look at me.'

'Course you can. Loads of people sing when they're preggers.'

'Not at fifteen—'

'No one will know. It's only four weeks.'

'And we need you,' adds Debs.

'And we want you,' says Lottie.

So I say, 'Great. Fattypuff in a sack. Well, why not? Madonna did it. But then she started getting all mumsy and writing sad children's books. That's what happens to you when you become a mum. You start off a rock chick but then you get old and tired and worried about healthy food and schools and female role models . . .'

'Like Lottie you mean?' says Mad A.

STYLISH CHICK TIP

Customize your clothes! Never turn up in the same dress as your arch rival in Lurve!

Horrors, mighT There be anoTher girl in an XXXXL denim sack jusT like mine?

Midnight

I am, in fact, very worried about school.

I will need all the GCSEs I can get if I'm going

223

to support three people.

And I've got to break the news to Dad.

Wherever the hell Dad is.

Dad phoned first thing to say things were going slower than expected at Ken's house – you know how it is, etc. – he'd have to stay a couple of extra nights. No, the phone wasn't connected yet – bloody telephone companies, what's the use of them, etc., and mobile reception's crap, too. But he'd ring again to report how things were going.

And Emma Dearest's car is still not there.

I'm already feeling pretty weird, and I don't need this. But then neither does my poor mum. Maybe it's just a coincidence. Perhaps he's doing something innocent like attending a Festival of Rubberware or something, and there's a perfectly harmless explanation for Emma Dearest's absence, like she's got pissed and driven her car into a canal.

But suppose there isn't an innocent explanation? Suppose Dad and Emma Dearest are grinding their wrinkled cells together in some condemned hotel somewhere, and proclaiming Undying Lurve? Yeeaccch, what a thought. I caught myself bursting through an imaginary door and shouting, 'That's my dad's willy you've got there!'

But at least this gives me a break.

We can tell him on Sunday.

If he's really back on Sunday.

If he's really back ever.

Tracey Hardwick rings to tell me the arrangements for her wedding. *Espinacas fritas!* It's tomorrow! But at least the party's only in the Weasel's Trousers. It'll be just like home. Tracey wants me to sing old pop songs I could sing in my sleep – although I wish I couldn't – and her Uncle Ron has apparently fixed up a band. Not too sure about that – can't imagine singing without Mad A and Lottie and Debs.

'Would you come to the ceremony too?' Tracey asks me, about as near to shyly as she ever asks anything.

'Isn't that . . . just for your family and mates?' I say to her, surprised.

'You are a mate,' Tracey says. 'It'd be nice if you came. An' Lottie an' all. But not those slags Alice and Debbie.'

Tracey has such a simple way of putting things.

Saturday July 26

Mrs Penelope Hardwick
invites you to a knees-up to celebrate the

WEDDING

of Tracey Hardwick and Gareth Foreshaw
SAT JULY 26
Weasel's Trousers, High St.

7.30-11.00

Tracey's Wedding

Lottie and I stand at the back in this little place like a dentist's waiting room round the back of the town hall. We've made a bit of an effort for Trace. I've pulled my hair back behind one ear and I'm wearing posh-looking pearly earrings and a nice cream-coloured kind of mini-smock Mum lent me from her own days as a budding mum, classy enough not to look as if you're just trying to cover a bump. Lottie is wearing a man's dinner jacket, black trousers and a bit of make-up and looks magnifico.

A guy in a suit mutters some stuff we can't hear to Tracey and Gareth Foreskin, and they mutter something back and then kiss, while a handful of ancients looking as if they've been dry cleaned with their clothes on smile at each other and us. Tracey looks really nice. She's wearing about as tight a black skirt as she can get away with in her condition, with a sparkly pashmina draped over her bump, glam strappy shoes, and her hair braided in about a million colours.

Then after about five seconds of people signing things – *caramba*, I didn't know you could get married faster than you can get through the check-out at Tesco – we all take off for the Weasel's Trousers, which is heaving with people all hoping for a free drink, including quite a few people from KFC.

'Hello, my darling,' says a strangely familiar voice.

It's Kath, the cleaner at KFC who used to babysit me when I was little and who I never see now because she comes to work when everybody else has long gone home. We hug.

'Great to see you,' I say. 'Are you one of the family?'

'I'm Trace's auntie,' Kath tells me. 'Didn't you know that? What you reckon to that Gary?'

'He's all right,' I say, as enthusiastically as I can manage. 'Nice, really.'

'He's a prat,' Kath says with feeling. 'Trace could've done better than that. He spends most of his time going drinking with my brother. Think the world owes them a living, both of them.'

I ask Kath what she does when she isn't sweeping up after us lot at school. She doesn't want to tell me at first, but when she does it makes me feel dizzy to think of it. Kath works in Argos all day and at the school at night. Her husband Ron was laid off years ago and stays at home looking after a son who's too disabled to even go to the loo by himself, and she still has that ear-to-ear smile that takes me right back to a time of my life when things seemed a lot simpler. I find myself offering to help her – maybe babysit the boy . . . But she pats my tummy and winks. 'Trace has got her suspicions about you,' she says. 'You're going to be up to here with baby-sitting, I reckon. Who's the boyfriend?'

'I . . . haven't really got one,' I say, after a bit of thought.

Auntie Kath looks at Lottie in her dinner jacket

and trousers and then back at me, raising an eyebrow. 'That's clever then – how did you manage it?' she asks, hooting with laughter.

I grab her arm, laughing too. 'No, no, we're just mates,' I tell her.

'Well, don't get me wrong,' Kath says. 'Standard of some blokes these days, it's a wonder us girls aren't all cuddling up together. Come and meet my Ron. He's got your backing group all ready.'

Backing group? What are they called, The Flintstones? We push through the crowd towards the bar, where Uncle Ron, a Clint Eastwood cigar in one corner of his mouth, is sharing a laugh with some other big men with pints.

'And this is Alf and Francisco and Dom,' Kath says, pointing to the others.

I haven't really taken them in, they just seemed to be . . . well, pub guys. But they're the band. Yikes. I look desperately at Lottie, with a daft stuck smile on my face. She squeezes my arm and gives me a little thumbs-up.

Tracey comes steaming over. 'Let's have some *music*!' she squeals. 'And take good care of my star guest, Uncle Ron.'

Ron pulls a crumpled piece of paper out of his pocket and shows it to me. It's almost illegible from beer stains, but I can make out things like *I Will Survive*, *Johnny B Goode*, *She Was Just Seventeen* ('You can change that to "he", if you like,' Uncle Ron says helpfully) and – hell's bells – *Wonderful World*.

I start to feel cold feet spreading all the way up my legs. I try to catch Trace's eye but both of them are rolling in her head.

'Look,' I say to nobody in particular, 'I don't usually do this kind of music . . .'

'That's all right,' says Uncle Ron. 'Neither do we. We usually do a Roy Orbison tribute act down the Duck's Head of a Sunday lunch time.'

'Get it over with,' Lottie hisses in my ear.

Aaargh! There's no way out! Tracey is already up on stage introducing us as Beauty and the Beasts. Uncle Ron and his mates climb up too, giving V-signs all round. I follow them sheepishly, wondering by Tharg's Imperial Egg Whisk how I'd let myself get into this.

I hardly dare look out at the audience, but I can see it's very different from the last time I sang in the Weasel's Trousers. There are old ladies with blue hair sitting in corners telling each other what look like bluer jokes. A toddler is trying to stick an ice-cream cone in the ear of its little mate, misses and sticks it on the bum of an unsuspecting fat lady instead.

I look round at the band. Things don't look good. I'm just beginning to wish for the hell-freezing sound of Mad Alice's famous opening metal-howl, when Francisco winks at me, clicks his sticks together, and they all rattle off into a surprisingly tight boogie that even I know comes from *Johnny B Goode*. In his and my younger days, I must have seen Dad mime to this song a hundred times. I have a glimpse of him dancing with my mum in our living room one Christmas years ago, while I clapped and hopped about. Is he dancing with Emma Dearest at this moment?

Suddenly the audience just start dancing all at once, as if somebody has flipped a switch – it's amazing. An old couple who look like they should be queuing for hip replacements are jiving like lunatics. I spot Ruth'n'Van gyrating near the front, all in black, as if they've wandered in from a Halloween party. *Johnny B Goode* turns into *Just Seventeen*, with the band singing it in bellowing, football-fans' voices until I find the sheet with the right words, just in time for the last chorus.

I'm enjoying myself. The crowd really make me feel like somebody. The band play everything right on the nose, but we get through all the songs without me having to hum the words more than about six times, and we end up with *Wonderful World*.

I see Tracey lurching slowly about, her head on Gareth's shoulder. He's treading on her nice tarty shoes. I see Kath dancing with Ron. I see the toddlers chasing each other through the crowd like kittens. I see the two old dears stop jiving for a moment and throw their heads back in a big display of laughing false teeth. And I feel a strange little thumping inside my big belly that catches me completely by surprise.

And as I belt out the last bars I seem to be hearing the words for the first time: *What a Wonderful World*. Yes, I think to myself. It is.

And to think I used to just dismiss Tracey as a stupid slag. What a snob I was, back then. It seems like a lifetime away.

Dad came bouncing in at 6.30, in a horribly cheerful mood. Amazing how much fun being up to your neck in plaster dust in Blackpool can obviously be.

Dearest's little car was back too.

'Nice tan,' I said.

'Marvellous weather in Blackpool,' he said. 'Got you a prezzie.'

He got me a stick of rock. He got the Puddings two fluffy crocodiles. I wished I was three. I would like a fluffy crocodile.

He got Mum some perfume. ''S gone up a lot since the last time I bought it,' he said.

How romantic.

'You've never bought it for me before,' said Mum, but she giggled in a girly way. She may have run around a bit once, but she has eyes only for him now. I have to get him to give up this mad thing. It would break her heart.

Mum and me had decided to break my news after the Puddings were in bed.

But they did their Puddingy thing for hours, making Dad read them nineteen stories because they hadn't seen him for a week.

'Got to kiss Mrs Marmalade night night. And her babies,' the Puddings commanded. They would make good prison governors, I think.

Mrs Marmalade and her babies are a row of marmalade pots in knitted bonnets.

Mum had made kippers for supper, as Dad loves kippers. 'We'll give him kippers first, then we'll tell him,' she had said.

I pushed my kipper round the plate a few times. Then I made a face in the mashed potato. Peas for eyes and a little tomato sauce mouth. I was just styling the lettuce hair when I caught Dad giving me a funny look.

'Dad, can we talk?' I said desperately.

'What's up?'

'It's something . . . important. But you're not going to like it.'

He looked at me strangely, as if he was trying to guess. ''Spect I've heard worse.'

'Not from me, you haven't,' I said.

'You're not ill?' He looked really worried.

'No, not . . . ill.'

'Mum ill?' He looked panic-stricken.

'No, I'm fine,' squeaked Mum.

'What is it then?'

'Think of the worst thing you can.'

'I have. You said you're not ill.'

'Think of another really terrible thing.'

'You're a lesbian?' he said, and roared with laughter. 'Don't worry, it takes all sorts – as my mate Ken says—'

'Yeah,' I said wearily. 'I spoke to your mate Ken the other day.' It sort of came out before I could stop it.

'Did you?' my mum asked brightly. 'You never mentioned it.'

'Dad!' I said, to change the subject.

He peered at me. His eyes came to rest on my stomach. Slowly, I began nodding my head.

'How long have you known?' he asked, after what seemed like hours.

'Not long.'

Silence.

He turned to Mum.

I wouldn't have minded so much if he'd gone ballisticus. But he just went white as a sheet.

Then he shook his head, as if he'd just learnt something that made everything seem pointless.

And he got up and went out of the house without saying another word.

11.30 p.m.

The stick of rock he gave me has SOUTHEND written all the way through it.

I haven't pointed this out to my mum of course.

That is tragic.

Not even Gay Paree, or a little nest in Cornwall.

Saaafend.

I hope the furry crocodiles do not have

SOUTHEND written on their bottoms. Mum will notice if they do.

11.45

Sneaked into Puddings' room to examine crocodiles, which just have MADE IN TAIWAN. NOT SUITABLE FOR CHILDREN UNDER 36 MONTHS.

Well, that is a bright side anyway. It would have been hard to lose two two-metre-long emerald crocodiles.

Midnight

He is not back.

Poor Mum is sitting in the kitchen pretending to read a leaflet called 'Bathrooms You'll Never Buy'.

I made her a cup of tea.

'He's never out this late without saying,' she moaned. 'It's his religion,' she said. 'He fights against it, but you know he was brought up very strict. He thinks the world's full of loose women, but not his own daughter.'

'Honestly, Mum, what's a loose woman? Somebody who isn't a nun? Don't be daft. Did half the people on the planet only get to be here at all because some loose woman couldn't say no? What about *you*?!'

Mum gave me a grief-stricken look which grief-struck me.

What is happening to us?

Just when I really need both my parents to be

proper grown-up parents, they are behaving like children. Maybe that's what a crisis does, throws you straight back into that helpless time of your life when you didn't know what to do unless somebody told you, and just sat on the floor and yelled if nobody did.

'He'll be at Jack's,' I said. Dad has only one bit of his own family left apart from us and that's his brother, Uncle Jack.

'Maybe I should phone the police.'

'Get a grip. People don't phone the police because their husband's out after midnight! They'd laugh at you. A lot of men do that all the time!'

She did raise a sad smile. 'You're right. He's probably staying with Jack. And he'll tell Jack everything, and Jack will tell Jan . . . and Jan will tell your gran. Oh, I did want to tell Mum myself,' and she got all weepy.

So much for the happy announcement of a new life. Lives.

'Eighteen years of marriage and I've never not known where he is,' she said, sniffing.

Oh no? Poor Mum.

But I am thinking, How much I do want him to be around . . . ?

Alice's dad hasn't been seen for years.

Ruth has got three 'dads'.

Van doesn't even have a photo of hers.

And now I was hurling my own dad into the arms of another.

7 a.m.

The phone is ringing.

Arg. Dad!

I hurtle downstairs and collide with Mum and the Puddings.

It stops ringing just as we get to it.

Mum dials 1471 and then calls the number it announces.

'It's the police . . .' she mumbles in a pale mumble.

Oh no – has he walked into a lorry? Or a river?

I grab the phone off her.

'You phoned this number . . . yes. Yes . . . Mr Baker, yes . . . I see. Yes . . . this is his daughter speaking . . . I see . . . Oh dear. Oh dear, oh dear . . .'

Then there's a strange thud, which is Mum falling off the wonky chair.

'He's all right!' I shout, laughing. 'They just locked him up for being drunk and incapable. He's been on the piss. He's just got a bruise or two on his bum.'

And we both laugh as though laughter has just been invented.

CHAPTER FOURTEEN

In Which Emma Dearest Encounters Mr Slithery Dithery

<u>**Wednesday August 6**</u>

Alice has just rung to say the company who signed up Mind Bandits are coming to the mega-gig on Aug 30th.

'Maybe you should get the Atomic Moron to sing,' I say. 'Suppose I throw up?'

'Well . . . we might have her on standby,' says Alice.

Terrific.

<u>**Friday August 8**</u>

I am happy and sad.

I am happy Dad isn't furious. After Mum told him how miserable I was and that I'd wanted to get rid of it and then found it was twins he didn't go on another bender. He told me later he was sorry he'd stormed off but it wasn't just my news – he'd been thrown by my speaking to Ken and he hadn't wanted to tell Mum he was doing up the house of a woman she didn't know: he thought she'd be upset. He thought I might have told her he hadn't been with Ken. He was dead relieved when he found I hadn't. Of course, I told him I thought he might have been with Emma Dearest, and he laughed and said I must be joking. Maybe I really did imagine all that. Being preggers plays funny tricks on your mind.

I am happy that no one at school except my BFs, who I trust with my life, knows I am up the duff without a paddle. I am happy that Mum has agreed not to tell Crazy Craven till next term. I might miscarry. Who knows?

Who cares?

I am happy that I sing in a band with a group of geniuses who will Change the World and that we are doing *Love, Fifteen* because that means I will be a song writer and make bare amounts of enormous dosh.

CAREERING AHEAD TIP

Practise writing your c.v., then find the number of your dream company and say they need a girl like you!

Mother of Two, can sing a bit . . .

But oh, desolate howling wolverines, I am sad about everything else. What have I got going for me apart from a bubbly personality? And where has that gone?

I hate my exploding boobs.

I hate my head.

The top and back bits – OK, some of the sides as well – used to be covered in curls. 'Your hair is like a bunch of black grapes,' Tom used to say, doing his hair-nuzzling thing. His hair-nuzzling thing was taking a strand between his lips and rearranging it. 'It is like a bubble fountain – let me nest in it.'

Now it rivals Lottie's in the depressed mouse department. No, more like suicidal spaghetti. The front bit of my head, where my face used to be, is having a zit party. It was invitation-only at first, and they didn't wreck the whole place, but then some little pluke must've printed flyers, and zits from all over the UK flocked to pack every available centimetre. I thought you were supposed to look awfully well when you were in the family way.

Well awful is more like it.

Worst of all, I hate the twins. The ones inside me. I cannot imagine why anyone, ever, would want to be a mum . . .

We have all talked ourselves into the ground about this and I guess adoption is the best thing. It's clear neither Dad nor Mum feel they can help raise another two kids and I don't feel I can, either.

One set of twins per household is more than

enough . . . It is the Puddings' birthday tomorrow. I will have to give up sleeping with the elephants I bought them.

To: Zlm

Araminta and Abigail are

FOUR

please come to ur party with

Mr. Slithery Dithery

SAT 3·00 till 6·00

Puddings' BirThday

The whole house is turning upside-down getting ready for the dreaded birthday party in the afternoon. Balloons are tied to everything, including the Puddings themselves, who run round the house squealing and trying to bump into sharp objects. Mr Slithery-Dithery is coming to be the entertainer – he's really Roger Nadger, the science-lab technician from KFC, who puts on a plastic cobra's head and brings the most disgusting collection of

240

giant snails, stick insects, snakes, frogs and other creepy-crawlies, including a real python the length of a bus – he makes everybody lie down and lays it on top of them.

The Puddings' little fiends from their playgroup will all be there, a terrifying assortment of budding teefs, liars, drama queens and psychos, who are far worse than Mr Slithery-Dithery's monster collection.

From now on, things start getting out of hand. Actress-over-the-road pops over, wearing a couple of silver stars on springs on her head, and presents the Puddings with a signed photo of herself in some ancient budget production of *Peter Pan*. This quickly finds its way to the floor, where it's trampled on by all and sundry until picked up by Dad, who slips it – lovingly, I would have said – into his jacket pocket. Mr Slithery-Dithery arrives with two bulging and rather smelly suitcases, and tells Mum that his cobra's head is unfortunately locked in a left-luggage compartment at Euston for which he's lost the key, and he will have to do the show in a Spiderman mask instead, but at least he's been able to paint a couple of fangs on it.

Gradually the playgroup contingent arrives – their parents drop them and take off like greyhounds, obviously delighted to make them somebody else's responsibility for an hour or two. Actress-over-the-road takes one look at them all, and vanishes with a look on her face like somebody in *The X-Files*, stars on springs bobbing wildly.

Dad takes off after Emma Dearest but is waylaid by Mr Slithery-Dithery in his Spiderman mask, asking the way to the bathroom. 'It's not for me,' he tells Dad, as if it's something to be ashamed of. 'It's for  me mates here,' he says, pointing at the suitcases. 'Some of them like to be kept wet.'

Wednesday August 13

Every night this week I have the same conversation with Dad and Mum.

They insist on confronting the father and I do the whole killing-him-them-and-myself number that had worked so well on Lottie. But my ancients are made of tougher stuff.

'Amy, it's his responsibility too,' said Mum.

'But I hate him. I don't want him anywhere near me or the babies.'

'But what about them? They need to know who their dad is.'

'*No!* They don't! Ruth doesn't know. Loads of people don't have dads.'

'But it's better if they do, darling, you know that.'

'I do know that, as it happens. But it's just tough. I can't face it. And I can't face anyone else knowing. His fiancée will leave him. It will wreck both their lives! I'll never tell you, never tell the babies, never tell *anyone* who he is! I won't tell him, ever ever ever.'

'But one day they might want to know – they have a right to look for their parents when they're eighteen. What are you going to put on the birth certificate?'

I have decided what I am going to do.

I am going to lie to the bitter end. I am going to pretend to the kids, for ever, that their father was a wonderful man who I'd loved passionately, but who had died in tragic circumstances. I have worked out his last words: 'I'll never see our darling babies, but I'll look down on them from heaven . . . I'll watch over you and them for ever, beloved Amy.'

I am going to write this in a letter to whoever adopts them.

Thursday August 14

AnTenaTal appT.

Back to Big Victorian hospital. This time the midwife gave me a teeny little bottle.

'It's empty,' I said to her, hoping she wouldn't shout at the nurses for forgetting the medicine.

'Yes,' she said, as if addressing a lunatic. 'You're supposed to fill it.'

'What with?' I asked, before being dragged away toward the loo by Mum.

'You're supposed to wee in it, for goodness'

243

sake,' Mum said, laughing.

I looked at the bottle. 'Who do they think I am, David Beckham? I couldn't squirt a water-pistol into there, let alone hit it with a gushing torrent of wossname . . .' I got a big jug thing at the GP's.

'You just have to position it carefully. Do you want me to come and help you?' Mum asked kindly.

'No!' I said unkindly.

The midwife asked my shoe size!

'Nine,' I whispered and she gave me the first smile I'd seen from her since I came in.

'It's not funny,' I said.

'No, no, it's just that shoe size can be an indication of pelvis size. So if that's true in your case, that's brilliant!'

Oh, goody, my giant's feet will be useful for once.

The midwife sat me down to take my Personal History. 'In case there are any diseases or conditions which might be passed on, like sickle-cell anaemia, or twins.'

Goodness, are the Puddings a disease, or a condition? Whatever, they've passed themselves on all right.

Did I smoke?

I said I hadn't looked down there since conception, but I didn't think so.

The midwife was looking well hacked off. 'Because smoking can be very harmful to baby,' she said, 'and can reduce birth weight.' Then she asked if I'd been pregnant before.

I nearly hit her.

'I'm sorry,' she said, quite gently this time. 'Lots of women hate answering these questions but it does mean we get to know things that will help in an emergency. People specially hate talking about terminations, but you know, one in four women has had one.'

'Really?' I was amazed.

I was given a lot of leaflets about not drinking, smoking or having any fun. And a big diet thingy about fruit and veg and fibre and protein. It seems spinach and marmalade alone may not be enough.

'Don't worry if you get food fads,' said the midwife. 'My mum used to nibble coal.'

I am very disturbed by this news. Suppose I develop an urge for something even harder to get? Dog soup with octopus? Quick-fried postman?

I was so relieved when we'd done all the form filling but then the midwife told me to go and get undressed and a doctor would see me.

I had to have a full physical examination. Inside!

'Don't worry, they only do this on the first visit. It will just be a hand on your tummy to feel baby – er, babies – after this,' said the midwife, ushering me into Dr Trough's lair.

Dr Trough was a fierce, bustling woman who needed a shave on just about every part of her I could see. She did the whole business briskly and silently, except for muttering a few things I didn't understand about uteruses and funduses and placentas. She used a rubber glove to feel inside me (not just a rubber glove, obviously – her hand was in it), and I lay there realizing I would rather be on Cliff Richard's knee. Or anywhere.

When she'd finished she said cheerfully, 'You're in excellent condition,' as though I was a prize cow, 'but in view of your age and because you're having twins, we'll have to keep a close eye, especially around twenty-eight weeks, as there is an increased risk of miscarrying twins during that period.'

Wouldn't a miscarriage be just what I need? I thought.

But I kept my lip buttoned.

I wobbled out with clucking Mum and we went straight to the pub for a lemonade. Mum has cut out boozing in solidarity. I am touched.

Friday August 15

Swanage tomorrow.

Lottie comes over to check out my wardrobe for our huge mega-gig in two weeks' time. She must be worried about how fat I'll look by then.

'Maybe I'll find something in Swanage,' I say.

'Yes, but let's sort it out now if we can.'

Ah. I see. She wants to borrow.

She burrows through the pile on the floor and finds a deep purple crop-top and some black hip-ster flairs in size ten. I was never size ten. I must have got those years ago in one of my hopeful moods of losing puppy fat.

'Hey, these would really suit me if I take them in a bit,' she says in fake surprise. She's into them in a flash and looks like a supermodel. Except for the owl glasses and the depressed mouse.

'What about me?' I finally ask.

We look again.

I have my denim sack.

And my flowery sack.

'I'll have to give them away, Lottie,' I say.

'No, you'll need them when you are nearly due.'

'Not the sacks, you pretzel, the babies.'

'Ooooooh,' she says.

'It'll be OK,' I say bravely. 'I'll live my life just like everyone else, then, and get ten A stars at GCSE because I will be so wise and caring after my toil and trouble.'

'Maybe they'll be adopted by someone rich and famous,' she says.

'Yeah. Sure,' I say. 'A rock star and a super-model, who have tried to get pregnant for ten years and fall in love with my babies on sight.'

11 p.m.

Holy guacamole, Lottie has persuaded me to exploit my Eurotrash cleavage. We found an old sparkly number I wore at the school disco in Year

Nine. It used to be a mini dress but it now works just fine as a top. Have to admit I look like a sex queen. As long as the slimming black joggers with elasticated waistband don't burst. Will I be much fatter in a fortnight?

Lottie said, 'Because your boobs are so gigantic, your bump hardly shows. Yet.'

Couldn't have put it better myself.

Saturday August 16

Off to Swanage.

Well, sitting in my room with Lottie, occasionally looking out the window at Dad's feet sticking out from under the car, actually. We don't care much – we have an ear each plugged into Lottie's minidisc player listening to the Mind Bandits' great new album *Don't Stamp on That Braincell* and eating Maltesers. Every now and then my mum sticks her head round the door and says something we can't hear, but which I think is 'He's nearly fixed it,' or maybe 'Eels are nearly fish, innit?' or more likely 'He's really f****d it.'

Two hours later

The Puddings are jumping up and down and waving their hands in the air. Eventually we realize the car is fixed. Swanage ahoy!

Dad was quiet on the journey, listening to some old radio station broadcasting pop music from Roman times when records were carved on round bits of stone. Mum tried to make conversation now and then, in between reading *The Elephant Goes Faaart*, or something, to the Puddings.

Eventually we all shut up. The Puddings finally went to sleep, Mum started reading *Cheerio!* – the magazine for the newly-divorced – Dad turned the radio off with a snap, mysteriously hissing, 'Bastards!' under his breath, and Lottie and I started playing Spot the Bum whenever we passed through any busy towns. You get ten points for spotting a really nice tight, peachy one first, six points for a vast, hippo-like one. You forfeit three if a nice bum has a really minging-looking face at the other end, and twenty if it turns out to be attached to the opposite sex to the one you thought it was.

Lottie was ahead by fifteen and I was feeling a bit sick when we arrived at Swanage. We were staying at Granny Meg's as usual – she has a little tiny cottage full of cobwebs and about a hundred cats. Cat hair makes Lottie sneeze.

'Hello, dear, nice to meet you,' Granny Meg said, peering in Lottie's direction (she doesn't see too well, or remember too well either – Lottie has been coming to Swanage for ten years . . .).

'Acaaaaaarrrrrrr!!!!!' said Lottie, dislodging her glasses with a sneeze about a million miles off the top of the Richter scale, and peering just as mystified back at Granny Meg. They attempted to shake hands, and missed.

Lottie and me were in our old attic room, which has a panoramic beachside view of the outside loo of a pub called the Goat and Pilchard, and the wheelie bins at the back of the Oriental Mysteries Sushi and Burger House. I sat down on the bed, suddenly feeling gloomy.

Lottie put an arm around me. 'Achaaaaaarrrrr!' she said. I wiped some nose-projectile stuff off my arm.

'Hope you're still going to like it here,' I murmured, snuggling up to her, feeling suddenly incredibly sleepy. I must have drifted off then. Occasionally, I heard voices saying, 'Dinner!' and 'Millis!' and 'It's all right, it's not broken,' and 'Achaaaarrrr!' And I had a dream I was running after two little figures walking hand in hand towards the sea.

Wednesday August 20

The first few days of our stay in Swanage are always a bit strange – we all have to get used to being on top of each other in Gran's little house, the cats have to get used to being chased around all day by the Puddings, and Dad has to get used to Granny Meg asking him if he's got a proper job yet. Mum spends all her time in the kitchen, trying to clean up all the cat fur, dirty plates and mouse droppings without Granny Meg noticing.

This time, of course, there was the extra question of My Little Bit of News. It's been weighing on my mum for weeks. When to tell Granny Meg, and how.

Luckily the weather is fanzuminous, Tharg be

praised for He/She is Great, etc. Lottie and I just go to the beach with a bagful of minidiscs and a picnic, while Mum and Dad take the Puddings on rides.

Friday August 22

I am happy here. It is like being a child again. Have said to Mum, 'Why bother telling Granny Meg? It'll only upset her.'

At which Mum just rubs her hands together in a worried, kneading sort of way. As if she is kneading dough.

Our ancestors must have kneaded, and that is why we are called Baker. Like blacksmiths are called Smith.

But then Mum wasn't a Baker, was she, until she married Dad?

'Maybe Dad's ancestors kneaded,' I say to Lottie, while she is trying on a kiss-me-quick hat.

Saturday August 23

I am even happier. First, am beginning to feel ludicrously healthy. Is it the sea air? Or could it just be being preggers? I get these daft moments of bliss, where I think, after all, I can imagine keeping the babies and being a mum.

As if reading my mind, Dad suggested we had a little walk together and a 'chat'. We linked arms in a cosy Daddy-daughter way and I thought, Why don't we do this back home? Is it because I'm embarrassed? Or because he is?

'You OK, sweetheart?' he said, when we had reached the shore and were gazing at a far-off liner.

Dad hasn't called me sweetheart for years – probably not since the Puddings were born.

'I feel great, Dad. Never better, except . . .'

'Missing your Tom?'

'Badly,' was all I could say.

'Love is hard. Love is very hard. It comes at the wrong time . . . and goes at the wrong time . . .' he said, gazing far out to sea at the dwindling ship.

It was great that he was acknowledging, again, that I loved Tom, but I couldn't help feeling he was trying to say something else, probably about Emma Dearest. And I just couldn't bear to ask.

'Amy' – he turned towards me anxiously – 'do you want to keep the babies?'

'Yes.' I said it without thinking, but Dad's face crumpled, which scared me, so I gabbled, 'No. Maybe. I don't know.'

'It's a horrible thought, giving them up,' he said. 'But you don't realize how tough it would be for you. You have no idea what it's like – so much responsibility, so much worry, so much money. Mum never really recovered after the Puddings, you know. She used to be such a . . . a playful person. They wore her out. We haven't been out together alone since . . .'

'Valentine's Day? The day I met Tom?'

'And look what that led to . . .' He smiled grimly.

'Dad, you know Tom isn't the father. If he was, I'd be keeping the babies, no problem.'

'I know, I know, but you wouldn't have, you know . . . gone off with someone else, would you? It was only because you were heartbroken, wasn't it? I mean, you're not that sort of girl.'

'Dad, I'm not really sure what that sort of girl is any more.'

Dad looked chastened. 'You are a hundred per cent sure the babies aren't Tom's? Did you, er, sleep with him? I'm only asking because I've . . . been wondering whether you're trying to protect him – and giving away babies by someone you loved – maybe still love – would be very hard for you.'

'Look, Dad, I did sleep with Tom once, just once, because I couldn't bear not to as he was going away, and if you really want the details, Dad, it was two condoms, spermicide, the Pill and during my period.'

Dad blushed bright pink.

'I know it's hard for you, Dad, to see your little girl turned into a woman overnight, but I'm not sure you and Mum have noticed me much since I was eleven – too busy with the Puddings.'

'Oh Amy. We should have done more. It's all my fault.'

'Dad, it's not your fault. You may not have noticed I was growing up, but I was. I chose to do what I did. It's just . . . life.'

'But you're right about us ignoring you. That's what twins do, you see. They addle your brain. They're exhausting. If you keep them, you'll never be free again.'

'Isn't there an old song that says freedom only means that you've got nothing left to lose, Dad?' I asked him.

He hugged me. 'Fancy you remembering that. I used to play that to you when you were two and wouldn't go to bed without me reading you six stories.'

'Well, I don't know what to do, but I think there's some truth in that old song . . .'

'I'm afraid there probably is,' Dad said very thoughtfully, and we turned to walk back to Granny Meg's as a biting wind blew up.

I was grateful for the wind, because I felt unable to say anything else, as though my emotions had collided, and happiness and sadness were the same thing. Dad had actually listened to me as though I was a grown-up too. And maybe that's what I've got to do now, somehow. I've got to grow up, if I can . . .

Sunday August 24

Well, I'm fifteen, and I can't be grown up all the time, especially as the beach is an excellent place to play Spot the Bum. I realize Lottie looks a lot sexier on the beach than I've ever noticed before, particularly wearing a bikini and two drum-practice pads strapped to her thighs, which make her look like something out of *Tomb Raider*. We've been clocked by some quite fit-looking boys playing football, but they seem a bit shy. We've given them a smile or two to see what happens, but all it's done is make them try to do fancier things that don't work with the football.

Monday August 25

Bought some rock. It had MARGATE written all the way through. The rock delivery people have obviously gone doolally.

Goody. That means Dad *did* get his rock in Blackpool, not Saaaafend.

I knew it.

Being preggers has made me subject to fantasies, obviously. Dad would never leave us – of course he wouldn't.

Managed to prise Mum away from Puddings and mouse droppings to go up the pier with me and Lottie. Lottie zoomed straight into Madame Orb's clairvoyant tent while me and Mum had a go on the rifle range. She scored six bull's-eyes with seven shots!

'Mum, how long is it since you've fired a gun?'

'Not since I took out those injuns back in Dakota, when they was a-tryin' to kidnap you, honey,' she drawled. 'Let's do the bowling.'

I don't know if it was the sea air that brought such a sparkle to Mum's face, or if it was just having a bit of useless fun instead of washing and cooking and working and worrying all the time, but she looked really pretty, suddenly. Much prettier than me, if I'm honest. I could see what Dad meant. I could remember it, too. Mum had often rough-housed with me and swirled me round her head when I was little. And she'd been brilliant at dressing-up games and make believe. But recently I'd only seen her lighten up when she was drunk. And now she'd stopped doing even that in solidarity with me. What had happened? Was it really just the Puddings?

'You know something, Mum? You should get out more. I haven't seen you like this since rabbit safari.'

She looked baffled, then burst out laughing. 'Rabbit safari! When we used to go hunting for the Easter Bunny. Goodness, I'd forgotten all about that. How awful, I never did it with the Puddings . . .'

'Oh, stop blaming yourself for things you didn't do, Mum. You need more fun now. You should get out with Dad more. I'll babysit. I should do it more. Sorry.'

The last time they both went out, I'd taken the Puddings with me, and . . . Oooh dear, everything leads back to that Valentine's night . . .

'OK, I'll make a resolution to go out with Dad more. You're right, it'll do me good.' Mum paused. 'You do see, that's why I can't face bringing up another two, don't you?'

'I do, Mum, I do. And I really don't think I'm ready for it either. Unless we can win all those coins at once!'

We charged over to the shove penny machine, which seemed to be stuffed with 50p pieces. We had about twenty tries and got 4p back. Why is it that only the 2p pieces come back out? Maybe they are all just glued on . . .

'Don't waste any more on that – you've got to go and see Madame Orb! She's amazing!' yelled Lottie.

'Really? What did she say?' I asked. Maybe crystal-gazing was what I needed.

'Oh, loads of things, all true!' said Lottie. 'Best ten pounds I ever spent.'

'Ten pounds!' said Mum. 'Daft. Let's spend it on fish and chips instead.'

So we did. All I want is their mushy peas, which are the nicest things I've ever eaten in my life. Dad was baffled. 'You've always hated mushy peas,' he kept saying. Mum just smiled to herself, and nodded.

Tuesday August 26

Hormone alert.

Fit beach boy and his mates asked us to go surfing. Lottie said I was recovering from falling down a man hole, so we made sand sculptures instead.

We made a giant willy, as it happens.

We were just putting on the finishing touches

(pubic seaweed) when a party of ancients in puffa jackets strode towards us.

Lottie and me locked eyes in shock. Lottie whispered, 'Say it's a dolphin.' Fit beach boy and pals disappeared in puff of sand as though their swimming shorts were on fire.

Ancients paused to admire sculpture.

Then they realized what it was.

A little old lady as skinny as a leaf started laughing so hard I thought she'd blow away. Between chortles she said, 'Shame they don't come in that size.' And the party stomped off, cackling fit to bust.

Goodness.

1 a.m.

I can't sleep. I really want to see Madame Orb. I could ask her if Tom will come back. If I should keep the babies. If they will be born OK with two eyes each and so on. If I will die in childbirth. If . . . if . . .

2 a.m.

Woke Lottie. Felt really bad about it, but I just couldn't get Madame Orb out of my mind.

'What did she say, Lotts, do tell.'

'I've been thinking about it since, and it wasn't much good, really. I feel a bit daft,' said Lottie.

'But do tell.'

'Erm . . . she said I needed to stop thinking about others so much and spend more time on

myself . . . that I'd been looking after someone else
. . . that there was love in the air for me if I could
only open my eyes to it . . . that I would cross
water . . . Oh it was just stupid waffle really.'

'But you thought it was good at the time. You
thought it meant something. Was it me you
thought you were spending too much time on?'

'Yes. It was. But that's not the point. I know
fortune tellers always tell you that you're spending
too much time being kind, because they think it'll
make you feel like a good person. And everyone
crosses water if they're on a pier, don't they?
Anyway she also said there were two men in my
life. And that's not true.'

'That would have been true for me though. She
probably says that to everyone as well. It's probably
true for most people—'

'Oh shut up,' said Lottie with feeling.

'I didn't mean that – I meant, it could be a
brother, or a dad, or whatever.'

'Can I go back to sleep now?' asked Lottie.

'Course. I'm sorry. I'm really sorry I've been a
drag. I really want to get back to being how I was
. . . before all this.'

'Amy, you've been great these last few days – we
had all that fun on the beach and everything. And,
well, you know the surf boy?'

'The fit one with the baseball cap?'

'Um, no. The quiet one.'

'Oh yeah, what?'

'He put this in my bag.' And she pulled out a

little card. It had a heart on! Inside he had written:

> *I like your hair. But it is your mind*
> *I'm after.*
> *Dan*

And then his mobile number!

'Lottie! It's love! But how do you know it was him, and not the fit one?'

'They told us their names, you loon,' she said.

'Anyway, he is fit too, very fit,' I said quickly, although I couldn't remember what he looked like.

'Do you think so?' she asked dreamily.

'I do, I do! Ring him tomorrow!'

But she had nodded off.

Wednesday August 27

KEEP FIT TIP

Take a beach ball to volley on the beach. Check out all those fit boys in teeny shorts.

Unless you resemble beach ball, in which case build sand willy.

Dreamt about fit beach boy.

Maybe rollicking hormones are because of being preggers? I suppose when you are preggers, that is the only time you can't get preggers, so that makes the preggers female feel like a powerful sex goddess who can do it all the time?

Or maybe it's just being fifteen?

Neither *Teenacious Tips* nor *Your Developing Child*, which I got from the library, are good on raging hormones.

I made Lottie ring Dan the minute she woke up.

'He does sound a bit young,' she said when she came off the phone. 'But he wants to meet up at noon by the pier. You have to come too.'

'Right,' I said, and we spent an hour choosing her bikini and doing leg waxing.

We spotted fit beach boy and his mates over by the pier.

'Which is him?' I asked.

'That one.' She pointed to a boy who looked about thirteen.

'You go,' she said. 'Say I'll meet him in the chippy at one. Please.'

So she sat down on her towel and I wandered up to the boys, trying not to ogle fit beach boy.

Dan came racing up to me, all eager. 'Did you get my card?' he said, his face breaking into a sweet smile.

'You mean did my friend get your card?' I said.
'Yes, and—'

'No, it was for you,' he said, and turned a lobstery pink.

'Oh. Sorry,' I said. I seem to be saying sorry rather a lot just now. 'But, honest, how old are you?'

'He's eleven and a half, he's my kid brother, so don't you go baby-snatching,' said fit beach boy.

'Oh, er, ah, er, see you in five years then,' I said as nicely as I could, and scarpered back to Lottie.

'Lottie, he's adorable, but he's eleven and his brother said you were a baby-snatcher,' I lied.

She took it really well. 'I did think he was a bit young for me,' she said. 'But he does look old for his age and it was sweet he liked me, wasn't it?'

'Oh very,' I said.

Oooh.

Boys are weird. Lottie looks amazing at the moment and I look crap. I think my hormones must be showing, somehow.

'You know, Lottie, you are better off not getting too involved with anyone yet – it's been a bummer for me.'

'But I am the only one who's never . . . even kissed anyone,' said Lottie.

'But look where a kiss can lead,' I said.

'You sound like your gran!'

'No, I just mean, there are other things in life. Although I can't remember what they are . . .'

'Friendship?' she smiled.

'Yes! And music!'

In the evening everyone else watches telly while me and Lottie read. Granny Meg's telly is black and white, has a picture about the size of a postcard,

and goes on and off at strange intervals. At 8.30
every evening she makes us all cocoa, and then
goes to sleep in an armchair at about nine o'clock,
usually in the middle of a TV programme she's told
us she absolutely *has* to watch. The Puddings are
put to bed, but keep creeping downstairs, giggling.

Thursday 28 August

Dreamt me and Tom were surfing. We were each
carrying a twin. But the twins were growing about
a metre every second. Then they turned into Lottie
and . . . Iqbal!

What does this mean?

It means Lottie should be with Iqbal, obviously.
Intellectuals together. I nearly tell her, but decide to
do some sneaky matchmaking instead.

We're going home tomorrow. Oh. Real life.

And it's our big gig on Sat. Can't face it.

I want to stay in Swanage for ever.

Later

No. I don't want to stay. Mum
has just beckoned to me to say
the time has come to spill the
beans to Granny Meg.

I feel terrible about this.
Granny Meg is a mad old flake but nice
in her way, and I've never done anything to upset
her and don't want to.

At cocoa time Mum signals it is The Moment

and Lottie and I pretend to do something busy in the kitchen, while the pyjamaed Puddings jump up and down shouting, 'Millis! Wotcha doin', Millis?'

We creep to the door of the living room, the Puddings under our feet screaming, 'Ssshhhh!' at each other and the cats, who are just chilling and looking as if they're above it all, as usual. There's a murmur of voices from the room. And then . . .

Oh no!

We hear a terrible choking scream coming from behind the door followed by a strange rhythmic creaking sound, which is probably Granny Meg breathing her last. We burst in, and there she is, collapsed in the armchair with Mum flapping a dishcloth up and down in front of her, and Dad heading for the telephone. Granny Meg has tears rolling down her face, and she's feebly flapping her arms about like one of those puppets in *Thunderbirds*.

My mum looks at me, distraught.

Granny Meg looks at me too. And reaches out her wobbly arms towards me, waggling her bony fingers in what I think must be an invitation to a hug.

Dad freezes in mid-lift at the telephone.

Granny Meg does her best to hug me, which works sort of OK, as relationships between stick insects and expectant mammoths go. And amid all the gasping and creaking and hissing and flapping, Granny Meg seems to be trying to tell me she's . . . ecstatic.

'I never thought I'd live to see great-grandchildren – and two of them,' she finally manages to say, and a big beaming smile spreads across her strange dried-walnut of a face, making her look for a split second about as beautiful as anyone I've ever seen.

'Clever, isn't she?' Lottie says to Granny Meg, who nods so fast her old head looks about to fall off.

'Bring them down here to see me, won't you?' Granny Meg says, gripping my hand. Lottie and I look at each other, and I give Granny Meg the most hopeful smile I can. My mum looks at me anxiously.

'I'm really tired, Gran,' I say to her, squeezing her hand back. 'I'll see you in the morning.'

Granny Meg nods, and lets go. Lottie and I go upstairs.

'Your gran is amazing,' said Lottie simply.

'You too, Lottie. You too.'

CHAPTER FIFTEEN

In Which Amy and Emma Dearest Both Get Caught Short

Saturday August 30

The mega-gig

A bit nervy all day.

Why? We had a good rehearsal last night and we have done half a dozen gigs.

But this is the biggest yet.

It might only be in the old Ferret and Flugelhorn, but they've opened up the front too, so there will be three times the number of people there were at our first gig. Ooooh.

I need a little lie down.

7 p.m.

Squash myself into sex goddess gear. Mini dress just long enough to cover bump. Put six safety pins in elastic waistband of XXXXXL joggers just in case. Lottie and me link arms and off we go, sex-queen rock stars, to our biggest gig yet.

Yesterday, Mind Bandits. Tomorrow, Black Hole!

Midnight

Quel disastre, in
every possible way.

At first it looked
like it was going to
be our best gig ever.
The Ferret and
Flugelhorn was
opened out to
include all four bars,
and people were

queuing to get in! Duane was saying our instruments
would be in glass cases in the front bar thirty years
from now, with little plaques saying this was where
we started out on our world-dominating careers!

And what happened?

Yrs Truly got caught short in the middle of the
third number, Mad Alice's *Just the Way You Lick,
Tonight*.

I suddenly wanted to wee so much, I knew I'd
have to get offstage or disappear like something
out of Harry Potter in the blue flash of some
bizarre water-and-megawatts incident. I lost the
last two verses and let out a terrifying scream
instead – it got a huge cheer from the crowd, and I
dived off for the hell-hole that is the Flugelhorn's
loo, looking as if I was fleeing the flashing blade of
Mad Alice's guitar, which anybody with any sense
would anyway. This was Mad Alice's moment. She

went off on an amazing one, as I crashed through the bog door letting out a squeal of relief. As I sat ecstatically on the pan, I could hear her solo, going on for chorus after chorus.

I wanted to get back out there more than anything. But when I'd finished, I just burst into tears. After a while I could hear the music stop, and a roar from the crowd, and not long after that a lot of banging on the door.

It was Lottie. 'You've got to deal with this,' she said. 'There's a cab coming to take you home.'

'No! Don't want to go!' I was beginning to sound like the Puddings.

'You've got to, you're a mess. Don't worry, we'll manage.'

'You can't manage! Who's going to sing?'

Lottie cleared her throat. 'Well . . . the Atomic Moron's here.'

'Are you serious?! That's like sticking Britney in the Manics!'

Lottie squeezed my hand. 'We'll get away with it. Most of the audience is pissed anyway. She looks all right, and we'll just play loud.'

'There's nobody home,' I said pathetically. 'Mum's taken the Puddings to WeightWatchers with her, and Dad's out hammering something.' Suddenly I couldn't face being home alone.

'My mum's in the same WeightWatchers group, remember?' said Lottie. 'I've tracked your mum down already. She's on her way up here in the cab.'

The taxi soon showed and Mum swept me up

like a lost kitten. The Puddings were asleep in the back, clasped together.

By the time we got home, I felt better, but as I was stumbling into the hall I heard a horribly familiar laugh, like a chandelier hitting a tin can. I glanced round at Mum, who was struggling to haul the still sleepwalking Puddings from the taxi. I slammed the front door and shot upstairs in the direction of the giggle. There was a light on in the loo but the door wasn't locked, and I wasn't in the mood for asking polite questions. Before I knew it I was in there, and before I knew it Emma Dearest, wearing only a thong, was reaching for a towel.

'Jeez!' was all I could say.

'Aaaargh,' was all she could say, grabbing my hand in what felt like a vice. 'I've been robbed. Darling, it's been a nightmare. Everything gone, everything. I came home to find the house a shambles. Thank God your father is a saint – he rescued me. Can you lend me something to wear?'

I just stared at her.

Emma Dearest made for the window. 'Will this drainpipe take my weight?' she squawked, before squirming out pretty fast, considering. It must have been all the jogging that kept her in shape. The thong didn't look that glamorous on the way out, but maybe the situation wouldn't have flattered even Kate Moss. Somebody was turning the door handle as she disappeared, and I jammed my foot against it, thinking Mum might have heard something.

'Piss off!' I squawked, surprised at myself. 'Can't anybody get any privacy in this house?'

'It's me,' came Dad's voice urgently. 'Is that you, Amy?

'Is Emma in there?' comes his voice again, when I don't answer.

'No. Fell out the window,' I say, grinning fiendishly to myself. 'Dead, mos' prob'ly.'

'My God! Let me in!'

I can hear Mum calling for him from downstairs.

'Amy, for God's sake,' Dad hisses at me. 'Where's Emma?'

I relent, sort of. I don't know why. 'She's gone home in her knickers. You're disgusting.'

'It's not what you think. Don't tell Mum. Please don't. She won't understand.'

There's a long silence. I think Mum is coming upstairs, because her calls for Dad sound louder.

'I won't tell her,' I whisper to Dad. 'But we've got to talk about this.'

Sunday August 31

Dad has done a runner.

I stomped downstairs to find Mum looking like a dog's dinner.

'It's not so bad,' I said. 'Girls have been having babies since the dawn of time.'

'It's not that,' she said. 'It's this.'

And she handed me a letter.

Dearest Puffball,

I hate doing this to you all. I'm not sure I know why I'm doing it either, except it's a chance to earn some proper money and be of some use for once.

A decent job has come up in Wiltshire, doing up a farmhouse for a woman with more money than sense. It's a nice part of the world, and maybe it'll give me a bit of space to come to terms with what's happened to Amy. I don't want to make it harder for her but I have to admit this hasn't been easy for me to handle. You try to do your best, but they're growing up in a different world. It doesn't seem a better one to me, but maybe we should have done more to help her.

It's best you should be with Amy at a time like this, woman to woman. She's a woman now – I should have realized. I'd just be in the way now. But I will help, once I've got things sorted out, I will. Please understand.

I'll ring every night.

Love you,

Harry

It's horrible to see Mum smiling like a loony and telling the Puddings Dad has gone to do a job for a few weeks.

Does she believe it? I can't tell.

Mondragon's blundering underpants! 'He's running away just when I need him,' I can't help saying.

Mum tells me that's nonsense and poor Dad has been under a lot of strain – isn't that obvious from his note? And then she tells me I don't know what earning a living is like.

I have to bite my tongue not to tell her about Emma Dearest. Instead I storm upstairs and ring Lottie.

'Oh my goddess,' she says.

Great.

But she agrees it's better not to tell Mum. 'It'll only send her bonkers and then you'll have to look after her, too,' she says. 'You've got to look after yourself a bit. How many things can you worry about at once?'

Thank you, Madame Orb.

School starts in two days and I am a whale.

CHAPTER SIXTEEN

In Which Lottie, Amy and Mrs Moon
All Face Facts

<u>**Tuesday September 2**</u>

First day of school. I am now officially in Year
Eleven!

Have persuaded
Mum to write a
note saying I am
unwell and asking
for Lottie to bring
me homework. I
asked her to say
I have glandular
fever, but she
didn't want to tell
a porky. Unwell is
OK, she says, for
a couple of days,
but they will ask questions soon.

Dear Mrs. Moon,
   Amy is unwell and is likely
to be off school for the next
few days. We realise, that
with GCSES approaching,
she must try to keep up
with her school work and
have therefore arranged for
Lottie Halford to pick up
and deliver homework.
   Yours Sincerely
      Anastasia Baker

You spend your life wanting to be free of
school, then you miss it.

273

What will Mrs Moon think? And Ms Corman?
I am even missing Mr Fish.
Come back, PE, all is forgiven.
Has Iqbal finished *Dude, Where's My Country?*
Who is ogling Señor Mondragon?

DREAM ROOM TIP
Try moving around your furniture
for a quick new look!

Yes . . . I could put my bed against the door
and, er, that's it really.

6.30 p.m.

Mrs Moon came round! Lucky I was in bed. Mum
ushered her up, clucking in a pretend-unembarrassed
way and looking like she was saying, 'My daughter's
in the club, what a silly slag she is, no one in my
family's ever had anything like this happen before,'
even though what she was actually saying was: 'We're
wondering whether it could be glandular fever.'

I pulled my legs up to my chin and tried to look wan.

I have in fact for the first time in my life got a nice
complexion. Not a zit in sight and cheeks as pink as
the old damask rose. My eyes are all clear and shiny.
What a waste. I look about as ill as Noddy.

274

Mrs Moon is very kind. She has brought me some work and some marked homework from last term and just wanted to see how I was getting on.

I think I fooled her.

But I wanted to tell her.

Best-laid plans . . .

As Moony was making for the door, the Puddings were arriving.

'Hello,' said Mrs Moon. 'You must be Amy's sisters.'

'Amy havin' a baby!' came the crystal-clear voice of Pudding One, up the stairs.

I put my head under the duvet.

Tell me it's all a dream.

Poor Mum, but Moony couldn't have been sweeter. She told Mum she had guessed, which is why she had come round, of course. So Mum brought her back upstairs again. I could have gone through the floor without a paddle, but Moony said I would be welcome to come back to KFC for as long as I can, although she will understand if I don't feel like it.

But she has to get in touch with social services – it's her duty, she says.

So now I will be 'at risk' and a health and safety issue and a statistic. Pukerama.

Should I go back to school? And prove it can be done? After all, I'm only having a baby. Everyone was a baby once. Why do people hate teenagers for having babies?!

Yes! I *will* go back.

Bad night. Dreamt I was at school, fat and stark naked, and everybody else was thin and dressed in fantastic clothes. Horrors! Lottie, Debs and Mad Alice were all pointing at me and laughing. I was in hysterics and trying to run away, but every corner I turned they were there.

Then I woke up. And remembered I was going back to school. After this summer it was going to feel so strange.

I was pretty quiet all through breakfast, but the noise of the Puddings made up for it. My mum was quiet too, between missing Dad and probably worrying as much about me going back to school as I was.

Then there was a ring at the doorbell. It was Lottie, Debs and Mad Alice calling for me. They weren't pointing and jeering, and they were about the same sizes and shapes they usually were. I was so chuffed they'd made such an effort to support me, all arranging to be in the same place at the same time and everything – it's no joke for Us Yoof. We linked arms and walked chattering to school four-wide (well, five- or six-wide, given the shape I'm in), probably forcing all manner of toddlers and dogs and pensioners into the road, but we didn't notice.

'How're you feeling?' they all squawked at me at once.

'Pregnant.'

'You slag! Why didn't you tell us? Were you abducted by aliens?'

'Yep. Big green dribbling slurpy ones with eight arms.'

'How many willies?'

'Just one tiny one. But I didn't comment on it.'

'Good call, you might never have got back alive otherwise.'

'Glad you reminded me about this,' I said to the BFs. 'That's going to be my story if anybody asks.'

Everybody did ask of course, and that's exactly what I told them. Didn't work, unfortunately.

'Yaaaah, piss off! What really happened?'

'All right, I met Johnny Depp in the Dog and Duck and we realized we were meant to be together. I'm just over here having the baby cheap on the NHS. After that we're going to live in a Hollywood mansion – er, in France.'

Choruses of 'Nyaaaaaahh,' 'Botox,' 'Your mum's Johnny Depp,' and 'Bog off,' followed this, and one of 'Corrrr' from a girl on the fringes who looked like a small bedraggled soft toy.

I was getting people I'd never spoken to in my life before coming up and asking. Some people lurked suspiciously, mingling with the crowd, but you could see their faces peering round people's heads or over their shoulders, following me about and peering at my bouncy-castle middle when they thought I wasn't watching. The soft toy I vaguely recognized from two years below me did it all through break and as we were about to go back in started trotting along beside me.

'Hello,' she said, trying to keep up. 'I'm Amy.'

'Don't be rude. I'm Amy.'

'I know. But I'm Amy too. Funny, isn't it?'

'Hilarious.'

'What does it feel like?'

'What?'

'Having a baby inside you. What does it feel like?'

'Fat.'

'You've done it with a boy, haven't you?'

'No, I watched a porno movie and got too close to the screen.'

'My boyfriend keeps saying we ought to do it. He says all the other girls he knows do, except for the dogs, who can't get anyone.'

I stopped and looked at her. 'How old are you, Amy?' I asked.

'Thirteen.'

'Listen, I didn't want this to happen, and if I could go back and start again I'd make sure it didn't. If I think I'm too young to be a mum, where does that leave you?'

'But I wouldn't be one. He's got those things. He keeps showing me them every chance he gets.'

'Well, it's none of my business,' I said to her. 'But when you do decide

LIES LIES LIES

Arrrrgh! These are some of the LIES boys tell girls:
YOU CAN'T GET PREGGERS IF

You do it standing up.
You do it during your period.
Your boyfriend smokes dope.
You don't snog first!

what to do, make sure it's your idea and not just his.'

Lunch time. Me and the BFs were sitting round the back of the girls' loos, listening to Ruth'n'Van sharing a spliff in the cubicles and slagging off just about everyone at KFC. Before they got to us, Debs did her amazingly lifelike copy of the geog teacher Miss Flint's scary voice, warning them that drug use was illegal on school premises between the hours of midday and two. There was a dead silence, then a bit of whispering, then the sound of a loo flushing. We clutched each other, hooting with laughter until Ruth'n'Van heard us and we had to flee before they came out.

'You know that other Amy in Year Nine?' I asked the others once we thought we were at a safe distance.

'The one who looks like a failed textiles project?' Mad Alice asked, grinding her teeth.

'That's her. She was asking me advice about doing it with her boyfriend. It's weird, I think I'm becoming an agony aunt more than a mum.'

'I know her boyfriend,' Lottie said. 'He's the big brother of Howling Hettie, a terrible junior school nutter who lives in our street. He offered me a bag of Skittles to show him my bum when we were little.'

'When was that?' Debs asked.

'Oh, last year sometime,' Lottie said, straight-faced.

'Heh heh,' said Mad Alice.

'Should she let him unpick her stitching?'

I asked nobody in particular.

'Nah,' said Lottie. 'She doesn't need him, he's out of control, he tries it on with everybody. Even me, and he didn't even offer the Skittles this time.'

'What d'you mean, even you?' I said, giving Lottie a squeeze. 'You're made to be a sex machine. You can do different things with all four limbs and you've got natural rhythm.'

'Great,' said Lottie, a shadow crossing her brilliant owl-face.

'What's up, Lotts?'

'I don't want to be a sex machine. I want to be me. I want somebody to like me just for that.'

We all shut up at this and thought for a bit.

'What do they really think of you? That's the question,' Mad Alice finally said, striking a fancy Shakespeare pose with her elbows out.

'Who?'

'Boys. You know, those aliens that keep their brains in their willies Saturday nights,' Mad Alice said, frowning with the effort of making herself understood. 'I mean, we all know which bits of us they like. And sometimes we play up to that – it's fun, like being in the driving seat. But then other times when you try to tell them how you feel, they start talking about football to their mates, as if you'd started going on about tampons or something.'

'I think somebody did a book about boys and girls being from different planets,' I said. 'Neither of them was this one, which was a bit confusing . . .' I tailed off.

'I think one sex came from Uranus,' said Debbie.

'So much for what they tell you about reproduction in Year Six then,' said Mad Alice, cackling.

'The old jokes are the oldest,' we all said in chorus.

'No, it's Venus, you spittoon,' hooted Lottie. 'Girls are from Venus.'

'How did we get here, then?' enquired Debbie. 'I mean, my mum's always hurt I can't remember going to Blackpool when I was little, but you'd think I'd remember Venus.'

'Look, this is all botox,' said Alice. 'Question is, do boys think your feelings are just not as interesting as your sexy bits, or do they actually get turned right off if you let on you've got any feelings?'

'Well, they want you to have feelings about them,' Lottie considered. 'They want you to think they're wonderful.'

'Right, but not about anything else,' said Alice. 'They get all grumpy and neglected if you care about anything else. Like music, for instance.'

'Mikey likes me playing music,' Debs said. 'He says he's proud of me.'

So did Tom, I thought.

'Aaaaahhh,' the rest of us went. Debbie stuck her tongue out.

'Well, you're lucky about Mikey then,' Alice went on. 'He's an exception. A lot of them don't like it if you . . . well, play guitar for instance, and do songs about boys and sex and that. They say you're flaunting yourself, or you look as if you don't care who you do it with, an' anyway you're not a proper musician really.'

'Who says?' I asked, getting interested.

Mad Alice went all shifty. 'Nobody special,' she eventually said. 'Jus' . . . someone . . .'

'Go on! Who?'

'Nobody, I'm telling you . . . I'm just . . . giving an example.'

'Leave it out! Somebody's said all this to you – who is it?'

Mad Alice looked cornered. 'I can't tell you now, it's a bit complicated. But it's true what I'm telling you. It's worse when you like the person,' she finished, rather sadly. I thought I saw a tear in her usually glinting eye.

Lottie squeezed my arm. 'Amy knows all about that kind of boy, don't you?'

I wriggled my nose. 'I don't ever think about him,' I said.

Mad Alice stared hard at me and got up. 'Come on,' she said. 'Old Moony'll be getting all aggy if we don't turn up soon.'

Alice charged on with Debs, looking as if she was trying to cheer herself up. They linked arms and broke into *Just the Way You Lick Tonight*.

Lotts and I linked arms too, and mooched along behind them.

'Sorry to bring him up,' Lottie said to me. 'You know, when you get all moony about somebody, you don't always say the right thing.'

'I thought something was up. What's the matter?'

'Tell you on the way home.'

And on the way home with Lotts it all came out.

Poor Lottie. She is in love with Señor Mondragon.

'Lottie,' I said, with the wisdom of a teenage mum-to-be, 'you know crushes on teachers never work. You know it is opening up the road to perdition and so on.'

'No, no, it's worse than that.'

'Eh? Nothing happened, did it?'

'I . . . I asked him if he was married!'

'And . . . ?'

'And he said no.'

'Yes . . . ?'

'And then he took one look at my face and quickly said he had a partner.'

'Oh, well, it's not surprising, is it?'

'No. But then I asked her name. I said, *What's her name?*'

'Mmmmmm?'

'And he said Antonio.'

'Mmmmmm?'

'You're not listening! He said Antonio!'

'Mmmmm?'

'That's a boy's name!'

'Oh. Yes. So he's gay?'

'Which means I will never get him. He will never ever be mine! Even in Year Twelve!'

Pasta frites. I didn't realize she had it so bad.

'Look at it this way, Lottiekins,' I said. 'No other woman will get him either.'

This cheered her up a bit, I think.

'And there's always Flubber,' I added generously. I felt I could hand Flubber over to Lottie now I had more important things on my mind.

'He's back with the Atomic Moron,' sobbed Lottie. 'She lets him feel her bits and keeps saying tomorrow night's going to be his big night. It's been going on like that for weeks, but it works. Why can't I do that? If I'd said that to him he'd have just said "big loss" and bunked off.'

For a minute I regretted not taking the same chance to wind the helpless Flubber around my little finger.

Wednesday September 17

My mum says time passes more and more slowly when you're pregnant, as if the way you drag yourself about as you become huger and huger somehow gets into the clocks. I've been finding the opposite happens. I'm in a daze most of the time, or I keep falling asleep – and I have weird dreams about my dad and Emma Dearest wheeling a baby in a buggy, while my babies are gone and I can't find them.

Last weekend just went in a blur, but some bits I remember were something like this:

MUM: Dad rang last night. He's fine, the job's going very well. I'm so glad – it's been very hard for him lately.

ME: I'm sure it has.

MUM: Sorry?

I wish I could get that gross image of Emma Dearest in a thong out of my head.

PUDDINGS: Play with us, Millis!

ME: Can't. Too tired and fat.

PUDDINGS: Boring fat Millis! Play Psycho Frogs with us!

(*Phone rings.*)

LOTTIE: Amy? It's Lotts.

ME: Oh, hi.

LOTTIE: Wanna do something?

ME: Great. Maybe next week.

LOTTIE: What?

ME: Bye.

And lots more like that. I lurch through school as if I was sleepwalking.

Wednesday September 24

Just when you think life is as boring as it gets . . . Lottie looked very grumpy at break.

'Is it Señor Phoghni Bologni?' I asked. 'Let him go, he's not for those born without the third leg.'

'Noooooooooooo,' said Lottie, letting the word out very slowly, as if she can't bear to get to the bit that comes next.

'What then?'

Long silence.

'My parents say I have to get rid of the kit,' Lottie finally said.

'*Whaaaaaat?*' I said, keeping cool as usual.

'I know,' said Lottie. 'It's terrible.' She looked as if she was about to cry.

'Why?' I asked her. 'I know they don't like it, but they've always put their fingers in their ears and let you get on with it.'

'We've got my crumbling gran coming to stay with us – she's got too old to live on her own,' Lottie said. 'The kit's in the spare room, and my room's only just big enough for me. Anyway, Mum says Gran won't be able to stand the noise.'

'I thought grans were all deaf,' said Mad Alice, who has overheard and come to join us.

'She's supposed to be deaf,' Lottie said, 'but Mum says even dead people could hear me playing.'

'You could test that theory out,' Mad Alice said fiendishly, baring a fang.

'Anyway, that's it,' said Lottie despairingly. 'I'll have to self-destruct, like the drummers in Spinal Tap. My life is over. The kit has to be packed up by the weekend and put in the loft. It'll be horrible thinking it's up there above my head all unloved, missing me beating the crap out of it. I think I'd rather take it out and burn it, like one of those Indian funerals.'

Debs arrived and we put her in the picture. The BFs all stood in a circle, staring at their feet in silent sympathy. Lottie looked at us, and her little face seemed to brighten.

'But . . . s'pose . . . one of you looked after it for me?' she asked. 'I could fill it with duvets and things and come round and practise very quietly.'

'Sorry, Lotts,' said Mad Alice sadly. 'Simon the Stockbroker is wound up like a harp, except he doesn't sound nice. He says he wants to strangle Hendrix, and he's just a bird. He hates everything, except doing it with my mum, and he doesn't sound nice then either.'

Lottie didn't argue with this. We all knew this was a Not Good part of Alice's life.

'I'll ask at home,' Debs said next, putting an arm around Lottie. 'But my mum's a bit funny about drums – she says you sing for Jesus but dance for the Devil. There's a lot of relatives living at my house too, and a few people I don't even know. I'm not sure there's room for a drum kit but I'll try.'

'I'll do it,' I said without thinking. 'I can get it in my room.'

They all looked me up and down.

'You're kidding,' Alice said. 'Another couple of weeks you won't even be able to get you in your room.'

'No, it's fine,' I said. 'My dad's away—'

'Helping with a bit of screwing and erecting,' nodded Alice.

'– shut up, thanks – and my mum's OK about things like that. Drum kits, I mean. Long as you don't practise when the Puddings are asleep.'

So that was settled. We were going to move Lottie's kit at the weekend.

Major problemo. Lottie's long-suffering parents usually carry the kit to gigs, but their car isn't working – probably fainted with relief at the thought of never having to carry it again. Simon the Stockbroker won't help move it in his big fancy car made of solid silver and luxurious dead cows because he says the dead cows will get torn. My dad's taken ours on the screwing and erecting expedition. Debs's parents don't have a car. What's the use of parents? Somehow we have to move the kit on our own.

Believe me, getting an elephant on a bus would be easier than a drum kit. We couldn't find where Lottie's mum had put most of the cases in her preparation for the gran's arrival, so we had to carry everything except the bass drum as it was.

We stopped the 212 at the end of Lottie's street for about five minutes while we tried to load it on. The bus was full of toddlers and people with shopping. The bus driver was cool, fortunately.

'Take your time, man,' he said, stretching. 'Hurry is the curse of modern life.' People were yelling at him but he just put some headphones in his ears and opened the newspaper.

Somehow Lottie fought her way on with the bass drum case and slung it in the luggage space next to a buggy. I was carrying the hi-hat and cymbals, Alice the snare and the stick-bag, and Debs had slung the side-tom on her back like a rucksack and was carrying the other two in front of her chest.

'Them uplift bras do the business all right,' said a guy to his mate. Debbie stood on his foot, and he stepped back onto the hi-hat pedal, which I'd parked behind him. The hi-hat snapped shut on the exploring fingers of a small child in a Spiderman suit.

'Waaaaaaaahhhh!' said the child, in the usual way they do. Its even smaller sister kicked it unsympathetically on the leg, then made its escape among the passengers while what looked like the nanny read *Hello!* Debs, parking blind, backed into a posh-looking woman carrying a pot plant, which fell into the shopping basket of somebody else who'd given up and was getting off.

'Hey, wait . . .' protested the posh woman, but the doors closed and the plant and its innocent thief were gone. 'You stupid lump,' the posh woman said to Debs, 'you owe me twenty pounds for that.'

'Very sorry, it was an accident,' said Debs, smiling the smile that usually fixed everything, but not this time. 'I'm afraid I haven't got twenty pounds.'

'She has to spend everything on her crack habit,' put in Mad Alice helpfully. 'She often kills people for money, but it's nothing personal.'

The posh woman screamed and started struggling to get off the bus, causing people between her and the door to start falling over like dominoes. Eventually the driver took pity and opened the doors, dumping a heap of passengers on top of each other on the pavement, the posh woman waving her arms and legs about on top. The bus set off.

'It was a horrible plant anyway,' said a spotty guy with a cropped head. 'You a band?'

'Yes,' said Lottie and me proudly. 'We're on a world tour.'

'Going to take you about ten years to get round it like this, innit?' said the guy. 'Ain't you got limos or nothin'?'

'We like mixing with the people,' I told him. 'For inspiration.'

'Shame more bands aren't like you,' agreed the guy. 'Most of them get all up themselves.'

'Scuse me, have you seen a little girl?' the nanny-person reading *Hello!* eventually said to nobody in particular.

We'd reached my street. Struggling and panting we somehow got the kit off the bus, dragging only a few swearing passengers attached to various bits of it in our wake.

'This bass drum's got heavier,' groaned Lottie. 'Give us a hand.'

It certainly had. The lid was slowly coming off by itself. We all screamed and clutched each other. Then a little girl with a fountain of blonde curls stuck her head out. Tharg! Spiderman's sister!

'Allo,' she said. 'My nameth Ruby.'

'*Oh no!!*' we all moaned at once.

'Ith a nith name,' said Ruby, looking hurt.

'How did you get in there?' asked Lottie through gritted teeth.

'Got in the nith bocth on the buth. Don't like my brother or my nanny . . .'

But her little voice was drowned by the screeching tyres of the 212.

'Rubeeeee!' The nanny-person shot out of the bus like a thunderbolt, grabbing a protesting Ruby and giving Lottie the evil eye.

Ruby wrestled free of the nanny and ran up to us. 'Want to stay with you,' she whimpered with her arms up.

'It's a custody case,' a large woman shouted out of the bus window at a policeman.

'Glutton for punishment, aren't you, darlin'?' the policeman said to me, looking at my large middle.

Lottie gave Ruby a sweet, which placated her, and carried her back to her nanny, who was now weeping into a mobile, presumably talking to her boss. It didn't look as if it was going well.

'All aboard!' shouted the bus driver, laughing. 'Nothing to see here!'

The bus drove off to cheers. Ruby waved excitedly out of the back window at us while the nanny stroked her hair but generally looked pretty unhappy.

I felt a kick inside me. I could still just see Ruby's little face in the distance, her arms waving like a windmill around it.

And it dawned on me that this childcare business is a big, scary new world, full of dangers I'd never thought of before. I suddenly found myself shaking uncontrollably.

Monday September 29

We had a lesson with Señor Mondragon today. He's gone all anxious about not encouraging poor Lottie, so he ignored her whenever she put her hand up, and went red every time he was anywhere near her. I could see his problem, but this wasn't the right way to deal with it, and Lottie was very unhappy at break.

'He hates me,' she wailed, blowing into a tissue.

'No he doesn't,' I said. 'He's just embarrassed. He doesn't know how to handle it.'

'Lotts could show him, couldn't you, Lotts?' nudged Mad Alice.

This made Lottie wail all the more.

'Please yourself,' Mad Alice said, unwrapping a piece of chewing gum.

We wandered past the playground, where a lot of boys were playing football and yelling.

'Look at them,' I said, taking Lottie's arm. 'All that testosterone. There must be one of them you like.'

'Do you?' Lottie asked, looking me straight in the face.

'No, not really . . .' I tailed off. She knew what I really felt, that no one came anywhere near Tom – but surely it was different for Lottie?

'You know, I don't really give a monkey's about it, all this boy–girl stuff,' Lottie said, disentangling herself and going into a hunched-shoulder mooch. 'Most boys just seem like babies – they can't control their bodily functions. I'd rather read a book. But it was different with Señor Mondragon. We could have . . . shared things.'

'What about Iqbal?' I said. 'He's just your type – kind, gentle, gorgeous. He's got the most beautiful eyes – like treacle wells. And he's clever – he likes Confucius and *Catch 22*, and Natasha . . .' I was going tell her about Iqbal being gifted and talented but I had the feeling maybe I was going on a bit, so I wound down lamely with: 'He's got amazing marks and he's only been learning English for a year.'

Lottie looked at me thoughtfully. 'He's not ready yet,' she said. 'He's got too much to forget.'

Just then I saw Stanley Maul down in the playground, missing an open goal I could have hit even in my condition. Mad Alice gave him an ironic cheer and he gave her a just-my-luck shrug, grinning broadly. She gave him a big grin back, friendlier than he deserves.

'There's somebody who can't control his bodily functions,' Lottie said.

'Right,' I said with feeling.

'You're too hard on him,' Alice said. 'He's OK when you get to know him.'

I gave Lottie a sharp jab in the ribs before she said that I'd got to know him a bit too well.

'You should be more open with people,' continued Alice and I felt myself getting angry with her for the first time.

'Everywhere I move, this goes with me,' I said, patting my bulge. 'You try opening up to people when somebody's left you with one of these.'

'You could have got rid of it,' said Alice, turning away.

'*I couldn't!*' I shouted at her. People looked round. 'It was too late!'

'Well you should have known, then. You run your own body – you can't blame anybody else for not looking after it for you. And you can't blame a boy for getting the message wrong if you didn't make it clear in the first place.'

 'What do you know about anything?' I said to her, almost crying. 'You just take the piss out of everything. You call that friendship?'

Alice was silent. 'I'll see you later,' she finally said, and headed back into school. Debs and Lottie looked helpless. We all went back to class, not saying a word.

At break, I offered some crisps to Iqbal. He flinched.

'Sorry, don't you like barbecue flavour?' I said. 'They're not to everyone's taste.'

He took the crisps and we sat crunching away in companionable silence. Then he said: 'So, Madam Amy, you are having a baby?'

'Bab*ies*,' I said.

'Babies!' he whispered. 'So, this was your little worry? You are happy now?'

'No.'

'But you will love them, one day,' he said firmly.

'No, Iqbal. I'm going to have them adopted.'

He looked blank.

'I'm going to give them away. To a family who will love them.'

'Who are they?' he asked innocently.

'I . . . I don't know.'

'You will give them away.' He gazed through me, as though he was looking into his past. 'It is a strange world. I lose my family. You give yours away.'

He wasn't angry, he wasn't even judging me. He was just making an observation, trying to make sense of his life.

'Oh, Iqbal. Tell me about your family,' I said.

'If I started, I would never finish,' he said. He pulled a huge old-fashioned white handkerchief from his pocket and dabbed the tear that had started trickling down my cheek. Then the bell rang.

11 p.m.

I can't get what he said out of my head: *You will love them, one day.*

Will I?

Wednesday October 1

Alice and I haven't spoken since Monday. Debs and Lottie are doing what they can to patch things up. I still feel mad at her for being so unfeeling.

Fell asleep in maths today. No BFs to keep me going in maths since I got dumped into the bottom group. Suddenly felt an agonizing pain down my leg and woke up with a squeak.

'What's the matter, Amaryllis?' asked Old Tangent wearily.

I sat there, mouth flapping silently.

'Must be thighatica, sir,' piped up Ruth. 'Pain in the leg you get when you're preggers. Tracey H used to get it.'

'I think you mean sciatica,' said Tangent, turning back to the whiteboard. I think we heard him muttering something like 'School, not a bloody maternity home,' but we weren't sure.

I looked round at Ruth and saw she'd poked me with the sharp end of a set-square to wake me up. She and Van and me all left the lesson together at the end.

'Coming down the bogs for a fag?' they enquired. 'Mind you, we have to be a bit careful – old Flinty was hanging about outside last time.'

I stifled a giggle. 'No, it's OK,' I said. 'Got some homework to catch up on for this afternoon.'

'Just say no to homework,' they said. 'Glad to see you're still singing though. We're all coming to see you Friday night. Got any new songs?'

Amnesias inglesias! We're playing Friday! I'd forgotten all about it! Mad Alice fixed it up last month and I'd forgotten all about it – this brain holiday is going on too long.

Thursday October 2

We had a rehearsal at my place after school. Alice didn't come.

'We can't go on like this, it's ridiculous,' Lottie said after the first song. 'What are we going to do tomorrow?'

'She said she'd come to the gig,' Debs said quietly. 'I saw her and she told me she wouldn't let the band down. But she won't talk to you unless you apologize to her.'

'Apologize? What for?'

'For saying she doesn't care about anything and she isn't a real friend.'

'Why doesn't she apologize to me? She as good as said there was nothing to choose between me and bloody

Stanley Maul! If we're talking about apologies, Stanley Maul's an apology for a human being!'

There was a knock at the door. It was my mum.

'Could you do us a small favour, dear?' she asked.

'What?' I said rather grumpily.

'I think Ken's at the door. You know, Dad's building friend. He keeps leaving messages asking if he can come round with a takeaway in case maybe I'm feeling a bit lonely with Dad away and all that.'

'Cheeky bugger,' said Lottie.

'Can you tell him I'm out?' Mum asked.

'We'll send Debs,' I said.

Debbie slipped her T-shirt off one shoulder, shoved her jeans a bit lower and went to the door. We all sniggered on the landing. 'Wot you all doing?' asked the Puddings loudly. I fell on top of them. A smell of chicken biriani wafted up the stairs from the front door. We could hear Debs's silky voice:

'Sorry, she's out. I'm the babysitter. Mmmm, that smells nice. Do you want to come upstairs and make yourself . . . comfortable? My boyfriend's up there but he's very broadminded.'

We heard a bit of muttering and then the door slamming. Debbie came back upstairs chortling. My mum was laughing too, but looking a bit anxious.

'I feel a bit sorry for him,' she said. 'His wife's apparently an alcoholic.'

'That's no excuse,' I said. 'Your husband's

apparently his best friend.'

We all sighed at once. After a brief silence the Puddings both sighed too, so as not to be left out.

'They all do it,' said Lottie disconsolately. 'Except Señor Mondragon. He has eyes only for one . . . guy.'

'I think I might give Alice a call,' I said, getting up.

Friday October 3

Patched it up with Alice, sort of. The gig went OK.

Just as we wound up the first half I saw Stanley Maul in the front row cheering loudly. But he wasn't looking at me. He was looking at Mad Alice. He'd even clapped when she tuned up.

At the interval Lottie was buried, as usual, in miniature drum nerds asking about flims and flams. Mikey, wearing a very sharp black suit, came up and slid an arm round Debs.

'Why don't you do some Bob Marley songs, girl?' he complained, but not very seriously.

'Cos nobody did them better than him, stupid,' Debs said, bumping him with a curvy hip.

Alice and I had a hug.

'That last solo blew them all away,' I told her.

'There's something I didn't tell you on the phone . . .' she began and I had a nasty feeling it was going to be something I didn't want to hear.

Luckily Tracey H came bouncing up to us looking even more enormous than me to tell us what stars we were and the moment passed.

Moony arranged for me to go to a special council-run teen mums class. There are six of us and one is only fourteen and she has had her baby already . . . Learnt following amazing facts:

Britain has more teenage pregnancies than anywhere else in Europe! Around 7,700 of these girls are under sixteen, and although about half of them have abortions, that's nearly 4,000 little kids every year trotting off to Infants with mums still under twenty! Imagine all those teen mums squashed together – we could start a little country all of our own. And to think I've been feeling so *alone*.

Our teenage birth rates are twice as high as in Germany, three times as high as in France and six times as high as in the Netherlands.

Why? Because we're sexier? Sexier than the French? I don't think so. Maybe we're just daft? Teens often use contraceptives the first time they have sex and get pregnant the second!

But all those statistics about being poor or stupid just don't add up when I look round the teen mums class. One's hoping to be a doctor and another's already got an A star in GCSE Eng Lit. I wonder if statistics are taken from real people?

A woman from MakingLinks tells us about how to stay at school, or get GNVQs and stuff and jobs and college and how you can do anything you like. You can pay a child minder a hundred quid a week to look after your baby and get money for this from the government!

'Suppose your own mum wants to look after the baby?' says Yasmin. 'Can she get a hundred quid a week?'

'Er, no,' says the poor lady from MakingLinks. 'Unless she goes on a child-minding course.'

I learn more being with other teen mums than I have at all the antenatal appointments. It's because doctors don't talk in English.

They all speak Doctorese, which is a special language designed to stop patients asking awkward questions like 'Does being cleverer give you the right to make me feel like an unsuccessful ant?'

Yasmin has been chucked out by her family and is living in a B&B. She is just sixteen! Her boyfriend has gone off with her best friend. Bernadette has been chucked out of school, because it is a Catholic school.

I feel really thick. I know nothing about life.

11 p.m.

The Puddings are in bed with me just now, like two little hot-water bottles.

Crêpes suzette! There are five people in this bed.

CHAPTER SEVENTEEN

In Which Gandhi Discovers True Peace and Amy Gets a New Home

<u>**Friday October 10**</u>

Scumbags.

I have to go into hospital! My blood pressure is up! I have protein in my wee!

What does that mean? Have they found traces of T-bone steak, or boiled egg, or double-cheese-burger in my urine sample? What is protein in your wee, and what does it want?

'There is a risk of miscarriage with twins between twenty-eight and thirty-two weeks, and in view of your age, and blah-blah-blahdy-blah . . . blood pressure . . . risk of pre-eclampsia . . . protein in urine . . . blah-blah-blah,' droned the doc, in fluent Doctorese.

Mum sat there with her lip quivering. I thought it was because she was about to cry but in fact she was over the moon when we came out.

'They'll look after you so well – it'll be such a weight off my mind,' she fluted, merry as anything.

Great.

I am going in on Monday.

My life is over.

6 p.m.

Got home to find the gerbil has died.

Have to have elaborate funeral with everyone dressed in black. Pudding Two insists on music: *Teddy Bears' Picnic*. Oh, well.

Pudding One is inconsolable. 'He never had any friends!' she cries.

'Why not put a little friend in with him, in his coffin?' I say.

'Not a coffin! Is a shoe box!' she splutters.

'Shoe boxes are coffins in gerbil heaven,' I say.

We spend a long time looking and find a dead bluebottle.

'There, we'll put Bluebottle in with Gandhi and then neither of them will be lonely,' I say.

Pudding One calms down a bit, from a thousand decibels to those little shaky sobs that wring your heart out.

Pudding Two is very solemn and says a few words at the graveside: 'Bye-bye, Gandhi, you was a good gerbil.' Then she looks pensive. 'And bye-bye, bluebottle.'

Rang Lottie and howled.

9 p.m.

Lottie, Mad Alice and Debs have bought me two pairs of outsize pyjamas. They are the nearest to cool you can get. One is black with a little row of luminous green skulls on the collar and cuffs and the other is luminous green with little black skulls. Outsize goth pyjamas. I detect the hand of Mad Alice.

And a big bag of make-up. And hair products galore!

Yessssss!

11 p.m.

Puddings in my bed again. I think they find me cosy just now. Or maybe they are missing Gandhi. Or Dad.

2 a.m.

Marmalade family now in bed too. Pudding Two said they were crying outside the door and had to be let in. Have compromised by putting them in a carrier bag.

'Not s'posed to put bags on heads,' says Pudding Two.

'It's OK for Marmalades,' I say. 'It's cosy for them, like a sleeping bag.'

It rustles a bit, but it's leak-proof, I think.

At least I will get a decent night's sleep in hospital.

Tues Oct 14

Marie Stopes Ward, 10th floor

Marie Stopes is supposed to have been a big campaigner for contraception about a million years ago when they used pigs' bladders or iron thongs or whatever. Naming a ward for mums-to-be after her is a bit fake, isn't it? It's like calling a cruise missile Gandhi or something – no offence to gerbils. Why didn't they just put big posters up saying

THIS IS WHAT COMES OF NOT KNOWING ABOUT MARIE STOPES

everywhere?

But how *could* I have forgotten my diary? Scribbling this on the back pages of my English book.

Am trying to do essay on *King Lear* in the front. Maybe I could go out on a heath and go mad, like him.

Thought about asking Mum or Lottie to fetch diary but can't. They might read it.

K.F.C.

Amy Baker 10M
English
Ms. Corman
Rm 204

Wed Oct 15

This is sooo boring. Am in ward of fatties, all having 'bed rest' and desperately trying to keep their babies in.

Then there are some new mums at the other end of the ward.

And a few poor souls who creep in for abortions and cry all night.

Why do they put sad abortion people in with happy new mums? They are all ancient.

I am going up the walls.

Thurs Oct 16

I have nicknamed the ward sister, or matron, or dictator, Attila the Hen. I get butterflies in my stomach whenever she comes near.

I think she hates me for being so young.

But the nurses are kind. Specially Nurse O'Connell, who is all pink and cheery, and Nurse Ibrahim, who is all kind and gentle. Perhaps I will be a nurse. It is more useful than singing.

I think I will be a sort of Florence Sparrow figure.

Or was it Blackbird?

Nightingale! That's it!

Will my brain ever come back?

Sat Oct 18

My high point is visits from Mum and Puddings, every day at 5.30.

Mon Oct 20

Amazing shrieks in the night, sounded like *Scream 2.* Nurse O'Connell came rushing up to me at 6.30 after I'd snatched six winks' sleep. 'Lovely little boy, and the mum's your age, Amy. Do go and see.'

Oooh good. Another loony teen.

Couldn't resist though, so I stumped off down the ward and there was Tracey Hardwick.

And Gareth Foreskin.

And a little red squealing thing.

'Isn't he lovely? Isn't he gorgeous?' Tracey squeaked.

It is a shame when a baby has a chance of looking like Tracey, who is OK looking, or a traffic cone, and they choose the traffic cone side of the family.

'Doncha want a cuddle?' she said.

So I had a little cuddle with Troy.

And then about a hundred of Tracey and Gareth's relations came flocking in and it was all 'You're the singer' and 'You should get a recording contract' and 'Female Tom Jones' and all this. And how nice it was of me to come to see Tracey and hadn't she done well.

They didn't even notice I was preggers too.

Maybe they thought my skeleton pyjas and bunny rabbit slippers were just what rock stars usually wear.

Tracey went home at four.

Maybe I'll get my life back soon too.

I want to go to a party.

And sing.

Tues Oct 21

Tharg, what a depressing book *Your Developing Child* is. Have just been reading about labour pains. I might be able to duck out of looking after my kids, but I can't duck out of having them.

Will the pain be double for twins?

I wish I had just had a late abortion now.

I'm going to have to go through labour and give my babies away.

They might as well be dead, if I'm never going to know them. Have been trying to read *Jane Eyre* but I can't seem to concentrate. Is my brain going to mush?

Wed Oct 22

The Big Top Dog, Prof Huff, and his little flock of docs swarmed round the ward today and prodded me about.

Prof Huff talks like he has plums up his you know what and never looks me in the eye. He neighed on about 'presentation' and 'placental function' and Tharg knows what while I lay blinking like a rabbit in his headlights.

He is suggesting a Caesarean on Dec 14, when I will be thirty-eight weeks. He says it will be safer.

A Caesarean is what Julius Caesar had. Well, of course he did. That's why it's called a Caesarean.

Well, *he* didn't have it, of course. His mum did.

I think Macbeth came into the world by Caesarean too. Or was it Macduff? Will I ever be able to stop thinking about babies for long enough to remember who is who in literature?

One thing I do know about all those things you learn in school re stamping-about-shouting guys with Great Visions for the World is that their mums hardly ever get mentioned. You'd think they just dropped in from outer space. Perhaps it's because if we started to think too much about their mums we'd all get very anxious about Human Failings. After all, Hitler and Genghis Khan and Vlad the Impaler and Stalin all had mums too. And they probably smiled when their mums went itchy-coochy-coo to them and thought they would be happy for ever playing with their teddies.

If I never see my babies again, how will I know this hasn't happened to them too?

A Caesarean . . . What would the Earth Mothers say?

I wonder if Oedipus was a Caesarean? He murdered his dad. And married his mum. I don't mind too much what my babies do to Stanley Maul, but I don't want them to spend the rest of their lives in prison.

And I couldn't marry both of them, either. Must remember to tear these pages out before I hand in my homework.

Mon Oct 27

I am knackered.

They take you into hospital for a rest and then send lots of little medical elves to take your

temperature and blood pressure every five seconds
and a lot of other hygiene elves to whisk about
with mops and more elves with tea trolleys and
then there's the wailing and screaming of mothers
and babies and the stomping around of Attila and
you don't get a wink of sleep.

Wed Oct 20

7 a.m.

The voice of Attila is bellowing down the ward.

'It is not visiting hours! *Who let that man in?*'

Oooh, there's a flurry in the beds. Is it a baby-
thief coming to whisk away the newborns?

No.

It's Dad.

'Dad!'

'Amy!'

Attila is apoplectic. She advances towards us
with her turret whirling, all guns at the ready. Her
face is purple.

'It's my daughter . . .' Dad starts saying to her.
'I've been away . . . haven't been able to get to see
her . . . just a few minutes . . .'

Attila the Hen comes to a halt, puffing.

'Never seen this man before in my life,' I say to
her, without thinking.

She swells up, about to explode over Dad.
He gives me such a pathetic look – not critical or
aggressive any more, a bit lost really – that I think
twice.

'No, sorry, I'm dreaming. It's all right, it's my dad. Can he stay for a minute?'

'Please, Doctor,' Dad sighs.

Calling her 'Doctor' did the trick. She primps her steel curls and says we can go to the visitors' room.

'I don't want to bump into Mum,' hisses Dad, as though poor old Mum is going to materialize from the tea urn.

'Come home, Dad,' I say, and burst into tears. I don't mean to, it just happens.

Dad is mortified. 'You haven't told her, have you?' he asks desperately.

Great. Is that all he came to say?

'Bye, Dad,' I say and stumble out blubbing like an onion peeler. Well, like someone peeling onions. Dad grabs my arm.

'Let go, Dad. I thought you'd come to see me, not to get me to lie to Mum. I bloody well will tell her.'

He sort of crumples up onto the visitors' settee. He looks all sad and old, like a sad old crumpled dog. 'Of course I've come to see you, I've been desperate about you! It's all just so difficult.'

He says he tried to tell Emma Dearest it wasn't working and she threw a wobbly and said she'd tell Mum everything. What a prize cowing aardvark she is.

'She's a prize cowing aardvark,' I say.

'Don't,' says Dad, his voice all crumbly. 'It's not been easy for her – life hasn't worked out the way she hoped. She's trying to find herself.'

'Find herself what? A job in a geriatric lap-dancing joint?'

'She's got involved in a lot of New Age stuff now. Maybe it'll help her sort herself out,' says Dad. 'It's not my sort of thing. But how can I leave her?'

'Like you left us?' I say, unmoved. 'Why did you lie to me?'

'I'm so sorry, Amy, I was trying to protect you all. I was trying to end it, but then you saw Emma in her—'

'Thong,' I say helpfully.

'And she wanted to spill the beans to Mum there and then. What else could I do? I just got in deeper than I meant. Just give me a little longer and I'll sort it out. Please?'

I relent. Dad seems to wind me round his little finger, just like the Puddings do with Mum.

'I'll help somehow,' I say. 'Just tell Mum you'll be back soon, OK? Or can I tell her? Please?'

SCHMOOZE YOUR FAMILY TIP
Take some time for that old dad of yours. When did you last tell him you loved him? Why not buy him a little treat for Father's Day?

Handcuffs? Ball and chain?

LaTer

I don't know what to think really.

Dad said he just didn't know where he was at or who he was any more. He said to give him a bit more time and keep up the pretence.

Well, I haven't got any choice really. I don't want to see Mum's face if she finds out about the actress-of-horror.

Bright side of Dad's visit: Attila plumped up my pillows! Said what a charming father I had. Dad has obviously got an invisible babe gene.

Fri Oct 31
Halloween

11 p.m.

Had a visit from Debs, Mad A and Lottie tonight.

That's nice, you might think. Not.

Mad Alice showed up with a plastic axe stuck in her head, a *Scream* mask and a very realistic-looking bolt through her neck. No change there then. Debs looked like a black Cruella de Vil, with a cigarette-holder, and an imitation dead cat slung round her shoulders. Lottie was dressed as a kind old wizened lady in little round specs, until she flung her coat open to reveal a grinning plastic skellington almost as big as her.

Most of the girls on the ward thought it was a laugh, but not Prof Huff, who unfortunately decided to show up at the same time.

In keeping with Halloween, he did a pretty good impression of Dr Jekyll turning into Mr Hyde, his comfortable Who's-the-Man smile changing into a snarl of fury. He looked so terrifying Lottie dropped the bag of trick or treat eggs and flour she was carrying and ran for it, hotly pursued by Attila the Hen – at least until the latter reached the spreading pool of egg yolks on the nice polished floor, a bad combination that sent her skidding into the advancing doctor.

Me, I am covered in Shame, with a capital 'S'.

Or I should be, according to Attila.

CHAPTER EIGHTEEN

In Which Amy Is Betrayed by All

<u>**Monday November 3**</u>

Freedom!

The babies have stayed put for thirty-two weeks, so I'm outta here! My mum came to collect me in a *taxi*. We got home to find the Puddings had made a

banner that they had hung across the front door. It's very visible from the street and probably from Outer Space too, so now not only our milkman but the milkmen on the Milky Way will know my secret. Puddings looked so pleased to see me, though, I couldn't stay cross about it.

Ooh. Bed. Lovely lovely bed. Hello, nice lovely diary. And Puddings. And ellies. And crocodiles. And Marmalade family. At least I'll have a good night's kip.

Midnight

I notice the Puddings are clutching the crocs very close.

Mum said they want to take them into nursery. But the nursery draws the line at fluffy animals that are bigger than their owners.

I suppose they are missing Gandhi.

Or maybe it's their way of feeling close to the hugely absent Dad. It's so strange that he isn't here. When he was here I hardly noticed him a lot of the time, and he hardly noticed me either – well, since the Puddings were born. That's when I stopped being the apple of his eye. And Mum too, I guess. But now he's not here it's like a huge great Silence in the middle of our house that somehow makes a massive deafening noise. I keep wanting to tell my mum what he's doing – it's like too big a secret to keep all to myself.

I can't decide who or what I am any more. I want to be like the Puddings and curl up with a soft toy and chuck every worry at Mum and Dad, knowing they'll be able to kiss it better. But now I'm going to be a mum myself, my dad has given up and run away, and my mum can only cope if she's living in a dream world where she hasn't a clue what's really going on.

I have to be a grown-up. Somebody's got to do it. If Mum asks later why I never told her, I can say I just thought it was for the best. After all, as Lottie said, how many things can you worry about at the same time? The babies are the most important thing. Getting them out into the world in one piece – well, two pieces – and giving them the best chance of happiness I can. And I know I need my mum operational to get that done.

If Emma Dearest blows the whistle and ruins this plan, I will kill her.

TEEN MUM SLAUGHTERS DAD'S MISTRESS
'I only did it for my mum,' says tragic Amy Baker,
clutching the still-bloody axe . . .

BABES IN THE CELL DOING WELL!
BARMY AMY SAYS SHE'D DO IT ALL AGAIN!

Hmm, maybe not. Emma Dearest isn't worth it.

Tuesday November 4

Mum suggested shopping to get something for the babies.

'What's the point?' I asked. 'I'm never going to keep them.'

'Oh, but they must have something nice to wear,' said Mum. 'You don't want them to be dressed in those little hospital dishcloths when—'

'When what? When their new parents come to take them away?'

I let Mum go on her own. And of course she got two identical sets of everything. I should have guessed she would. Two little cuddly toys, looking exactly the same – how sweet. But I don't want them dressed alike! How are they going to learn to be individuals if they just look like an ad for baby products?

I told Lottie this when we sneaked out for a latte.

'I want them to be individuals,' I said.

'No offence, but it's not up to you, is it?' she said.

I gulped. 'True,' I said. 'It'll be up to James and Sarah Simpson.'

'Who they?'

'The couple I've decided are going to be the parents.'

'You're not allowed to know who they are, are you? In case you go mad, or maybe sane, and try to nick them back again.'

'I know all that. I just like the idea of the babies being the Simpsons.'

'Do you think the mum'll have big blue hair?' Lottie muses.

'Nah. She'll have a mousy bob. Tired, worried. Old. Desperate. I will be giving her a whole family in one go, see? And when the kids are eighteen . . .'

'They'll be bored by their old adopting fogeys and desperate to find their real mum?' said Lottie.

'That's it, exactly,' I said, delighted. 'And I'll have gone to college and got a fantastic power-boss job and I'll be stinking rich! They'll love me as if they'd known me all their lives.'

'You don't want to give them away, do you?' said Lottie.

Don't I?

Bonfire Night

Mum and me do sparklers for the Puddings and I miss Dad. I miss the way he always nailed his thumb to the Catherine-wheel plank.

Lottie persuades me to go to the big fireworks display on the heath. Somehow the fireworks seem too loud. I think of Iqbal. Do fireworks make him think of war? Or of Confucius?

The babies go bananas. It's like having the entire Premier League in my belly.

'They're scared,' I say.

'They're dancing,' says Lottie.

Goodness. Is Lottie becoming bubbly?

'How is Iqbal?' I ask.

'Fine,' she replies. 'He lent me *Stupid White Men*. You should read it.'

'I have,' I say, feeling an odd pang.

Friday November 7

Have a little cry about adoption with the nurse at
my check-up. 'They'll have a much better chance
with a family that really wants them,' she says.
'And they may not have to be split up.'

May not? Not *won't*? How will they manage if
they're separated after all those months floating in
each other's arms? Will they always wander the
world with a sense of something missing? Like that
guy I read about who had a dream brother, an
imaginary friend he went on seeing all his life until
he was thirty? That was when his mum told him
he'd had a twin who'd died.

They've got to be together. They've just got to be.

Tuesday November 11

Note from Ms Corman:

Dear Amaryllis,
Was most impressed to see you had
done so much extra work, but then
realized much of it is a private
diary, so am returning it.
Your King Lear essay was of a
high standard – well done. If you
can continue in this vein I believe
you have a good chance of achieving

Double Tharg.

Friday November 14

A couple have been found who want twins!
'Isn't that wonderful?' says the nurse, while I'm
having one of my million check-ups.

'Great,' I say, and I don't feel wonderful, not
at all.

At least they'll be together.

Thursday November 27

The teen mum group is brill. Found out following
amazing facts:

1) In 1770, if breast feeding was impossible,
babies were put to the udders of goats or donkeys!
This still went on as recently as the nineteenth
century in French orphanages.

2) 300 years ago babies were not put to the
breast for three days. They were given almond oil,
rose-hip syrup or a glass of wine! (But as Candy
was quick to point out, just as me and Yvette were
nipping off to the off licence, nearly *half* the babies
born in the eighteenth century died before they

were five years old.)

3) A childcare book of 1775 offered four whole pages of advice on how to rock the baby's cradle. Maybe *Your Developing Child* isn't so bad after all . . .

4) The 'morning-after' pill is to be added to school medicine chests throughout France in an attempt to reduce the abortion rate among teenagers. Sounds like a good idea.

5) One *third* of girls aren't told about periods by their parents until they've started! One in ten girls hadn't been told by *anyone*! (Were they living in a cave?)

Friday November 28

I am thirty-six weeks preggers. In two weeks I may 'go under the surgeon's knife'. Will I wake up? Or will that be the end of me? And them?

Lottie came round and forced me to go to the cinema with her.

She's being such a good friend. Mad Alice and Debs have gone AWOL lately. I've probably bored them to tears.

The film was a comedy, I think. I cried all the way through. I am crying at everything. I cried when we got out of the cinema.

'What's up *now*?' said Lottie. She was sounding far from patient.

'I have trodden on a beetle,' I said.

'Er . . . did it hurt?'

'It *died*,' I wailed. Poor little dead beetle, whose life I have taken. Poor little dead beetle. How can Lottie be so unfeeling?

We went to the coffee bar after.

'Watch where you're walking,' Lottie said. 'You might step on a bit of paper that was once a happy laughing tree.'

For almost the first time ever, I couldn't think of anything to say to Lottie in the coffee bar. It was as if she and I were living in different worlds. In desperation I went back to what I knew best and started going on about my backache and swollen ankles and—

'Stoppit, I can't take any more,' Lottie said. 'I've got something serious to tell you.'

I looked at her. 'You're pregnant too,' I said. 'How wonderful! We'll have so much to talk about.'

'It's not about me. It's about Mad A.'

'She's pregnant? What do you think she'll have, a boy or a ghoul?' I find this so funny for some reason that I have to get Lottie to repeat these words:

'Mad Alice is seeing Stanley Maul.'

'What do you mean, *seeing*?'

'I mean, engaging in willy aerobics with.'

'What? But Mad A's cool. Why would she fancy

324

somebody who wears jumpers? And corduroy trousers?!'

'Well, you sort of liked him enough to go off with him that night.'

'What are you going to say next? That it takes two to tango, whatever that is? You know what happened that night. He took advantage of the state I was in. I hate him.'

I had stood up rather suddenly and realized my arms were flailing around like windmills. Lottie looked anxiously at the people watching us, and tried to get me to sit down.

'Listen, maybe you've got it all wrong. Mad A says Stanley Maul's really nice. And he asks after you—'

'*Bastardo frites!* Tell him I'm dead! Died in childbirth!'

'Oh, you're hopeless. I'm only trying to help,' Lottie said, jumping up.

'Tell Mad A all about it if you want to help,' I found myself saying to Lottie. 'Let her know what she's in for.'

'But you don't know for sure yourself what happened! You said you were pissed! You said you couldn't remember!' Lottie shouted. People were pretending not to listen, but their ears were all flapping like sails.

Lottie gave me a long, searching look through her owl glasses. And then she was gone.

My BF.

Gone.

I don't have a friend left in the world.

Except maybe the Puddings. But they don't understand anything except furry crocs and sweeties.

Everything is coming unravelled.

Will Lottie tell Mad A the truth?

Go back home and mope. Lottie's mobile is on voice-mail and she isn't answering texts. Her mum says she's 'out with friends'. What friends?

Tramp around the band's usual dives, realizing for the first time how small hunky Horst's latte bar is and wondering how I ever fitted into one of those dinky chairs. Cruise the late-shopping arcade, the Ferret and the Weasel's Trousers. Nobody there. Nobody anywhere.

Debs not answering.

Wondering about plucking up courage to call Mad Alice myself. Am just staring at the phone when it rings.

Lottie?

Don't recognize the number. But press answer, and hear a boy's voice.

'Amy?'

'Who's that?' I ask, in a panic.

'Stanley.'

Aaargh! Not him! My thumb hovers over the OFF button but I don't press it.

'What do you want?' I finally say to him.

'I think we need to talk, don't you?' Maul says. He sounds very calm, too calm.

'No.'

'Oh yes we do. If you're going to put these

stories around about me, then there's some things I need to get sorted with you,' Maul goes on, his voice really frosty, sounding quite different.

'I'm not going to meet you,' I say to him. 'I've got nothing to say to you—'

'But you've had plenty to say *about* me. Alice has just been giving me a bollocking because of everything Lottie's told her. It's all from you, and it's all bullshit. Meet me in the front bar of the Ferret and we'll have it out. You have to tell Alice the truth – and anybody else you've told all this.'

'*No!* I'm going to ring off!'

'Because the truth doesn't suit you? You're more or less saying I'm a rapist – do you have any idea how serious that is? I'd never do anything like that in a thousand years, not to you or anyone else. You're covering up for another guy. You're trying to pin it on me.'

'I'm not. You're a bastard. You were just thinking with your dick. I'm going.'

I'm almost in tears by now. But I hear Maul's voice change on the other end, and he almost sounds as if he's crying himself.

'Don't ring off! Look, we have to sort this out, for both our sakes. I'd fancied you for months, I don't deny it. You must have realized it.'

I hadn't. But then I hadn't realized anything like that until recently.

'I wanted to try it on with you that night, of course I did. When you said you were ready for bed, I thought it was a come on.'

My stomach lurches when he says that. He goes on: 'And we kissed, remember? Or have you forgotten you kissed me back? But then I realized you were muttering someone else's name and you were legless and then all I wanted to do was get you home. The next thing I knew you were hitting me and calling me names. I hadn't done anything. Well, hardly anything—'

'Exactly!' I shout down the phone.

'But nothing that would have made you pregnant, unless you can get pregnant by bloody telepathy. But you were making such a fuss shouting at me to leave you alone I got scared what people would think, so when you took off, I didn't run after you. I was scared it would look like I was attacking you. I know there are bastards who do that sort of thing – get girls drunk and then take advantage – but that's just not me. But I'm really sorry I never ran after you and sorted it out there and then. I've regretted it ever since. And I've wanted to talk to you about it, but you've given me the evil eye every time I come near you. But it isn't me, I swear it isn't me. I'll take a DNA test and prove it to you.'

There's a long silence.

'I have to go now,' I say.

'But you have to give me the chance to prove this to you – and to everyone else,' Maul says urgently. 'If my parents find out then you won't have any choice about it. Why don't we sort it out before that happens?'

'I'll call you back,' I say to him. 'Goodnight.' And ring off.

As I go home, I find I'm shaking uncontrollably, as if I've got the flu.

10 p.m.

In bed, still shaking. Have told Mum I think I'm coming down with something. Mum very sympathetic – gives me two hot-water bottles.

One for each baby?

My mind is spinning round and round.

Could what he said possibly be true?

Maybe it could . . .

Aha.

So I am a reincarnation of the Virgin Mary. And I am having not one Messiah, but two!

Excellento! Dad will be dead chuffed to find he is the grandparent of twin baby Jesuses. Or he would be if he was here. Oh stuffit.

Midnight

Or . . . could there have been a mistake? Could they possibly be . . .

Tom's?

1 p.m.

I'll have to contact Tom, somehow.

With the most embarrassing message of all time.
How many condoms were you wearing? Are you
sure everything was all right?

Because . . . because . . .

I'm having twins.

How can I say all that to him?

But how can I *not* say it, now?

1.30

Well, I am going crazy, obviously. I was taking the
Pill as well! And I had my period! No one could be
that unlucky.

Maul is a liar.

And my best friends *believe* him.

CHAPTER NINETEEN

In Which Amy Makes a Break for Freedom

<u>**Monday December 1**</u>

10 p.m.

Sent Tom an e-mail about ten hours ago. Asked him all those terrible questions. Have looked at my e-mails about every five minutes since. Two offers of penis enlargement (this definitely proves that if God exists He's got a weird sense of humour), one of Viagra, and a petition to save the last six surviving Giant Aardvarks or something. But no Tom.

Stupid of me to think he'd reply. He'll be thinking I was two-timing him, or just trying to use him to get me off the hook.

I've never felt so misunderstood in my whole life.

11 p.m.

Have just been weeping over Tom's last e-mail, the one when he said he still loved me. Of course I printed it out and kept it in my bedside table knicker drawer, where I used to keep his egg . . .

egg. Tharg. I haven't opened that knicker drawer for ages as I am now keeping my elephant underwear in my chest of drawers. Which is why I guess I hadn't noticed that faint smell of joss sticks. What was it? I rummaged around and found the culprit: it was the Earth Mother leaflet I'd been given at Glastonbury.

The EARTH MOTHERS

+ + + + + + + + + + +

New Age Birth
Birthing Pools
Aromatherapy
Aura Readings
Check out your
Karma!
Your Baby
Dances Within!

Wigwam Paradiso, Acacia Gdns
Stone Circle Lane, Bramblerow, WILTSHIRE

It all started to come back to me. I was happy then. I didn't believe what was happening was happening. I still had friends. I still had dreams of being a singer. I've hardly sung a note these past few weeks, even to the Puddings.

I could hear their voices:

'Come and join us, we will look after your babe.'

And, *patatas fritas!* It's got an address!

Fantastic.

Maybe this is the answer.

I could get away from check-ups and doctors and anaesthetics and Caesareans and missing dads and grumpy friends and hand-wringing mums and have a free natural water-birth in the wild. The Earth

Mothers will show me how to do it all. They'll probably adopt the twins, too. Then they can be part of the Rainbow Festival and laugh a lot, which is more than they'll do with me for a mum.

Dad will feel that his home has been restored to normality. Everything will be back as it was. I can tell him how much we've all missed him, that I've been a responsible person and taken care of my problem myself, that Mum is the one for him and always has been.

But there's no phone number. Well, of course not – it's a wigwam.

Midnight

I'm going to go for it. It can't be that hard. I think we went to Wiltshire to stay with some relative once – well, it was somewhere in England with 'shire' on the end anyway.

Look up the Earth Mothers' village in our map of England. Find the nearest town to it with a train station, and look the times up on the Internet. How did people ever get around without the Internet? How did Julius Caesar get around the Roman Empire without the Internet?

I think I can get there without never being seen again. It's just a place, near a station, and there's a station at the other end near me. I know I can do it.

Have a hundred and fifty quid in a purse at the bottom of my knicker drawer. Always imagined I might need it when I met the Love Of My Life so we could run away together like Eric and Barbara.

Never thought I'd need it to try to find my way to a place I've never heard of to have babies I never wanted by a father I'm not sure about with a bunch of strange women who might not be quite all there.

12.10 a.m.

It's great to make a decision.

Can't sleep, but can't face getting up and going out in the middle of the night, with nobody around but weirdos and bats and stuff.

Will go about an hour before the Puddings wake up.

Have to write a note. It needs to reassure my mum at the same time as showing I have to get a hold on my own life. Something like:

> Do not get upset that me and Dad have both left home, it is a coincidence and not your fault.

Perhaps not. Open to misunderstanding. Maybe:

> Dear Mum,
> I'm doing something now I should have done a long time ago. I've caused you and Dad too much trouble and worry already, so I've decided to go ahead and do what I have to do.

No, that's open to misunderstanding too. She'll think it's the river scenario all over again. What about:

Dear Mum and Puddings,
I love you always. I'm going away to have the babies with some very wonderful people who'll take care of us all, and I'll be back as soon as it's done.

I think that's best.

Tuesday December 2

4.30 a.m.

Check e-mails one last time. Nothing from Tom. Leave house very quietly, bearing rucksack stuffed with outsize bras and elephant knickers. Turn mobile off. Feel very grown up and free all of a sudden. Catch a night bus to the railway station. Hardly anyone's there, except people who live on the railway station until somebody comes along to chuck them out. My train is not till 7.43. I suppose the railway timetable people don't think many Londoners have jobs in Wiltshire.

Sit in station coffee bar, talking to a nice old tramp lady. She looks like the old dear covered in pigeons in *Home Alone*.

'I used to play the piano at the Festival Hall,' she says. 'Don't suppose you could spare a fiver?'

Well, I've got my hundred and fifty quid running-away money, so I can afford a fiver. The bottle she's drinking from is almost empty, so I have a pretty good idea of where that fiver is going.

Well, why not?

Maybe I will be like her one day, telling people how I used to sing in a band . . .

Calamitous tickidos! Have spent nearly half my running away money on the lousy ticket to Wiltshire! Who makes up these prices?

Think of nipping back and mugging nice tramp lady, but since my fiver is probably now inside her it won't do much good.

Catch the train, and immediately fall asleep. Fortunately nice conductor remembers where I'm going, and shakes me when we reach my stop. Only a twenty-minute walk, says nice friendly red-faced country person when I ask directions at the station.

10.30 a.m.

Look out for something that might be Wigwam Paradiso. A little cluster of tepees in a stone circle. A huddle of wood fires by a river bend.

But Acacia Gardens turns out to be just a street, and Wigwam Paradiso is just a house.

But what a house! It's like Tom's folks' house.

This can't be right – there isn't a wigwam in sight.

The Earth Mothers must be squatting here. This must be the perfect conjunction of leylines, or astral vibrations, or harmonies of the universe, or something.

Feel nervous. Do Earth Mothers get up before noon?

Still manage to see no tepees. Babies kick me, as if to agree with my own nagging worries about coming all the way out here. Suppose the Earth Mothers are really psychopaths, or sinister agents who murder people and sell their babies to childless millionaires?

Finally decide to knock on door of Wigwam Paradiso. A guy the size of a skyscraper opens the door in those stripy pyjamas posh guys wear.

'I've come to see . . . the Earth Mothers,' I stutter.

He looks at me as if it's the daftest thing anyone's ever said to him. Then he lets out a deafening roar.

EEEARCHHHHHHOOOOOOOOO!

I jump like pregnant elephant trying to jump.

But I realize it is only a sneeze.

Noon

The truth has all come out.

Melon is married! To Humph, the skyscraper. And Wigwam Paradiso is where they live.

Melon calls Plummella – I mean Jane – who lives in Tepee Dreams over the road, and they stagger about the house for a bit making infusions out of old leaves. They say I should have some herb tea because my karma is out of kilter.

'But I thought you'd be living in tents,' I say.

'Look, we're only Earth Mothers at festivals,' snaps Melon. 'You can't live like that all year round in this climate, specially with kids. They have to go to school, you know.'

'You mean those little Rainbow kids are not always running free?' I ask.

'Well, a lot of the time they are,' Melon assures me. 'The playing fields at their school are very spacious, fortunately, and they get most afternoons off for sport. That's the blessing of private education. It'll be even better when they get to Eton.'

'But they said they didn't go to school,' I say pathetically.

'That might have been Oberon and Titania. They're home educated,' says Melon, sniffing.

I think I have been a fool. Now I wish I was with Mum and the Puddings in our little cramped, untidy, friendly house. But I'm so exhausted, and the pain in my leg has started up again. I can't go back home today.

The Earth Mothers want to ring my mum. Somehow I manage to convince them I'll do it, and go back home tomorrow.

They give me a beautiful room, with its own washbasin and shiny gold taps. It's like a room in a fairy tale. Perhaps Tom will come and kiss me in the night and I'll wake up and find this was all a dream.

Could go to sleep right now and sleep for months. But can't resist finding out if anybody cares. Turn mobile back on, and there's a flood of petrified-sounding voice-mails from Mum, one with the Puddings wailing in the background. The last message says she's calling the police. Feel awful. I'll have to call them and say I'm all right, and that I'm coming home.

Before I can do that, Lottie rings.

I've never been so glad to hear from somebody in my whole life.

'Where the hell have you been?' she simply asks me.

I can't answer for laughing. I don't know why.

'Have you gone nuts?' Lottie says. 'Are you on drugs?'

'Yes to the first, no to the second,' I say. 'I came to find those Earth Mothers we met at Glasters. I thought it might be the answer to everything. But there isn't an answer to everything, is there? I'm coming back tomorrow.'

'Thank God for that,' says Lottie with relief.

'So you're talking to me again,' I say to her.

'Of course I am.'

'How did all that stuff about Stanley and Mad A work out?' I ask.

'He convinced her he was innocent. But he's desperate to talk to you again. He wants to do this DNA test and stuff. Are you sure you and Tom couldn't have cocked it up, if you follow me?'

'Impossible. We used loads of contraception. Two condoms, *and* spermicide. *And* the Pill.'

Silence for a moment.

'You know that's just the way to break them, don't you, you twat?'

Break what? Hearts?

Oh. Condoms. Oh.

I have just remembered a PSE lesson about that. 'Don't use two condoms,' they said. 'They can rub against each other and may tear.'

Anyway, there was the spermicide, and I had my period, and the Pill. But I didn't take it for very long . . .

'I need to have a think about a few things,' I say to Lottie. 'But it's been really great to hear you. See you tomorrow.'

My brain has gone so soft I can't think straight. Was Stanley telling the truth?

Want more than anything else to rest my head on a pillow in the Earth Mothers' guest room that's about as big as most people's entire beds.

But I need to send my love to Mum. And the Puddings. Will just turn off mobile and lie down for a second or two . . .

Wednesday December 3

6 a.m.

Was thinking about phoning Mum, but instead I fell into a sleep like Alice falling down and down the rabbit hole for ever and ever . . .

And now it's the brightest, clearest winter morning, and there's a frost in the rolling gardens of Wigwam Paradiso.

Feel a bit strange inside. Will have a bath and get my stuff together, and ring Mum when she's awake. Terrible I didn't do it last night. But Lottie will have told her I'm OK and coming home.

Melon and Plum have given me some soothing potion to put in the bath. It smells of loo cleaner. I wonder if they've opened the wrong sachet.

But oooooooooh! Just to be in a big fat hot bath with no marmalade in sight and no Puddings battering the door down. This is the life.

Later, much later

I don't think it was anything to do with the bath potion, honest. Or even all that thinking about water-births. But just about when I was thinking, This is the life, I had a pain rolling over me like a humungous wave of, well, pain. Then another. Then another. These couldn't be contractions, could they? At thirty-six weeks? It was much too early. My waters hadn't broken. But of course, they might have. How could I tell, in the bath?!

I screamed.

Melon came running to the door. 'Amy? Are you all right?'

'No! No! I'm having the babies.'

'Get out of there quick!' She rattled the door. I'd locked it!

Melon called Humph. He barged at the door. It wouldn't budge. A skyscraper was attacking it, and it wouldn't budge.

'Stay calm, Amy!' he shouted in the calming

341

tones of an apoplectic banshee. 'We're calling an ambulance.'

An ambulance? Where was the shaman? What about my karma?

Stay calm? My pains were coming at regular intervals, just like they're supposed to. But much too strong and much too close together. I was completely panic-stricken. My babies would drown! I had to get out! I tried to pull myself out but I sank back each time – my legs had turned to jelly.

'Get Mum! Get Lottie!' I yelled.

I tried to get out of the bath to unlock the door, but I might as well have been trying to climb Everest.

Then I blacked out.

I came round to a lot of harrumphing and shouting and swearing coming from the bathroom window. Humph's head and shoulders and bright purple sneezing face were framed in it. I wasn't much concerned about my modesty by this stage, but he was, and immediately closed his eyes when he saw I'd woken up, which made the whole picture look even odder.

I was laughing and crying hysterically at the same time. Humph seemed to be stuck, and somebody – Melon by the sound of it – was pushing and pulling him from behind. Eventually he shot through the window like a sneezing cruise missile, flung an arm over his eyes to avoid looking at me,

and hurtled over to the bathroom
door to unlock it.

Two complete strangers in green
overalls carrying bags rushed in.
Stupendous stethoscopes!
Paramedics! For me! Somebody
cares after all!

I was past embarrassment, but
one of them hauled me out while the other
modestly offered me a towel, pretending to be
very interested in his feet. I was doubled up every few
seconds by now. And scared as a loon. This was even
worse than the mother-to-be handbook. I was certain
it was all going wrong.

Melon bundled me into an old towelling
dressing gown and pushed me into the ambulance.

'Aren't you coming?' asked the paramedic.

'I don't even know her,' she said. 'Anyway, my
little Thomas is being the back legs of a horse in the
Nativity play this morning – I can't possibly miss it.'

So much for the Earth Mothers.

So there I was, all alone except for paramedic
number two, who looked like Sean Connery in
Dr No, or maybe *Dr Yes Yes Yes*. What is it with
me and Scottish medical people?

He gave me a nice thing to breathe, to calm me
down, or help with the pain or something. We
hurtled along with the siren blaring, exactly like in
Casualty. I started to enjoy myself. Wahey! Amy
Baker, Teenage Mum! The centre of attention at
last! Whoooooopeeeee! Wow! Whatever was in that

gas mask thingy was rather jolly. Whooof! Yippedy dippedy!

Seconds later I felt panicky. Why was he giving me this stuff? To knock me out so I wouldn't know the worst? 'There's something wrong, isn't there? What is it?'

'No, hen, it's fine,' came the soothing voice of Sean. 'But we don't want baby born in the ambulance, do we?'

'Babies,' I hissed, as another contraction swept over me – a rolling pain that starts from the end of the world and the beginning of time, drags you over there and then rolls you, very slowly, over hot coals, spikes, dragon's teeth and a continent of porcupines, back – back into the present.

'Go away. I want to go home. Stop the ambulance. I've decided not to have them.'

'It's a bit late for that, hen,' he said kindly, while he was scribbling down as much about me as I could remember.

'Phone Mum!' I shouted.

Twenty-first-century teenagers, especially Britgirls, have been told they are empowered, they can make decisions. Stand tall, don't step aside for anybody, you're in control of your destiny. Well, by now I was quite simply out of control and realized, perhaps for the first time, that I was unable to do anything else but have two babies, dead or alive. And for the first time since my scan, I hoped against hope that they would be alive. For the first time since my scan, they were more important than me—

Aaarghhh! What in the name of Jupiter's jock-strap was that?!

I think I must have exploded. This is the end, it's going to be like *Alien*. There's been a massive bang and the world has started spinning round, and I'm sure the twins have just battered their way out of my middle, murdered the paramedics and charged off on an orgy of destruction.

I must be dying. The world is going deep purple, people are shouting, glass is breaking, big lumpy things falling on the floor. One of them is me!

But I can still hear Sean's voice. Not as calm as before, but at least he doesn't seem to be dead: 'It's OK, it's OK. You're all right, don't worry.'

I clutch him frantically. 'What's happened? Has God sent a thunderbolt because I'm such a bad person?'

'No. We've bloody crashed. Hang on.'

He gets up, flings open the back doors, and disappears. I can hear a lot of yelling and screeching outside.

Ages pass.

Everybody seems to have forgotten me. Even the babies. The contractions seem to have stopped. Maybe they're going to stay inside after all. I can't stand this. I squeak a little protest, but nobody hears me. So I take a deep breath, undo the belt on the stretcher and crawl along the floor to the open back doors. It seems like a mile down to the ground, but I manage it, as if I'm a drunk person trying to work out how to get out of bed.

Am just thinking, Why does this have to happen to me? Why, with people having babies all over the world every minute of the day, can I not do it without ending up alone in a houseful of loonies only pretending to be Earth Mothers, nearly drowning in a bath, terrifying my lovely mum and Puddings, and getting in an ambulance driven by Laurel and Hardy – when . . . when . . . the Most Bizarre Scene in World History meets my blinking eyes.

A little red sports car is perched at an angle in a ditch, its back end jammed under the bent front wing of the ambulance. Four people are gibbering and flapping away like Hendrix the Parrot on Ecstasy.

Two of them are Sean and the ambulance driver.

One is a sleazy-looking guy with long hair I've never seen before.

And the fourth, limping around in circles like a peroxide poodle on one leg, is Emma Dearest.

'You stupid bastards!' she yells at Sean and his driver. 'Haven't you heard of speed limits?'

'In case you haven't noticed, this is an ambulance,' Sean says to her. 'We're on an emergency call. You could hear the siren in the next county. It's you that was speeding, and you were on the wrong side of the road.'

'Well, Emmy, maybe we shouldn't have had the

346

stereo up so loud,' says the sleazy longhair, smiling a sickly smile.

'*Shut up!*' Emma Dearest yells at him too, then sits down in the middle of the road and starts screaming like a smoke alarm. 'Take me to hospital!' she howls. 'I've broken my leg.'

'No you haven't,' Sean says. 'Cuts and bruises. I can see that from here.'

He suddenly remembers me and turns round. 'My God. Amy! You shouldn't be up!'

But me and Emma Dearest have caught each other's eye, and neither finds the other a pretty sight.

'Oh my God,' groans Emma Dearest. 'I might have known it would be you.'

Even in the state I'm in, this seems like a pretty hot contender for the 100 Maddest Things Ever Said poll, along with 'The Third Reich will last for a thousand years,' and 'Families are where our wings take dream.'

It seems to spark me off. I feel my own big Tidal Wave of Madness approaching from somewhere in my beach ball of a middle, rising up through my chest and roaring into my head as if it had burst through a hole in the *Titanic*. I start bearing down on Emma Dearest, and suddenly the only thought in my thumping mind is killing her where she sits trilling away.

'*Where's Dad?*' I start hissing at her. 'What have you done with him?'

'Who?' Emma Dearest says, pulling frantically at her hair.

'Who?' says the sleazy guy, his smile sicker still.

Sean grips my arm. 'Get back inside,' he says gently to me. 'You have to keep calm. We'll be on our way as soon as we've sorted this.'

'No we won't,' says the ambulance driver. 'The wing's stoved into the front wheel.'

I struggle free of Sean. I'm surprised how strong I feel. 'Where is he?' I shout. 'Where's Dad?'

'Never heard of him,' Emma Dearest sniffs.

'All right, Harry then! My dad! He was with you, wasn't he? Where is he now? I want him!' I wail.

'I thought you said Harry was your husband,' Sleazo says to her, the smile slipping a bit. 'The drunk you were trying to leave.'

'Ohhhhhh shut up! All of you shut up and leave me alone!' Emma Dearest groans, rubbing her leg.

'Look, none of this is my fault,' Sleazo starts saying to the paramedics, who are writing things down in a notebook. 'I wasn't driving, you could see that. We haven't known each other long. I didn't realize there was a problem . . . Look, I've got rather a lot on today, I think I might call a cab.'

In the spinning top that is my head, a little picture starts forming. Sleazo's face appears in it, a bit younger, not so sleazy-looking. 'I've seen you before somewhere,' I start saying to him.

'No, I'm sure you haven't,' he says nervously, fiddling with a mobile phone. 'Don't mind if I use yours, do you?' he says to Emma. 'My battery's dead. Anybody know the number of a taxi service round here?'

Emma Dearest lets out such a loud shriek birds start rising up from the trees, squawking.

'Yes I have,' I say, getting interested despite myself and mad Emma Dearest. 'Ow.' The babies have woken up again and given me a little iron-fist squeeze, but I ignore it. 'Weren't you Vlad Slivowicz, the lead singer in Naked Ambrosia, which had such classic nineteen-eighties hits as *You've Got to Be Soft to Be Hard* and *Leg Over the Moon*?'

Vlad simpers a bit. 'Well, yes I was, actually.' He looks proudly at the ranting, hair-tearing Emma Dearest. 'It's like I told you, the younger generation has more taste than we think,' he says, his voice hardly audible over the din.

'I'm a singer too,' I tell him. 'My friend Mad Alice has got your first albums on the original vinyl.'

'Really?' Vlad says. 'They're worth a bit now. But I'm relaunching my career, you know. I'm going back into the studio next week – in fact I . . .'

The rest of the sentence is drowned out by a squealing of tyres and another metal-crunching thump as a speeding people-carrier roars round the corner, jams on its brakes and slides into the other end of Emma Dearest's little car, pushing it completely into the ditch.

'Oh, no,' groans the peroxide poodle. 'That car was a present from dear Nigel.'

'*Who the hell was he?*' yells Vlad Slivowicz.

I suddenly have to sit down in the road. The white-hot razor blades are at work inside me again,

349

and muscles I didn't know I had are twanging away like harps. Emma is wailing, 'I'm dying. I've got a brain haemorrhage and a broken leg. Get me to a doctor.'

The driver is getting out of the people-carrier. Vlad looks at the TAXI sign on its roof.

'That was amazing,' he says, looking at the mobile phone. 'I've only just turned this on.'

Sean rushes over to the baffled taxi driver. 'I'm requisitioning this cab for the Health Service! You have to take this girl to A and E! She's going to give birth any minute!'

The taxi driver starts rubbing his chin. Another great crime wave of aggers flashes through me.

And then a great wave of amazement.

The passengers are getting out of the back of the taxi and running towards me, shouting, 'Amy! Darling!'

I must be in a coma. Maybe I've died and gone to heaven.

But Emma Dearest is howling, 'Oh no!' and 'Oh my God!' again, and if people like her get let into heaven then it can't be much of a place.

I think I'm really here. And I think the two figures running towards me are my mum and Lottie.

They fling themselves on me, kissing and hugging and both talking at once.

'Careful, careful,' says Sean. 'This girl's on the verge of giving birth.'

'I know,' says Mum, smiling through tears. 'I'm her mum.'

'Are you the one who's got my vinyl albums?' Vlad asks Lottie, who stares at him blankly.

'We have to get her to hospital immediately,' Sean tells my mum. 'Your driver knows where to go. Help me get her in.'

'You're not leaving me here!' squeals Emma Dearest. 'I'm coming too!'

'No you're not,' Sean says. 'There's nothing wrong with you.'

Emma hits a new level of noise-emission, and the birds that have just settled back in the trees all grumpily take off again.

Sean and the ambulance driver look at each other and shrug. 'Might be easier,' the driver says, raising an eyebrow.

'Hello,' my mum says to Emma, as we all hobble towards the taxi. 'How did you get here?'

'It's a long story,' I say to Mum, through gritted teeth.

'Yes,' says Emma, going quiet for once.

'Room for one more?' Vlad says, running up. 'I've got to be back in the smoke by two.'

'No you haven't,' Sean says, gripping his arm. 'We've got the details of this accident to sort out. The police are on their way, if you need persuading.'

'Emmy!' he wails at the now thoughtful-looking Emma Dearest. 'Don't dump me in this! Tell them what happened!'

'They'll know where to find her,' Sean says. 'Get going.'

And we did.

'How'd you get here – fly?' I gasp to Lottie and Mum as we whiz through the country lanes.

'Thank God you spoke to Lottie last night,' Mum says, squeezing my hand. 'And thank God you dropped the Earth Mothers' leaflet in your room. We caught the first train down here and we were on our way to Wigwam Paradiso when we crashed into you. There must be a higher power involved in all this. It's too amazing to be a co-incidence.'

'Yeah, right,' says Emma Dearest, wiping her smudged make-up.

'Yes, and you here as well,' says Mum. 'I can't believe it. My husband's even down this way too, working on a house somewhere. I'm surprised he didn't show up, ha ha.'

I look closely at my mum to see whether her nervous laugh has anything else floating under it, but I don't think so. She really does live in a dream world. Here's the marriage-wrecker sitting right next to her and she doesn't get it. Or doesn't want to.

'Ow! Stop it!' I say to the babies, who are getting excited again.

Lottie smiles at me. Emma Dearest is fidgeting, and looks as if she wants to say something to my mum.

'Down here on holiday, were you?' Lottie asks her casually. 'That your boyfriend? He looks cool.'

I give Emma Dearest a little kick you could almost mistake for my foot slipping.

'Yeah,' Emma says after a bit. 'Used to be a rock star, you know. We're thinking of moving out of London – it's all such a hassle. I'll miss you all, of course, but it's about quality of life, isn't it? And the air is much better for Giselle's asthma.'

Giselle? Oh, yeah, her ludicrous little dog.

I give a sigh of relief and wince in the same breath. Emma Dearest's platinum-coloured finger-nails rest on my clenched fist.

'I hope it goes well with your babies,' she says. 'I'm sorry about . . . you know . . . everything . . .'

'Take me home,' I pant, to no one in particular. 'Take me to marmalade heaven.'

The next hour made my worst nightmares seem like sweet dreams.

We got to the hospital and I was wheeled into a little room.

They hooked me up to a monitor, which bleeped away quite happily for a while, then suddenly changed its pattern. Like in those movies where you know someone's died because the line goes straight.

And the line went straight.

I thought it was me that was going to die there and then.

'One of the babies is very distressed,' said a midwife. 'I'm afraid we'll have to do an emergency Caesarean.'

They come out of nowhere, these medics, when

their little bleepers sound. What seemed like a
football team of scurrying, measuring, scrutinizing,
chattering, scribbling people in green coats and
masks were ferrying me along the corridor and
putting a mask over my face. I fought, for about
three seconds, and then plunged into darkness.

Down I dived, down, down. I didn't care if I
never woke up.

Down in that dark space I met Tom.
'I'll look after you,' he said, very quietly.
I came to in the recovery room. Just like
Casualty. But of course, Tom wasn't
there at all. I cried and cried and
cried.

But Mum was there, and Lottie.
'Amy, oh, Amy, thank God you're
all right.'

I tried to sit up and felt a searing
pain in my stomach.
'Don't move – it's where they've cut you. It's
ever so neat, though – below the bikini line,' said
Mum.

Whaaaat? Bikini line? What did she think I was
going to spend the rest of my life doing, posing for
Page Three? Did she think I'd ever wear a bikini
again? Did she think I cared? I gazed at her in
amazement.

A nurse bustled about taking my temperature
and pulse and stuff. 'Fit as a fiddle. We'll wheel
you up to see the babies in a minute.'

354

Babies? What babies? She wanted me to see two little corpses?

'I don't want to see them!' I shouted. 'I'm not ready for this!'

'Come on,' she said briskly. 'They're just gorgeous!'

Gorgeous?

'Are they alive?'

'Gorgeous!' (She seemed to think my question was so ordinary it wasn't worth answering.) 'A darling little girl and a big bouncy boy! Whoppers! Your mum and dad are in love already.'

'What you mean, my mum and dad?' I managed to say.

And then I gazed in amazement at the person who had come into the room and was standing sheepishly behind Lottie and my mum.

Who was Dad.

I couldn't say anything – I just stretched out my arms to him. My mum smiled and Lottie clapped her hands together. We had a big hug and he was crying as well as me.

'A girl, and a boy,' Dad said to me. 'Do things properly, don't you?'

'Come on, come on, out you go,' said the nurse, shooing everybody towards the door. 'I'll get her ready and bring her up to see the babies.'

Lottie and Mum went out, and the nurse stood at the door, tapping a foot. But I hung onto Dad.

'What happened?' I whispered to him. 'Why are you here? Does Mum know where you've been?'

Dad looked shamefaced, like a little boy. He couldn't speak.

'You knew, didn't you?' I said ecstatically to him. 'You felt it. You knew what was happening to me. It pulled you here on invisible wires.'

'Well, not exactly,' Dad said. 'You see, Emma and me had a bit of a bust-up last night. She didn't come back, and by this morning I was getting really worried – her phone wasn't on. But eventually I got through, and got some guy—'

'Vlad Slivowicz,' I said.

'Who?'

'Nothing. Go on.'

'Come on, Mr Baker,' barked the nurse. 'Time to go upstairs.' But Dad went on anyway.

'– who said there'd been an accident and that she'd come here. When I told him my name was Harry he got all nervous and said he was just a friend. I said I was just a friend too. We've arranged to have a drink and a chat about it when we get back to London. Sounded like quite a decent guy. He thought I ought to come and visit her rather than him – said something had come up. And then I got here . . . and saw Mum . . . and . . .'

'Come on, Mr Baker,' said the nurse, even louder this time.

Dad gave my hand one more squeeze and went out.

A girl. And a boy.

Nurse wheeled me through acres of corridor back to the maternity ward. I had been given a bed in a little double room. There was one other mother in there, bottle feeding a squealing bundle.

I was feeling bonkers. 'I'm seeing coloured lights. And why are there little trees everywhere?' I asked the nurse.

'Christmas decorations,' she giggled.

And there were two plastic cots beside my bed, empty.

And there were Mum and Dad, each holding a tiny bundle.

Looking at my dear old folks, I was too relieved and weepy to care about anything that had happened.

They had scrunchy little faces like little old men. (The babies, not my folks.) Wisps of black hair. Tiny hands! Well, of course their hands were tiny. I mean, they'd look horrible with adult hands, of course. But really tiny teeny weeny hands, hands that make the word tiny quite different from that moment on. Tiny, tiny, tiny, weeny weeny little hands!

Everyone who ever sees a baby goes on about this.

Look at their tiny hands!

With little fingernails!

They were all there.

They were whoppers, though. For twins anyway. And born at thirty-six weeks too! They didn't even have to go in incubators! I was dead proud.

A boy one.
And a girl one.
Bart and Lisa. Lisa and Bart.

CHAPTER TWENTY

In Which the Truth Is Revealed

<u>**Wednesday December 3**</u>

ConTinued

'We can't give them away now,' said Dad. 'We'll look after them.'

The right words at the wrong time. Better late than never. I thought of Yasmin and Bernadette from the teen mum group, going back to their B&Bs, or nunneries.

But I felt a rolling wave of protectiveness when I first saw my babies. I had brought them here, to begin whatever journey they would take. I felt I couldn't give them away to strangers. I had to do my best for them. They were here because of me.

I was going to have to be tough about the adoption. I knew I wasn't going to do it now they were here.

Lottie arranged me and them like a window display, a baby on each arm, for a thousand photos. Me and them. Mum and me. Mum and them. Dad and them. Dad took me and them and Lottie.

I gazed at the twins. They were sharing a rare moment of mutual kipping, as if even they thought it was the Decent Thing to shut up while I came to terms with this complete reshuffle of my take on the whole business. Cherubic they looked – angelic, in fact. Then I remembered they were angelic. Twin Messiahs! One female, one male! And due more or less at Christmas, too . . .

I thought Dad would be thrilled to be Jesus' grandad, so I whispered to him that Bart and Lisa were the result of an immaculate conception, and that he was right about all that Catholic stuff. It's just that I hadn't believed in all this mumbo-jumbo before and now I did.

To my surprise he looked horrified. 'Er, people, um, I mean, women, um, go a bit funny after giving birth,' he said. 'Your grandmother decided to call me Cyclamen, just because there was one in a pot by the bed . . . She came round later,' he added, glancing at me in a frightened way.

'Dad! How can you? I've just told you you're Jesus' grandad!' I squeaked.

Dad gave me a very odd look and called Lottie, as the next best thing in the absence of a team of top psychiatrists.

'Um . . . Lottie has something, er, to tell you,' he said, vacating the bedside chair as if someone had put a rocket up his backside.

Lottie came back in and sat down. 'Hi,' she said.
'Hi,' I said.

She just looked at me, grinning like a loony.

'Is that it?' I asked.

'Um . . . you didn't happen to send an e-mail to somebody before you came down here, did you?' she asked in a casually-casual kind of way.

'I don't remember. I might have done,' I said, feeling more uncomfortable than I was already. 'Why?'

'Well, the person you sent it to got very worried about it and rang your house. When your mum wept all over the person and said she'd no idea where you were, the person rang me. And I told the person everything.'

I heard myself clearing my throat, a noise that sounded like furniture being moved around a room inside my head.

'And?' I finally managed to say.

'This person wants to speak to you, as it happens.'

Lottie, Mum and Dad between them managed to fix up for me to receive a bedside phone call from Japan, which seems to have involved filling in a lot of forms, making a lot of wild promises, rewiring the phone network for Wiltshire, and offering to fund the entire National Health Service for the next ten years. But it worked.

6 p.m.

My phone call with Tom went something like this:

    'Tom.'

    'Amy.'

    'Tom.'

'Oh Amy.'

'Oh Tom.'

And then a lot of crying.

And then roughly this, but I can't remember the order:

'The condoms *did* break. I didn't want to worry you – oh Amy, why didn't you *tell* me?'

'Why didn't *you* tell *me*? About the condoms breaking?'

'Because you had your period and the Pill and the spermicide and I thought you'd have let me know if anything happened and it wasn't till ages later that I found out about the other thing—'

'What other thing?'

'That the spermicide I used was KY Jelly. Bloody Damon told me to use it. He said it was great. Well, it *was* great, but it's a bloody lubricant, not a bloody spermicide.'

'And so what about the Pill?'

Long silence.

'I don't know how to tell you this . . .'

Longer silence.

'I think it was HRT.'

'What's HRT?'

'It's, you know, what women take for the change of life . . .'

Oh. Yes. I knew that.

Godfathers. HRT.

It could have damaged the babies.

'Amy, I'm so so sorry.'

'What do you mean, you *think* it was HRT?'

'Well, I've just checked with my mother . . .'

The thought of his mum's earwig eyebrows when he asked her that made me speechless.

Then there were a lot more sorrys and horrible long pauses and guilt and confusion in which he realized that I'd nearly got off with someone else very soon after he'd left and in which he hinted that he understood because that is what had happened to him too and in which we both said jealous things and angry things and sad things.

And then he said: 'Amy, I've got to see you, and the babies. I'm coming back to England as soon as I can.'

I couldn't speak.

'Is that OK with you?' he said.

'Yes.'

I put the phone down and my hands are shaking. Is it possible? I still have that packet of pills in my toilet bag, I know I do. I read it again, and it's like I thought. It says nothing about it being HRT. It says it has oestrogen and stuff in it and that you should take one a day! But it also says: *read accompanying leaflet* and of course there isn't one.

So the babies are Tom's, after all.

Thursday December 4

Best sleep I've had in months, even with waking to feed Bart and Lisa.

Debs and Mad Alice came bursting in wearing antlers and clutching two stuffed velvet parrots and a couple of babygros, one black with green skeletons on and the other lime green with a purple skull and cross-bones.

'We've written a song for 'em,' they said, hurling the stuffed parrots at the twins and cooing.

I told them about Tom.

'Great – Stanley's a big softy, he wouldn't hurt a fly,' said Mad A. 'He'll do the DNA test though, if you want,' she added. Cheek.

It is post-box heaven here. A little bunch of roses arrived from Granny Meg.

Two tiny white teddies came from Tracey Hardwick. She sent a card saying:

Welcome to this wonderful world, kiddos,
Troy is dying to meet you.

A card from Class Eleven M! Mikey has written, '*Make sure they join a string quartet so they can play in my ristorante.*' Ruth'n'Van put: '*Twins! So you forgot to take two pills then.*' Ho ho. Iqbal wrote: '*Madam Amy, I hope you are happy now. I think one twin will be bubbly and the other will be serious.*'

So he did remember. One day, if I ever get time off from changing nappies, I am going to cook Iqbal a beautiful meal . . . Maybe I could make him godfather . . .

A card from Moony all by herself!

A card from the teen mum group!

The Puddings came up for the day and started hurling Lisa and Bart about like soft toys. I suppose they think they will make quite interesting new pets.

Thursday December 11

The drugs have worn off. I have got over the disappointment of it not being a virgin birth. Just shows how when you've just had a baby your brain, which up till then you've believed to be an efficient grey squashy thing lurking about doing sums and stuff, goes on holiday – leaving its unsmarter brother behind, which is a hopelessly squidgy, weepy, spongy mass. The kind of mad spongy mass that thinks you're the Virgin Mary.

The hospital told the London lot that I wasn't going through with the adoption. I wonder whether James and Sarah Simpson, or whoever they were, got another baby from somewhere. I expect they went off to Guatemala and bought a couple off the peg.

Hope so.

I've got fond of hospital in a strange way. There are loads of nursery nurses to help you. They wrap the babies in little dishcloths and pick them up all the time. And they take the babies away at night and they change the nappies and everything!

There are two kinds of babies in here. Winston Churchill babies and mouse babies. There are two kinds of mums too. Long-suffering and not.

A long-suffering one was in with me for the first two days. Her baby screamed non stop. 'Isn't he good?' she said. 'Hardly makes a sound. Only cries when he really needs something.'

The next mum in that bed had an incredibly quiet baby who made little whimpers about twice a day: 'Ooh! She's got a temper on her, hasn't she? Never satisfied!' said the mum.

What different starts we all get in this life. What kind of mum am I? What kind of mum will I be?

But I'm fed up now. I'm longing for home. They won't let me go for two whole more days. Most mums are in and out so fast it's like being in a supermarket checkout. But Caesareans stay longer.

Tom couldn't get on the next plane, obviously. But his whole family is flying back tomorrow for a long Christmas visit. It's funny, but we seem to have an unspoken agreement not to phone each other again, as if this fragile thread that holds us together might break if we speak. We have to see each other again, before we can work out whether there's anything to work out . . .

Would like to say that Emma Dearest was

encased in plaster for a year, but she was off out of here the next day. She told Dad she thought she needed a new start with Sleazo.

'I was relieved, to be honest,' Dad said. 'I was desperate for him to take her off my hands. She wasn't a patch on Mum.'

Well, I could have told him that.

But I suppose Emma is just a fool over love, like me.

Or maybe like everyone.

I think I didn't really know what love was, till I had Lisa and Bart. The sheer physical shock of it overwhelms me. It is like a red-hot furnace in my chest every time I look at them, or cuddle them, or feed them – which is all the time.

Do I love Tom?

Tom, who thought KY Jelly was a spermicide? Who mixed up contraceptive pills with HRT?

Tom, who turned my bones to silk . . .

Am looking at Bart and Lisa as I write. Am always looking at them.

They are curled up clasped in each other's arms, like two halves of the same person. I swear they are smiling but the nurse says it's only wind.

And Dr Earwig-eyebrows is their granny, poor little things.

What in Tharg's name will we all do?

HELP

There are loads of organizations that can give
confidential advice on contraception, abortion and
pregnancy, and also financial advice and details
of benefits and housing. Here are just a few:

British Pregnancy Advice Service
0845 730 4030 (Monday–Friday 8am–9pm;
Saturday 8.30am–6pm; Sunday 9.30am–2.30pm)
www.BPAS.org

Brook Advisory Centres
421 Highgate Studios
53–79 Highgate Road
London NW5 1TL
0800 018 5023 (Monday–Friday 9am–5pm)
www.brook.org.uk
Information and advice for under 25s on contraception,
pregnancy and sexual health. If you use a BT landline
the call is free and the helpline won't show up on your
bill.

Childcare Link
0800 096 0296
www.childcarelink.gov.uk/index.asp
A website where you can search for childcare facilities
in your area. The free helpline also provides info on
local childcare, plus fact sheets about your childcare
options.

Citizens Advice Bureaux
www.citizensadvice.org.uk/index/getadvice.htm
Free, confidential and independent advice on benefits,
housing, legal issues, discrimination, employment,
immigration, consumer and other problems is available
from advisers at your local CAB office. Search for your
nearest centre on the website.

Family Planning Association
FPA UK
2–12 Pentonville Road
London N1 9FP
0845 310 1334 (9am–6pm)
www.fpa.org.uk
Advice on contraception.

Fathers Direct
www.fathersdirect.com
Information for dads, to help them get more involved
with their children.

Get Connected
0800 808 4994 (1pm–11pm 7 days a week)
www.getconnected.org.uk
Free, confidential helpline that aims to offer
young people the best help, whatever the problem.
They will listen, talk through your options, and
make suggestions for services that can help. They
can connect you by phone for free to local services,
and text key info to your mobile.

Gingerbread
0800 018 4318 (Monday–Friday, 9am–5pm)
www.gingerbread.org.uk
Gingerbread is for lone parents. It runs support groups
all over England and Wales, has a free advice line and
an e-mail discussion forum.

Having a Baby
www.bbc.co.uk/parenting/having_a_baby
The BBC's site on pregnancy and birth.
Includes a calendar that tells you what is happening
each step of the way.

Home Start
0800 0686 368 (Monday–Friday, 8am–8pm; free)
www.home-start.org.uk
Home Start's team of volunteers – who are usually parents themselves – visit families at home to offer informal, confidential support. There are 300 projects in the UK.

Jobcentre Plus
Correspondence Manager
Jobcentre Plus Secretariat
Level 6, Caxton House
Tothill Street
London SW1H 9NA
www.jobcentreplus.gov.uk
Help, advice and support in job-hunting and making a claim for benefit.

Like It Is
www.likeitis.org
Info for teenagers about sex and sexual health, including a 'dear doctor' page and info on pregnancy.

Marie Stopes
153–157 Cleveland Street
London W1T 6QW
0207 574 7400
0845 300 8090 (for advice on abortion; 24 hours)
www.mariestopes.org.uk
For advice on contraception and abortion.

Maternity Alliance
3rd floor West, 2–6 Northburgh Street
London EC1V 0AY
0207 490 7638
www.maternityalliance.org.uk/parents_to_be.htm
All the latest information on maternity rights, parental rights, benefits and tax credits for pregnant women and new parents.

Meet a Mum Association

www.mama.org.uk

This was set up to help thousands of mothers who feel depressed and isolated when their babies are born. The site gives a DAPeND helpline for advice if you're depressed after having a baby:

0208 768 0123 (7pm–10pm, weekdays).

National Childbirth Trust

Alexandra House
Oldham Terrace
London W3 6NH
0870 770 3236
www.nctpregnancyandbabycare.com

Website with loads of info about pregnancy, birth and babies, with a facility to ask questions by e-mail, and a section on becoming a dad.

Net Mums

www.netmums.com

Tips and information – like what to do on a rainy day – plus details of how to meet other mums in your area.

Parentline Plus

0808 800 2222
(free and confidential; 24 hours)
www.parentlineplus.org.uk

Support and info for anyone parenting a child.

R U Thinking About It?

0800 28 29 30 (every day, 7am–midnight)
www.ruthinking.co.uk

Info on sex, relationships and contraception. If you call from a BT landline the call is free and the helpline won't show up on your bill.

Ready Steady Baby

www.hebs.scot.nhs.uk/readysteadybaby
Straightforward site about pregnancy, birth and early childhood, run by NHS Scotland.

Teenage Pregnancy Unit

DfES
GD Caxton House
6–12 Tothill Street
London SW1H 9NA
0207 273 4839
www.dfes.gov.uk/teenagepregnancy
This website contains information about the government's Teenage Pregnancy Strategy, including guidance issued by the Teenage Pregnancy Unit as well as relevant publications from other government departments.

YMCA's Respect Young Mums Campaign

www.ywca.org.uk/youngmums
Very helpful website responding to the hard time young mums have, with loads of links. You can sign the Respect Young Mums charter here.

Your local council

Most local councils will have a team who support young mums and mums-to-be. Find your council details on this website
www.direct.gov.uk/QuickFind/LocalCouncils/fs/en

About the Author

Ros Asquith lives in North London with her partner, a jazz critic, and their two sons.

She has worked as a photographer and stage designer and painted murals in six countries. She was theatre editor of *City Limits* magazine and a critic for *Time Out* and the *Observer*. She draws regularly for the *Guardian*.

Ros has written over thirty books and illustrated lots more. The *Teenage Worrier* series starring fifteen-year-old Letty Chubb has been an international success, translated into eleven different languages and selling well over a quarter of a million copies in the UK alone.

Ros Asquith
I WAS A TEENAGE WORRIER

Letty Chubb is 15. Inside this slim yet sensuous volume she details her hopes, her fears, her joys, her tears (Get on with it – Ed) in easily the most brilliant, perceptive and comprehensive alphabet of teenage worry ever published.

'Exuberant . . . a mine of information about every anxiety known to teenagers' *The Times*

'Fearlessly opens up expensive new landscapes of anxiety' *Dr Bert Jung, Consultant Psychiatrist*

'The wit of Eddie Izzard, the moral strength of Gandhi, the tumultuous literary power of Tolstoy, Shakespeare and Jeffrey Archer' *Mrs Chubb*

'Over a million copies sold! Buy another one to help me feed my cat' *Letty Chubb*

CORGI BOOKS
ISBN 0 552 55280 1

Ros Asquith
THE TEENAGE WORRIER'S GUIDE TO LIFE

Bored? Fed up with yawning, day-dreaming, scuffing
your trainers on the pavement? Worry no more. Inside
this humble buke (blush) is all you need to know for
life-skills in the 21st century (yeech). A true voyage of
the soul from moi, Letty Chubb, aged 15.

'The ultimate A–Z guide on how to cope with those
traumatic teenage years . . . a laugh a minute' *Shout*

'Extremely amusing' *Time Out*

'A female Adrian Mole . . . a mine of
information and fun' *Daily Mail*

'Great advice' *The Times*

CORGI BOOKS
ISBN 0 552 55282 8

Ros Asquith
THE TEENAGE WORRIER'S GUIDE TO LURVE

Yes! Here it is! From moi, Letty Chubb, aged 15. A thrusting, passionate, juicy (phew, must hurl self into cold shower) look at every aspect of lurve. Buy now, and you too can swap yearning for spurning (heh, heh, mad cackle of triumph . . .)

'Will get all your romance worries sorted!' *Bliss*

'Hilarious' *Daily Telegraph*

'Will help you through any questions to do with the L-word!' *TV Hits*

'If you are a teenager worried about lurve, this is certainly the book to guide you through the best and the worst of it . . . giggle-getting humour . . . good for a laugh and great advice' *The Times*

CORGI BOOKS
ISBN 0 552 55281 X

THE TEENAGE WORRIER'S POCKET COLLECTION

Four Books in One!
The Teenage Worrier's Pocket Guide to Romance
The Teenage Worrier's Pocket Guide to Families
The Teenage Worrier's Pocket Guide to Mind & Body
The Teenage Worrier's Pocket Guide to Success

Worry no more! I, moi, me, Letty Chubb, aged 15, world-famous author of worry-free bukes for True Teenage Worriers, am on your side! Here, within this v. handy Pocket Collection, is all you ever need to know about Romance (from Attraction to Zits), Families (from Aunts to Zoos), Mind & Body (from Acne to Zombie) and Success (from Acting to Zest)!

CORGI BOOKS
0 552 54839 1